THE MISTS OF MBINDA

Kate's busy life concealed the soul of a woman lonely for love

CORRINE VANDERWERFF

Pacific Press Publishing Association
Nampa, Idaho
Oshawa, Ontario, Canada

Edited by Kenneth R. Wade
Cover art by Jacqui Morgan
Designed by Dennis Ferree

Vanderwerff, Corrine
    The mists of Mbinda : Kate's busy life concealed the soul of a
woman lonely for love / Corrine Vanderwerff.
        p.   cm.
    ISBN 0-8163-1404-7 (alk. paper)
    1. Women missionaries—Africa. I. Title.
PS3572.A667M5
813'.54—dc21   97-29678
                                                                      CIP

98 99 00 01 02 • 5 4 3 2 1

Contents

Dedication

Then your light shall break forth like the morning,
Your healing shall spring forth speedily,
And your righteousness shall go before you.
—Isaiah 58:8, NKJV

Preface

The names used in this book are not the names of individuals you'll find on any precise mission roster; nor will you find Mbinda Mission or the country in which it is located on any map; nor will you find the exact happenings chronicled in any specific historical records—but what you will find is truth. Everything in *The Mists of Mbinda* is a composite embodiment of people, places, and events that are as genuine as every day and as real as life.

May this book provide you with an insight into the personal struggles, heartaches, failings, happinesses, and triumphs encountered by the real beings who people foreign mission stations, and may reading these pages aid you in your own search for truth.

—Corrine Vanderwerff

CHAPTER
1

Kate Shayne picked her way across the cobbling of bricks, remains of someone's earlier ill-laid attempt at blocking in a patio where the bedroom ell jutted from the main house. Coffee-colored water—run-off from the downpour that had passed about an hour before—traced gaps between the bricks and trickled into a long puddle on the bare earth of the yard. The sun pressed around her, sponging moisture back toward the heavens and making the late November heat even more oppressive. As she started to step across the puddle, she became aware of four dark slabs.

"What . . .?"

She stopped, stepped back, then crossed to where they leaned against the off-white plaster of the house and reached out to touch one. "Mbayo!" she yelled, snatching her hand back.

An immediate clopping of hard soles against cement sounded from the direction of the kitchen, and in a moment a dark face appeared in the doorway. "Yes, Madame?" The two words spoken in accents of the local French held the appropriate balance between respect and question.

"These—when did they come?"

"The boy brought them this morning. I told him he should leave them there."

Kate nodded approval.

"He said the chairmaker himself will come to see you tomorrow in the afternoon."

Kate nodded again and turned her palm so Mbayo could see the brown smudge. "His boys didn't polish them enough." A quick smile erased her seriousness. "Ask Jonas to brush them."

Full lips broadening into a grin, Mbayo dipped her head in understanding and said, "Yes, Madame, I'll tell him."

Kate turned to resume her interrupted errand, then as if in afterthought added, "I'm going to get a pineapple. Jonas can gather the others after he's finished with the chairs. And . . . Oh, by the way . . ." With a start she realized what she'd forgotten. "Please tell Marie to see me."

"Marie?"

"The girl from Kato village. In fourth form. The one . . ."

In her mind Kate again saw the girl collapse across her desk, heard the thin voice, felt the too-thin arms.

"Yes, Madame, I know the girl."

"Tell her to stop." A warning cut across her mind: *What'll George say?* She knew what he'd say. Clearly knew. They'd agreed. Their budget was already stretched beyond its limit. Nevertheless, she continued to speak, pronouncing the next four words with determination. "On her way home."

When Mbayo disappeared into the house, Kate shoved aside thoughts of her promises to George and stepped back to study the chair pieces. Oversized eyes dominated the triangular mask face chiseled into each of the two backrests, their empty slits staring from between large, smooth lids, down past the pointed chin and onto the scene below.

"Nice."

She spoke aloud, though now she was her own audience. The simplicity of the work pleased her.

"Very African. Very . . ."

In one a woman, arms smooth and firmly muscled, worked at her pounding while in the other a man sat idly holding his drinking calabash.

"Typical."

Her one-word judgment included more than the artistry.

A pattern of diagonal chiselings framed the edge of the solid wood; a similar pattern covered the seats. Two pieces, back and seat, fit into a stylized version of a traditional village chair. "But of course he would bring them now when he can ask a higher price." She half laughed— money was always a topic to be discussed whether between husband and wife or between vendor and vendee—and she went back to the puddle and rinsed the sticky brown stain from her hand. Village markets were stocked with brown shoe polish, though few customers owned shoes to polish, and that quirk of third-world marketing gave local artisans a bargain-priced product for staining their woodcraft.

At noon, briefly, and in the later afternoon, Kate's was a familiar figure in the well-tilled garden filling the lower half of their large enclosed yard, and she turned now in that direction. She walked with a firm step, though her right foot tended to droop. "Anatomy's all wrong," a specialist had remarked jovially about it when she was much, much younger. "As long as you can walk and have no pain, don't worry." So she walked and didn't worry, and life had taken her many places, even to this mission station where now the full skirt of her cotton shirtwaister swished against the sides of her boots as she strode through the heat.

With the beginning of the rains, the banana plants along the edge of the Shayne garden had plumped into a robust green, their long, broad leaves fanning up and out into an almost impossible-to-see-through thicket between their place and that of their neighboring missionaries, the Parmers. A hoe lay at the base of the nearest plant, its handle jutting into the path. "Will that boy ever learn?" Kate muttered, bending to retrieve the tool Jonas had left lying where he'd dropped it. As she straightened, the handle pushed against a large banana leaf, folding it into a spout. A gush of collected rainwater

dumped against her neck, breaking into a dozen downward slithers.
"Oh!"

Her breath sucked sharply, and she lurched sideways. She heard another shriek, short and staccato. Hers! And she felt herself sliding toward the next banana plant. Her boots plowed the loose, damp earth, scooping a personal-sized slippery-slide, and when she finally scooted to a stop, she lay inches short of the banana plant, still holding the hoe.

"Oh!"

This time the single word was both observation and expletive. She sat there for a moment, then drew a long, deliberate breath, pushed herself to her knees, and stood. She swatted at obvious mud that clung in gross chunks to her dress. And then she turned again toward the pineapple patch.

A stretch of sandy soil flanked the mission houses. It grew excellent pineapples, and the new season's crop ranged from rosy pink flowerettes to robust, full-shouldered fruit. The spikes of several larger plants stabbed at her legs, but she pushed past them toward the far corner where she knew a particularly large pineapple waited, ready-ripe. She stopped short.

"Jonas!"

There was no answer.

"Jonas!" She yelled even more loudly.

"Yes, Madame." The gardener suddenly appeared at the corner of the house. "What is it?" He carried his mpanga, the thick-bladed, heavy-handled knife with which he cut wood, edged flower beds, weeded . . .

"Look!" Kate pointed.

Jonas broke into a run, his bare feet shushing through a puddle in the low swoop of the yard, the chest of his navy-blue work coveralls bagging open. When he reached Kate he, too, stopped and stared. "No! Madame! It cannot be!"

"When?" She fastened him with her one-word question.

A sudden sallowness flushed under the deep chocolate of his face.

"They were here yesterday. In afternoon. I swear." His words gulped in short sentences that tended to bump one into the other. "I came myself. And I see them. Right there." His gaze was fixed on the sharp-pointed milky-green spikes that flared out as protectively as always from the plants in the soldier-straight rows. But the pineapples were gone. He pushed through the spikes and stopped when the outlines of his bare feet met an interlacing of footprints coming and going. Then he pointed. Strands of wire hung loosely around a gap in the hedge fence.

"Thieves in night." He spoke slowly now. "In our village these weeks we having many thieves. Very bad these times."

"Very bad!"

Kate's eyes held her gardener's face, but he did not look up. He wouldn't, she knew that already. Among his people it was neither polite nor proper to look directly at anyone to whom you must show respect; neither to an elder, neither to a mother who was not your own; not even to an employer whose dress was caked with mud.

"You will repair the fence," she finally said after thinking through the futility of all the other things she would have liked to say.

"Yes, Madame. I will mend it." Then he looked up and almost met her gaze but instead looked past her to some distant point. "Thieves in night. They very bad."

CHAPTER

2

The day of the pineapple theft had begun abruptly for Kate, well before dawn, and earlier than usual she sat in her study, writing, words flowing clearly onto the pages in the brilliance of the twelve-volt solar-light system George had installed the year before.

"Voices."

Her pen slowed, and she twisted it to loop a heavy, oversized period. Beside her on the wide arm of her chair lay her open Bible and a devotional book. She glanced briefly at them, then deliberately wrote: "The truth of our lives is that they are full of voices. Calling, pleading, demanding voices. Voices we can't escape. Voices that need us. Voices . . ."

Sharp echoes of their guard's voice filled her thoughts.

"Mr. Director! Madame!"

His shouts had levered into her sleep less than an hour earlier. Then when metal had grated against metal, rasping in sharp, crude thwangs, her eyes had sprung into wide-awake openness. She'd seen nothing, though, except the thin pale line of moonlight edging the blind. More metal rasped on the other side of the window behind the blind. "Mr!—Madame!" The voice had insisted.

Kate had pushed herself up onto an elbow. "What is it?"

"The gate!"

"Gate?"

"Your front gate. It is not locked, and I have found it open."

Kate's jaw had tensed. Guards were hired to make sure that mission gates were secure, to keep watch, to . . . "Then, please! Close it!" She clipped her reply. "And lock it!"

"Huh?" George had stirred beside her.

"The watchman." She'd lowered her voice then and had turned and let her arm drape across her husband's shoulder. "Proving he's on the job and not sleeping, pounding his mpanga on the window grilling . . ."

"Mmmmm." George had twisted his pillow to better cradle his head then turned just enough to let his body fit against hers.

"To let us know . . ."

The *scuff-clumph, scuff-clumph* of oversized shoes plodding toward the gate had told her the guard was on his way to do as she had said. From the pillow beside her the sounds of slow, deep, rhythmic breathing had resumed, and she'd let further spoken words trail for lack of an audience. That's when she had decided to get up, to go to the study, to be alone. She often started her day early—reading, putting thoughts in her notebook. This day she simply started it a little earlier.

"Voices sent by God?"

She stared now at the new words she'd just written and slowly double-traced the question mark. Suddenly she was hearing echoes of her own voice, echoes of her unspoken words, and an almost physical pain slapped across her heart. Her thumb and fingers tensed against the pen.

"Liar!"

She pressed her pen hard against the paper.

"Liar!"

Her pen moved in heavy strokes. When she looked down she was surprised to see a series of Xs, dark, crooked-legged and uneven, and with an almost satisfaction she realized she was angry again, very angry.

"Trust me, he said."

Her pen continued to slash Xs across the page.

"Trust him?"

15

A creaking sound moved from the periphery into her hearing, grating on her nerves. She needed to move, to pick herself up, to take herself away from her feelings, and with a burst of resolution she made herself put her books on the floor and get up and go to the window and look out.

A bevy of junior guinea fowl filed by, tiny heads perched atop oversized bodies, dwarfing the little hen who was their foster mother and who was leading them to the breakfast they wanted. Obediently they followed and pecked spots she scratched along the edges of the flagstone walk. They belonged to one of the nurses and often strayed into the Shayne's yard of an early morning. Kate stared at the speckled effect of their black-and-white feathers and at the startling blue of the rumpled skin sagging from their cheeks; she didn't know if she liked or disliked the noisy birds whose beaks worked in time with their strides and produced the heavy creaking sounds. Lately she'd been feeling ambivalent about a lot of things—about Mbinda, about mission life in general, about George.

"He lied."

The effect of getting up and going to the window and focusing on the guinea fowl helped ease the intensity of the emotions that pressed in when she let herself dwell on what had happened. Intellectually she believed what she always had believed and accepted as fact: she and George for the most part had a good marriage, and they were good for each other in the ordinary day-to-day. More than that, they put their best efforts into trying to do a good work for the Lord, working long hours—George especially—not only at the school but in helping the poor and teaching truth. They'd given up a home they loved to come and to serve. That was what faith in God and missions was about, wasn't it? Sacrificing? And meeting needs? And sharing truth?

"Truth!"

She silently formed the word with her mouth. Just then a rooster crowed.

Usually the roosters and their crowings were nothing more than a part of her surroundings, but the sharpness of the bird's voice pierced her thoughts, pulling her from within herself and into awareness of the world around her. The morning mists hung more heavily than usual, muting

16

the light of the rising sun, draping the nearest palms and the mangoes with a misty haze, blurring the rest of the mission into an indistinct gray. And she found in her muted surroundings the vagueness of her own understanding. Already, though, the sun had begun its work, phasing away the mists, lifting them from the mission, unveiling the mud red termite spire across the road on which the rooster perched.

"I've got to go to the radio."

With a start she swung around and saw George standing in the doorway. "Oh?"

"Promised The Chief I'd talk to him this morning." George always referred to their mission organization's countrywide president as *The Chief*.

"Is it that time already?" She needed the rhetorical question to bridge her way to his sudden presence then quickly added, "Did you have a good committee last evening? I have no idea when you got home."

"Late. Usual problems. Lotsa talk." George's wavy brown hair hung longer on one side than the other, and his forehead pushed up and back into what once had been a thick covering of hair. He swept his fingers up through the long strands, pushing them across the bald area.

"Didn't you lock the gate when you came in?"

"Sure. Why?"

Kate had to laugh at the innocence of his response. "You sure do sleep like a log." The cliché rolled with deceptive glibness. "Didn't you hear the guard—4:15 this morning—pounding on the window and yelling that the gate was open?"

"Open? How can that be?"

Kate shrugged. "That's what I wondered. Anyway, breakfast'll be ready when you get back."

She rushed to have things on the table by seven; then when George hadn't returned by seven-fifteen, she ate by herself and prepared for school. From that point on, time flowed into a series of classes filled with students who seemed even less able to concentrate than usual. About midway through fourth period, Marie in the end seat at the middle front table folded forward, head dropping onto her arms. Kate crossed quickly to her and touched the girl's shoulder. "What is it?" she asked.

CHAPTER

3

Marie turned her head just enough so Kate could see one eye. The veins traced puffy lines under a murky white.

"Are you not well?" Kate spoke quietly.

"Hungry." The word was muffled against a thin, dark arm.

As Kate stood looking down at the girl, hand still resting on her shoulder, she noticed how the shoulder blade traced a sharp pattern against her palm, much too sharp, and something stirred in her memory from a staff meeting they'd had shortly after the beginning of the school year. *I should check into that,* she made a mental note to herself. Then instead of speaking directly to Marie again, she looked around the classroom. "How many of you ate breakfast this morning?" She'd taught in the school long enough to dare to surprise her students with blunt, not-to-be-asked questions.

Thirteen boys and nine girls raised their hands—all of them dormitory students. The other twenty-nine sat immobile. Village students. Had it still been her first year at Mbinda, Kate would at that point have launched into a lecture on the importance of starting the day with a nutritious meal, but she had long since learned that such would be equivalent to rubbing salt into open wounds. The school district she and George had left in North America seemed eons away with its before-school meals and adjusting rates that let all children have breakfast.

"What did you eat yesterday?" She looked back at Marie and again spoke in a low voice.

The girl said nothing.

"Before that?"

"Cassava."

"You should bring us something from your place." Jacques, red pullover as usual stretched tightly over his uniform shirt, made a bright spot among the others. A mischievous grin spread across his wide features.

"What would you like?"

"Bread."

"Bananas."

"Biscuits."

Repetitions of the three suggestions popped from various parts of the room. Kate listened. Even a full stalk of ripe bananas wouldn't have enough fruit to give them two each. She held her hands up for silence. "Well, I'm afraid that idea, as tempting as it may sound, is too late for today. Now . . . On with math."

Finally she was with the fifth-year group, her final class of the morning—the school schedule had for once been kind to her, giving her the last period free—and while she was at the board explaining a new equation, the room darkened as if someone had drawn blinds over the windows lining the east wall, their only source of light. She could hear the approach of dark, heavy clouds. More precisely, she could hear the rain, a drumming din, marching in, quickly closing toward the school and growing louder. A thick cloud settled overhead, hanging low, dumping its storm nonstop on the earth, pounding it against the metal roof. The racket forced through the thin ceiling, filling the room, obliterating all other sound. Even in her own ears her loudest voice became only a dull muffle that could not possibly reach even those students sitting nearest, so with a sweeping motion she lifted the eraser from her desk and brought it in a large arc across the notes she'd started on the black-painted cement chalkboard. Then in large letters she wrote: Do ex. 4, p. 56.

"They need the review," she thought, shrugging to herself. Rains might make impossible lecture conditions, but they did not postpone the examinations that would determine her charges' scholastic future. While the youngsters worked, she walked to the window and stared out. A streaming gray hung like a liquid curtain around the school. The far edge of the mission road, a scant thirty meters from where she stood, had vanished. "Hungry." The rest of the world was gone, leaving only the tiny island that was their school. "Hungry." Marie was not the only hungry one locked with her under the long metal roof.

"Bring us food."

Echoes of Jacques' voice followed Marie's, and it annoyed her. "That's not the answer," her thoughts responded harshly.

Through all the years they'd been at Mbinda, Kate had looked for answers. Solutions seemed easier when they first arrived. "Set up feeding programs for the hungry," she'd suggested, baffled by the head shaking among veteran missionaries. "That's not the answer," they'd responded, adding things about creating dependency and destroying initiative and about the actual mechanical difficulties of space and place and equipment and supervisors for preparing and serving meals. "Just for the hungriest of the hungry," she'd insisted, and they had asked, "Which ones of the hungriest?"

The passing years had given sense to their reasoning. Those same passing years had also brought them face to face with a new political era. Ceausescu's fall from the dictatorship of Romania startled thinking Africans into an attitude of "Why not here too?" A wave of change swept the continent, bringing in transition governments and talk of free elections. "Democracy!" The word sounded good. Leaders promised glorious new freedoms. At the same time, they schemed and bargained and jockeyed to get themselves into preferred positions of power. Money devalued, prices rose, and the people in the villages and the wage earners who lived in the cities had less and less.

"Hungry." The word continued to throb in her thoughts. Too

many people, among them even teachers, subsisted on one meal a day—or less. Only the double adobe bricks of the classroom wall separated her from Marie's class, and she wondered if the girl still drooped over her work.

"How can she learn?"

The question was the one any professional, conscientious teacher would ask; it was also the one with an easy answer: "She can't." Kate had no doubt about that. The girl needed adequate food; without it she'd be forced to drop out of school.

"Like so many others."

Most village youngsters could not both go to school and eat. Theirs was not to choose, and they did the only thing they could do—they stayed home and worked with their parents in the family fields and kept alive their heritage of subsisting.

And if she does leave school, how will she survive?"

That was the real question.

As abruptly as it had come, the storm moved on, taking with it the temporary relief from the heat it had brought. Before going home, Kate stopped briefly at the office to speak with the secretary.

21

CHAPTER
4

"My mother wore hers that way," Marie responded to Kate's compliment, and she unconsciously reached up to smooth her hair, which she wore poufed up and away from her face and not tightly braided as many of the other girls wore theirs. "She was a beautiful woman, Madame, very beautiful. And kind. I want to be like she was."

"You remember your mother very well, don't you?"

"She didn't die until my last year in primary school."

"And your father?"

Marie traced her finger along the scroll of the upholstery on the arm of the couch where she sat. "Dead. My mother says he went away when I was very little. That he traveled to another part of the country on business and that she never again saw him alive."

"Did something happen to him?"

Marie studied the floor. "The other children say that their parents say that my father had other wives and other children in other villages, that he left my mother because she . . . Because her tribe and her people are not good."

"And she stayed?"

"You know my mother was a leper. The disease was not bad, you could not tell by looking that she had it. But sometimes she was sick, and our village was where she was on the list for getting medicines. Sometimes she talked of going back to her old home, but she was afraid that because she had been away so long that she wouldn't be put on the list to get medicines there. And so we stayed. And now . . ."

Kate studied the girl as she talked. Mbayo had given her some bananas and a sandwich while Kate had changed out of her muddy dress and washed and then purposely kept herself busy so the girl would have time to eat. The restoring effects of the food were already evident. *And this is what they call democracy?* Kate's thoughts scorned the term flaunted before the people by the politicians. *Look what it does to children like this!* But rather than allowing any inkling of what she was thinking to enter the conversation, she asked, "Where did you stay after your mother died?"

"My mother had a very good friend who told me to come to her house and to stay with her girls. My mother had a large field of cassava. Also peanuts and bananas. We ate some and sold the rest. With that money I could pay to go to the secondary school near our village and to buy my uniform and notebooks. Then . . . Then . . ."

Kate didn't force the girl to continue. She'd verified the rest of the story in the office before coming home. The sudden openness of expression allowed under the transitional government, which according to promises was to take the country from a one-party state to multiparty democracy, had created new tensions. To observers it was obvious that would-be presidents were moving themselves into position to get what they could for themselves without concern for what might benefit the general population. It had also become overwhelmingly evident that the opposing parties were divided according to region and ethnic heritage. The largest geoethnic group would win any election. Marie's mother's tribe belonged to that largest geoethnic group. Many of them held key positions across the country—especially in the province where Mbinda was located. But because they were not members of the same tribe as the majority of the people in the province, the provincial political leaders quickly labeled them as "The Foreigners" while those of local heritage were called "Originals."

"Democracy offers freedom," the governor had enthused to the masses gathered to show their support for his party. "We are here to give you that freedom—and it is for everyone. If there are "Foreigners" in our province, we are not forcing them to stay. They are free— free to go home. In fact, if they find it difficult to find the way to go, we can find ways of helping them."

The intent of his speech was readily understood, and certain individuals initiated a "purification" process. Before long those in the city whose heritage reached into the unwanted tribe and who held a key post of any kind whether in government, in the school system, or in business, were suddenly suspended and given one week in which to pack and to leave for home territory. At the same time, self-proclaimed party adherents, mostly jobless young men, drifters with some academic training who considered it demeaning to be mere cultivators of fields, many of them on drugs, banded together, roving from village to village, issuing ultimatums. Stories circulated from many corners of the province telling how people stood back mutely watching as long-time neighbors were attacked and driven out, their houses looted and destroyed, their fields ravaged. The day came when the looters arrived in Marie's village, and now Marie described what had happened.

"All foreigners must leave! Today!" The surly-faced leader, about twenty-eight years old, a red rag looped around his head and knotted on the side, folded his arms across his chest and confronted the village chief.

"We have no foreigners in our village." The chief replied evenly.

"You know who we mean." Behind the spokesman stood a mob of twenty-six, all with similar red bands around their heads, all armed, some with mpangas and heavy sticks, some with hoes, a few with spears. "If you don't show us their houses and tell them to leave— now—we'll show you who they are, and we'll show you what we do to those who insist on staying and robbing us of our lands."

"I told you, we have no foreigners in our village." The chief stood his ground. "Everyone who lives here belongs to this village. We have no troublemakers, no robbers of our land." By then most of the villagers had gathered around to watch. Marie stood near the fringe of the crowd.

"HA!" The leader whipped a folded paper from his pocket. "This paper has names." He opened the paper and nodded to a stocky fellow standing to his right. "We have ways to find if your are lying; our magic will tell us whether or not those whose names are on this list are foreigners."

"I tell you, we have no one in this village who is either robbing us of our land or causing trouble." The chief stepped toward the band leader and held out his hand for the paper.

The leader stepped back, then flipped the paper upward and held it out for the chief to read. There were three names; Marie's was first.

"There are no foreigners on that list."

"You must live well from their bribes," the band leader sneered. "If you were not chief, I would show you how we make those who lie to decide to speak the truth." He lunged two quick steps forward, his face close to the chief's. "But you are chief, and the spirits forbid that we should touch any chief. Tomorrow we will return."

When it was dark, the chief called Marie and her adopted mother to his hut. "No one can accuse you of being a foreigner to our village. Your father was one of us, and among our people inheritance always passes from father to child. No one can harm you, but these people are troublemakers. Bandits. It is well known that the family fields now belong to you, a girl, and they will use any excuse to take your fields and rob you of your crops."

"What should we do?" the older woman asked.

"Keep the girl with you and go to your fields early tomorrow morning. But, my young one," he turned to Marie now. "For tomorrow, don't work in your own field. Work beside this mother and then, if there should be trouble, I'll send a messenger."

The next day Marie went with her adopted mother as the chief had instructed. About midmorning the same band of young men marched back into the village, and the villagers not out in their fields lined the road to see what would happen.

"We have returned." The leader thrust his chest forward, his unwashed jacket swagging back from his shoulders. "We know the houses of those on our list, and we have brought our instruments which will tell us the truth about these people." He nodded toward an assistant who held a skin bag. "If it becomes evident that you have been lying, we will find these people and bring them here to this very spot and execute them, one by one, before your eyes, and leave the cadavers at your doorstep. You will dig the graves." He stabbed a grubby forefinger toward the chief. "You will bury their bodies. Do you understand?"

The chief stood his ground. "I tell you, these people are our villagers."

"HA!"

"I am chief." The older man steadily faced the aggressor. "I have had no orders from the higher chief about any of my people, so now tell me by whose authority have you come to trouble our village?" As he spoke he shifted his feet slightly and raised his left hand to his hip, flicking it outward as he did so. At that moment a young man watching from the edge of the crowd stepped out of sight behind the others and then slipped along a path leading away from the village.

"We come in the name of the government," the leader yelled. "We are sent by the government that allows all you chiefs to wear your ceremonial feathers and your animal skins and to lead your people in all of your traditions. We have been called to clean away the filth, to purify our land so it might again be ours and so we can prosper."

"Our village is clean." The chief's voice was steady, his words measured. "The only filth I see are these bandits before me with red rags around their heads. No one has been given any authority by anyone to clean our village."

The leader flung his arm upward, bouncing onto his toes. "I'm Mpanga, the knife," he growled, "and it seems that you prefer that I request the one who is called the One-Who-Finds-the-Answers to get us the truth. Maybe we should start with a half-truth. Call for us this

Kunda Mbala Marie. If you won't talk, the spirits will."

"The girl is not here." The chief spoke quickly. "She is sick, in the hospital."

"You are lying."

"I tell you, she is not here."

Mpanga the Knife signaled to his assistant.

"Go to the hospital; see for yourself," suggested the chief.

"The others."

"They are none of your concern."

"We'll see."

"I would advise you not to touch them or their houses." The chief raised his right hand and at that moment many among the crowd of villagers bent to pick up objects which lay beside them on the ground. "What do you say?" The chief shouted the question.

"We say, leave our village! Don't touch our friends!" The message, momentarily clear, dissolved into impassioned shouting.

With a whoop, Mpanga swung about, loosening the club that dangled from his belt, hefting it. His men scrambled around him, twisting in and out among each other like a bunch of ants whose nest has suddenly been disturbed, waving their weapons over their heads. The villagers stood before them, a solid shouting wall, and along that wall were those who tensed into warriors' stance, spears grasped firmly.

27

"You will go now. By the way you came." The chief spoke with the authority of the one in command. He pointed, and the feet of those scrambling around suddenly understood the direction they should go. With the sound of many footsteps, they quickly carried out his order. Mpanga and the one carrying the leather bag soon stood alone in the center of the road.

"The governor's office will learn of this." Mpanga's words hissed out in a low snarl. "No foreign parasites will be left to leech our land."

The chief continued to stand where he was, but rather than respond, he simply lifted his arm again and pointed in the way the others had gone. Mpanga had no choice but to follow after his hurriedly departing followers.

At about the time they crested the hill beyond the river, the messenger, who at the chief's signal had slipped away from the crowd, arrived in the field where Marie and her adoptive mother worked. "They did return, and for now they have gone again," he told the women and the girl. "The chief has learned that we have spies in our village, informers, and for that reason you must go into the forest that leads to the other side of the village and hide yourselves until evening. As soon as it is dark, you are to return. You, Mama, must go to your house; and you, Marie, are to come to the chief's house where you will stay for tonight with his daughters."

At the chief's place that night Marie learned that plans for her future had greatly changed.

"And so it is best that you go away for now," the chief told her when he had finished explaining what had happened. "My church has a mission school that is closer to the border of the area of your mother's people. It is a very good school, a place where you can receive schooling that is worthy of the name education, and a place where you will be safe. A merchant will pass here early in the morning and for me he will hide you in the back of his truck. I have money to give you for the crops that are in your fields, and that will be enough to pay your school and to buy the necessary things they ask you to have there. But it is not enough to pay for a place in the dormitory for girls. I will send a letter to my friend in a village near the school—his name is Papa Clement—and though he's a poor man and old, he is very wise and has a good heart. He will give you a place to stay and will tell you what to do."

So it was that Marie had come to school at Mbinda Mission.

Kate drew a deep breath when Marie had finished her story. "I am happy that you are here—happy that you are part of our school, happy that you are safe. I also understand that you usually do well in your studies."

"I enjoy the learning that is to be found in books."

Kate found a certain charm in the village manner with which the girl still spoke. "If you wish to continue doing well, you'll have to do more than pay your school fees and attend class," she said. She paused in order to give the girl's mind time to prepare for the next words she spoke as a mother. "You must also be careful that you eat enough each day."

The girl studied the floor.

"This morning you were too hungry. You cannot be hungry and continue to learn."

"Papa Clement is very old, and he has children of his children living with him whom he must feed. He has been very good to let me make a little house on the parcel of ground behind his house."

"And the money from your own garden?"

"It is gone. I had to pay it all to the school. You know, Madame, these times are very difficult. We in the villages have our gardens, but it is very difficult to get money. The chief's wife and my adoptive mother gave me a sack of cassava to bring."

Kate listened as the girl explained. She already knew something about the hardships of everyday life and had dealt with many hungry people both young and old, but never before had she sat face to face with a school girl who had fled for her life because the blood of her mother's people flowed in her veins.

"Papa Clement is allowing me to cultivate a piece next to his fields, and he has given me a few beans for seed, and a neighbor has given me a few branches of cassava, but it is not yet time for the planting of beans, and the cassava will not be ready to eat for two years' time. I have asked for work, but no one in the village has patience for a student who can only work in the evening. And here at the mission . . ." The girl continued to study the floor. "I asked Mademoiselle Luanne and Madame Carole, but they already have all the workers they need. I wanted to ask you too, Madame. But I could see without asking that you also have more than enough workers."

"That is so," Kate agreed then quickly added, "but I still do need someone to help me mark notebooks for the younger classes, someone who is a good learner and quick. The problem is that since we already do have so many workers—I don't have enough money to pay for that work. If you would be willing to do it, though, I could pay you with food. Each week a quantity of rice, some vegetables, and some milk."

Marie looked up. "I would be very happy to do that." Her eyes looked hopeful. "And I would be very happy if you would pay me with food."

"Then if you promise to come to work on each Tuesday afternoon, I'll get some things for you now." Kate excused herself and in a few minutes returned with a bulging green plastic bag. "I've added some vegetable seeds," she said, holding the bag toward Marie.

"Oh, thank you, Madame, thank you so much. Oh, how can I even thank you enough when I have nothing to give you. Only God knows how to thank you enough." The words flowed almost nonstop as Marie stood and took the bag with both her hands as one always does when one wishes to show appreciation, and she curtsied in the polite way of her people. "May God bless you for your kindness. Madame, may God multiply His blessings upon you and the work you are doing here. Madame, I have no thanks to give you, only my prayers for you and your family." She curtsied again.

30

"You're very welcome." Kate was smiling, and her smile, as much as anything, served to cover her near-embarrassment at the profusion of words that tumbled from the girl's mouth. "Remember, though, this is not a gift. There is something you can give me in return, and that is work well done."

"Oh, Madame, I promise to work well. I'll be here on Tuesday as you ask. I promise . . ."

"I'm here!" George's voice sang in from the side door. "Sorry I'm late. Oh! I see you have company."

"Marie's just leaving." Kate nodded to the girl and walked with her to the door. "She stopped by to see about her new job—she'll be helping me correct math papers." Then before George could react she quickly added, "Mbayo has lunch on the table—waiting."

"You're needing more help?" George's comment came when they

were alone and at the table. "But I thought . . ."

Kate shrugged. "She collapsed in class this morning. Hasn't eaten for about three days."

"But we've already reached the limit to our budget for helping students, and you promised . . ."

"George, this is the girl they were telling about—the one a lake area chief saved from the "red bands" and sent here. If she has to leave school, she has nowhere to go. Besides, she's agreed to work for food, and we have that huge bag of rice, and . . ."

George sighed, but the unmistakable beginnings of a smile helped to soften the tiredness Kate saw in his face.

"Marie's special," she hastened to add, "and we're not going to be sorry about giving her a chance."

George raised one eyebrow and tipped his head, and the smile grew more definite. "They're all special, aren't they?" Then he quickly became serious. "I'm afraid, though, this business of geopolitics is getting worse. I've been picking up vibes from the teachers, and it seems certain staff members hope to see a wave of ethnic cleansing sweep through the mission."

"Here? Mbinda?"

"It seems so." George drew a long breath, "There's too much negative talk lately. For now the lid's on. For how long though?" He shrugged and spread his hands. "All we can do is to hope and pray that it'll calm and go away. If not. If politics don't change, this country could find itself with another war—and if it does, I'm afraid it'll involve our mission and our people and our school."

CHAPTER 5

"You should have seen them, Katie, you should have seen them."
George was grinning when he came in for lunch the next afternoon.
"It was *magnifique!* I tell you, it was absolutely *magnifique!*"

"What was so magnificent?"

Being in a French-speaking country, they, of course, used French
as their working language. Being of solid down-home American stock,
they, of course, spoke English at home; more specifically, they spoke
English of the earthy, West Coast USA variety. Both of them, though,
slipped easily from one language to the other and frequently and on
purpose borrowed words from one language to use in the other. They
called the resulting quaint expressions "Franglicisms."

"Doc and the pastor—and the pastor's been most severely *injured.*"

"What's our good doctor said now?" Kate did not bother to re-
strain her sarcasm.

Verbal insults—especially public verbal affronts—were the high-
est degree of offense one person could commit against another. More
than once George had been called to serve as the moderating influence at meetings between parties involved in a verbal confrontation.
If injured dignities weren't salved with these discussions, individuals
would retreat into hereditary groups and the resulting cold war be-

tween families and clans whose differences reached back many generations could effectively disrupt the work of the entire mission. Missionaries, especially those who were new or those whose personalities did not endow them with a sensitivity to the importance of cultural fine points, could easily transcend the limits of tolerated behavior. George and Kate, soon after their arrival, had learned that it was as important to know who was related to whom as it was to understand the boundaries between polite and proper censure and gross insult. The doctor, on the other hand, seemed to have no time for such niceties, yet for the most part, the people accepted his behavior.

"You know the pastor's son who was asked to take *his presence* away from the mission—the one involved in the drinking and beating incident earlier in the year," George explained. "Well, the mother's been quite sick, and the boy came to see her. With his very own eyes Doc saw the said young man walking by the hospital, and as soon as he finished rounds, he headed for the pastor's house. I happened to be at the primary school director's house next door, talking outside, when Doc marched into the yard and up to where the pastor and son were sitting."

As George detailed the ensuing sequence of events, Kate had no trouble visualizing what happened. Ryan Bellington, MD, was one of those enigmas who moved in and out of their lives, belonging, yet not belonging. The only doctor for miles in every direction, he couldn't have been more capable at filling the hospital post. A skilled surgeon, he was quick, aggressive, and sure in the operating room. Beyond that, he was an apt medical man known for his ability to diagnose difficult cases. As chief of the hospital, he did great, but as chief of the mission . . . well, she considered his being placed in charge as another of those quirks the higher administration of the church delighted in foisting on a remote mission, and as George continued his story, she could easily visualize Ryan, long white coat, businesslike over his trim frame, turning on the boy.

"What are you doing here?" he demanded. Then before the boy had a chance to speak, he barged ahead. "Into the house! Get your

33

things! Go! You know better than to be here!"

The boy, without speaking, got up and went into the house. Then Ryan turned on the father who by now was also on his feet, his short, rotund being blocking the path toward the front steps. "The boy has just come to see . . ."

Ryan didn't allow the father further time. "He's not to be on the mission! Committee action! And you know it!"

"But . . ." The pastor bounced upward onto his toes in the way he had when he endeavored to increase his stature before those who towered over him.

That was the moment when what verbal restraint Ryan had been employing vanished, and his words rushed out, loud, harsh, and fast. That was also when the neighbors, adults as well as children, began to collect around the perimeters of the pastor's front yard, standing along the low-clipped and somewhat ragged hedge of pencilbush.

"You know that drunkard's been banned from the mission and that you as father are to see that he stays off our property. What? Are you blind?" Ryan's arm pumped and his pointing forefinger shook in rapid rhythm to his speech.

Against the machine-gun staccato of the onslaught, the stubby pastor bounced on his toes like a diminutive boxer bobbing up and down. "But . . . But . . . He . . ." His efforts to speak became little more than one-word jabs.

"Are you trying to make me into a monkey?" Ryan stormed.

An almost audible gasp passed over the growing group which by now had worked itself through gaps in the hedge and pressed around the two men. That word. One must never allude that the primate to which it refers has any likeness to human kind.

"Of course," George added as he concluded his recitation, "that question was quickly twisted into a statement by those who belong to the pastor's side, and now mission undercurrents are buzzing with the fact that Doc called the pastor a monkey!"

Kate winced. "That's not good!"

"Yeah. Two years ago if the authorities had wanted to make a case, they'd have given poor Doc forty-eight hours to clear out of the country. Now. . . . That's why I've promised Doc I'd meet with them here at our place this afternoon."

"Who all's coming?"

"Just Doc, the pastor, and the Bible teacher."

"I don't know what would happen to this mission without you." Kate shook her head from side to side. "If you weren't here, who would help rescue Ryan Bellington from himself?"

That afternoon Kate had more than enough schoolwork to keep herself hidden away in the study when Ryan and the others came. For her, one of the major pluses mission life offered was Mbayo and the other workers who cooked and cleaned and washed clothes by hand and answered doors and kept the woodbox filled and ironed and ran errands and otherwise freed missionaries from a number of the tedious tasks inherent in running a household in an area that lacked most of the amenities one took for granted in everyday American life. As usual, she'd left the after-lunch cleaning up to Mbayo, and then on her way to the study paused by the full-length mirror that hung opposite the bathroom door. Sunlight angling through the bathroom window sharpened the reflection. What she saw brought her to a full stop.

"Sick!"

She'd aimed the word directly at the mirror. At the time they'd left the States it had been used to describe anything not good.

"You look sick!"

And her hands reached up to tug at the collar of her dress. She'd never before noticed how the pale yellows and muted grays of that material brought out the sallowness of her complexion.

"Mummy!" Memories of Kimmie's advice during last furlough cut through her shock at the aging reflection staring back at her. "Keep bright colors in your wardrobe. Pinks and roses and lilacs and greens— they're the happy colors for you."

Kate looked above the sallowness, and automatically her hand went up to poke back the clump of curls that insisted on drooping onto her forehead. As she did so, realization hit home that what all three of the children said was true—wearing her perm wash-and-wear did nothing to flatter her face. She'd grown up with ears full of repeated warnings that a woman's beauty must not come from outward adorning. Even now, the only extravagance of adornment she allowed herself was the simple gold band that circled her ring finger. Otherwise, the warnings that had shaped her way of thinking had made it convenient to slip into doing just the minimum to keep herself neat, tidy, clean, and. . . . Again echoes of Kimmie's voice broke into her thoughts.

"The Bible doesn't say you have to look bad, does it Mummy?"

The innocence of that question back when their second daughter was a just-turned teenager had startled Kate. "No! Not at all," She'd replied then.

"And if Christians look grungy or weird, that really wouldn't make others want to know about their Jesus, would it?"

"No."

"There's a difference, isn't there, between looking good and being too showy?"

Kate had agreed, though by that time she wondered where the reasoning of their petite little darling with her flair for the beautiful was leading.

"Then we shouldn't look too bad and we shouldn't look too good— so, we should use just enough makeup to make us look good, but not too good? Shouldn't we?"

After that day "Not too bad and not too good" became their catch-phrase.

"Not too bad and not too good." Kate repeated the words tentatively, and a slight smile helped to lift some of the dullness from the face looking back from the mirror. She took for granted that others saw what she considered herself to be—a rather average middle-aged, middle-sized individual, medium tall, moderately plump, slightly round-shouldered and round-faced, neither pretty nor, as her mother used to say, homely. But what she saw now . . .

Instead of going on into the study, she went to get the butane curling iron the girls had given her and her cosmetic bag, and twenty minutes later the mirror reflection she saw appeared years younger. She found a loose-fitting red blouse and a flared navy skirt, exchanged the dull cotton dress she'd been wearing for them, and slipped into a pair of navy pumps.

"Wow!" George's exclamation caught her just as she started back toward the hall mirror. "Is this the same woman I had lunch with?" He held his arms out to her. "Whatever you've done to yourself, do it again."

Kate felt herself blushing. "I . . ." Suddenly she realized that she didn't really know how to fit into words what she wanted to say. "I'm glad you like it," she concluded hastily.

"Doc's just come in the gate." George's reply seemed miles away from their conversation. "And I realized I'd better get a notebook. Who knows what notes I have to make." He caught her hand and leaned over and kissed her. "You look good, babe. And I like what I see." He raised his eyebrows in that special way he had.

"Thanks." Kate smiled, and the smile was an unconscious and natural part of her.

In the study, her journal lay open on the desk. A question she'd blocked in red letters the day before stared up at her.

"What is truth?"

She started to close the notebook, but the question had lately become such a part of her that she paused, and an underlined bit she'd added that morning caught her attention.

"Offer yourself as a living sacrifice."

Abruptly, she saw the two fragments as question and answer. She flipped the notebook closed, pushed it to the side of the desk, picked up the tan and maroon Kikuyu basket, the one she'd bought on their last trip through Nairobi and used for carrying her schoolwork, took out a stack of soft-backed notebooks, and set them in the middle of the desk. But rather than sitting down to her work, she went to the window and stared out. The afternoon was clear and sunny. Only a few fluffs of cloud dotted the sky, leaving the world a happy combination of blue heaven and green earth. Those details became lost to her, though, as she pondered over the parallel between truth and sacrifice. "If in Bible times the best of the flock, healthy and unblemished, was what God required, then those now who offer themselves to carry God's truth need to give of their best, and that includes looking good."

That made sense.

She turned, forced herself to go to her work, and before long became lost to her surroundings. Then she was aware of voices—two very loud and very harsh voices—filtering into the study from the direction of the living room. She recognized both of them—the strained nasal tones that could belong only to Dr. Ryan Bellington when he became unnerved and the charged baritone of their church pastor.

"No! No! No! No! No!" she heard Ryan yelling.

"Doctor!" The retort was explosive.

Kate forced herself to not listen, but she could not escape realization that battle was in progress and its heatedness caused her own nerves to tense. Sometimes a third and even a fourth voice joined the first two, though they were quieter and more calm. Then the discussion settled into more even tones, and she was again able to lose herself in her work. At last, she arrived at the bottom notebook, and when that was finished and all were neatly back into her basket, she realized that the house had become very still.

Curious about the outcome, she went out to find George, but near the living-room door she became conscious that someone was still speaking, though now in subdued tones, and she tiptoed quietly to peek around the corner. Four men, two white and two black, knelt in the center of the room with their arms locked around each others' shoulders.

CHAPTER

6

An envelope lying on the corner of the table caught Kate's eye. It was the thin, off-white, almost-square, red-and-blue bordered sort with "By Air Mail" stamped in a block of blue in the bottom left corner. Everyone used that kind of envelope—they were the only ones available at the markets, and Kate herself bought them in packets of twenty bound together with a paper strip marked plainly "Flying Eagle. Made in China." It wasn't the envelope itself that attracted her attention, though, but the return address. She could see that it had been opened. A slap of anger tightened across her heart.

"Trust me, he says?"

She reached out to pick it up then let her hand drop and forced herself to turn away from it and from the table. The sounds of Ryan's and the pastor's voices carried in from the porch with their leave-takings, and a moment later George came back into the room.

"Doc left this letter for you." He held out a proper business-sized envelope bearing the official mission imprint. "Says it's in your department and wants your opinion."

She choked back what she'd been thinking, took it, noticed it was addressed to Ryan and that it also had been opened, then pulled the letter out and read. "Grr-reat!" The word exploded through her lips, and she looked straight at George. "They expect me to teach full time—to classes so full that kids are literally sitting on the wall—and to run a household in this place with no electricity and with water that when it does run is so contaminated it can almost literally stand on end! And . . ." She clipped off the words that started to come and instead said, "And now . . .twenty-eight people are coming because . . ." She lifted the letter and began reading in stilted rhythm. "You'll be pleased to know that it has been decided that it would be refreshing to hold annual committees in the wholesome atmosphere of your Mbinda Mission."

"Refreshing? For me? And for Luanne and Carole? The ones who'll have to do all the work?" The questions came out like a series of punches directed at George as if he, alone, were responsible for the inconvenience. Then her eyes turned quickly toward the other envelope on the table, and she started to open her mouth again.

"It'll be a challenge!"

The positive lift to the way George said "challenge" pulled her attention back to the letter she held. "A challenge! It's challenge enough to live here without taking care of a week-long invasion of living-breathing-eating-drinking-and-expecting-a-comfortable-bed-to-sleep-in-every-night group of twenty-eight!"

"You've been wishing out loud for more stimulating company to talk to."

"Certainly not in groups of twenty-eight!"

"You have Mbayo."

"It takes her all morning just to sweep the floor and to get lunch for only two of us. Do they realize what they're asking?"

George started to lift his hands in mock protection from her tirade but let them drop.

"We can hardly find enough semicapable house help for the few mission homes we have here without which help, we spouses . . ." She emphasized the current mission cliché that had replaced the word *wives*. "We spouses would never be able to work because everything has to be done from scratch and on stoves that gobble wood that has to be cut and carried long distances only to give off unpredictable heat. And then the food has to be kept in one of these indescribable kerosene monoliths—that someone had the audacity to classify as refrigerators and that are as liable to be hot as they are to be cold." The fury that had gripped her inspired an eloquence she seldom aired. "We have no stores within a day's drive. We have no food like they have in the city except for the few things we've had shipped in and have kept hoarded for our families. And where'll they sleep—in hospital beds? When Ryan and Luanne can hardly find places enough to put all their patients?"

At this point George did lift his hands. "OK. I give." By experience he knew that once she'd worked through the outer layer of emotion, she would come to the place where they could discuss the issue. "They must have lots of confidence in your capabilities."

"Capabilities? What are they expecting—for us to perform a miracle of loaves and fishes for a group made up mostly of vegetarians who won't even eat the fish?" She clasped her hands together and unconsciously began to twist at the gold band which circled her ring finger. "You got a letter too." She swung her left hand abruptly in the direction of the table.

"Yeah." The word rode an aspiration of surprise. "Another pastor. Applying for the summer seminar."

"Oh." At the answer, the impulse to rapid-fire speech suddenly drained away, and she wished the sight of that envelope hadn't made her so jumpy. "If you happen to see Ryan tonight, tell him I think he should send a message to mission headquarters." Her voice was regaining its usual matter-of-factness. "I think they should rethink their plans for having committees here at Mbinda, but if they're adamant about that idea—preposterous as it is—they should at least make a workable proposal. And while you're at it, tell him that I want an inquest into the theft of our pineapple."

CHAPTER

7

Kate sat in the study, a book in her hands when George came in later that evening. "I talked to Ryan about your—uhm—reluctance—to have the committees here."

"Good." Guilt over her first reaction made the word sound strained.

"He's promised to send the message on in the morning." George set his briefcase on the floor, and as he dropped onto the study couch, he forced his eyes to open wider in that way he had. "Mmmmm." He drew the sound into one of satisfaction. "You do look good."

Kate felt herself flush.

"And I asked him to put your missing pineapple on the agenda. And the diesel."

"Diesel?"

"Someone cut the measuring stick in the mission shop—at the ten liter mark—and Lloyd got this great idea to check the barrels. Wouldn't you know it—every barrel measured exactly 200 liters—with the short stick! Twenty barrels! Each missing ten liters! Katie, some crafty someone's made off with enough of our fuel to fill a whole barrel!

"What'll they think of next?"

"Only time will tell, my dear. Only time will tell." George shook his head. "Oh, before I forget, Rene's coming next week. Wants to stay with us."

"Good. Which day?"

"Tuesday-Wednesday." Their itinerant development director's schedule was unpredictable at best. With the heavy rains and the condition of the roads, his timing would be even less exact.

"Is he bringing mail? Haven't heard from the kids since . . ." She let her voice trail.

"Hope so."

Now. This evening. Talk to him about it. An almost voice seemed to speak the command into her thoughts, and she twisted herself quickly about in the chair, drawing her legs up, tucking her feet under her body, and curling into herself as if in that position she could ward away the irritation. "Did you see the chairs?" she asked. She needed something to blot over the uncomfortableness she felt. "The ones from the Loma woodcarver."

"That's what I saw out on the patio?"

"Umm-hum. Jonas put them in the storeroom for now. I was thinking—if we moved that one out." She pointed to the large chair by the bookcase. "Rearranged things . . ."

"Mmmmm," George said again, but in a very different way from when he'd come in, for he'd already picked up a magazine. "Whatever." His voice barely cleared the edge of the page. "Sounds good to me."

"Maybe I'll get Jonas to help me on Sunday. You'll like . . ." But Kate found herself speaking to the magazine's cover, so she turned back to her own reading. Sometimes she wished their lives followed more closely the pattern of the characters in the books she owned. Caught in the words of a story, right looked so right and truth so evident and choices so obvious, so dramatic, that compared to their day-to-day lives . . . "Missionaries!" She found the word ironical. The saintly people she'd found in the stories of her childhood, well. . . . She could never dare put on paper all the reality of the mission life she had come to know.

She remembered a favorite teacher saying to her class: Reading a well-written book can take us to many places, introduce us to many people, and teach us many truths. It can bring tears, or it can bring laughter. It can even bring conviction, but the real test is this—does it help you to understand the truth of life?"

Truth? She considered the word.

"Know what I think, Katie?"

George's question from behind his magazine broke into her thoughts. "No! What?"

"Someday you should write a book."

"Me? A book?" The idea shocked her. "Whatever about?"

"Oh. About life. About the mission. You're good with words—always putting things in your journal. You've got a way of seeing into people. With your honest good sense, you could tell it—well, like it really is." He stopped, and a lopsided smile worked across his face, as it did when he had something he really wanted to tell her but was sort of embarrassed about putting into words. She waited, not just to give him time to say what he wanted to say but because of her surprise at how what he was saying overlaid her own thoughts. "You could write about us—the sinning saints of Mbinda."

44

"The sinning saints!"

She caught his eyes with hers, and suddenly she remembered that letter on the table and the address and the mention by a teacher of George's stopping at the pastor's home in that very town . . . and to her worry about . . . about those things . . . things they'd promised each other never again to mention. Then the prodding, moments before, to talk to him . . .

"The sinning saints?" she repeated.

And her mind saw beings with bent halos, smudged wings, and torn robes. She continued to hold his eyes with hers and then, impulsively, she forced a laugh. "Georgie!" she exclaimed, adopting his grandmother's way of talking. "If you don't just beat all!" Then: "About us—*The Sinning Saints!* Maybe." The idea grew as she thought about it. "Maybe someday I'll do just that. Write our story. Write a story that shows the real truth."

A few spatters of rain patted the window, thunder growled somewhere far to the south, and that, for her, provided a way to pull herself back from the caustic remarks she wanted to make and casually turn the conversation. "Thought we were finished with rain for today."

"Seems not."

A momentary glow lighted the distant clouds and faded. Just then a brilliance seemed to flare from one side of the house to the other, followed in an instant by an ear-splitting crash. The house went black.

"Wheeeew!" George whistled. "That was close!"

Kate heard him get up and grope his way along the wall. A moment later their fluorescent solar light blinked on.

"Must have hit the line somewhere and tripped the generator." George sounded disgusted. "Guess I'll have to go over and get Lloyd and then see if we can get it started again."

A stronger rain moved overhead, and another flash of lightning seared from east to west, and within seconds more thunder boomed and rumbled. "Maybe you should wait till the storm moves a bit," Kate suggested. "Kids in the dorms won't mind; the hospital has its backup solar system. Those've been a great invention for places like this—we sure do use the one you put in for us."

"Rene says they're on the way out for development projects."

"Whyeverfor?"

"High investment for short-term returns."

"Short term?"

"Upkeep problems. Carelessness. The usual other. Like the missing diesel at the shop. You know what they say: He who works at the hotel, eats at the hotel. So . . . project director has brother who has brother-in-law who has vehicle that needs battery. Solar systems operate with batteries. Battery disappears. System can't run without battery. New battery costs money."

"Yeah." Kate sighed. "George?"

"Mmmmm?"

"Do you think we—missionaries in general—the sinning saints that we are," and she paused and in the pale light saw that he smiled at her use of his term. "Do you think that what we're doing—here where ethics of some tribes say that to take something in order to help your family is not stealing—do you think we're having a positive impact? That we really are helping the people to understand Christianity? To understand truth?"

"I think . . ."

Footsteps running up the walk and onto their porch clipped short any explanation of what he thought. Someone pounded on the door. "Mr. Director! Mr. Director!"

Kate recognized the voice of Enock, the senior boy's prefect. Two other voices she could not identify echoed his calls.

"Mr. Director! Quick!"

Both of them were on their feet. Kate grabbed a flashlight off her desk and followed George to the door. Three boys, soaked and wild-eyed, stood on their porch. "Mr. Director! The lightning! It hit our dormitory! And Sylvanus! Fire came out of the walls! And he's not breathing!"

46

CHAPTER

8

When Kate reached the long, squat building that served as living quarters for a hundred fifteen boys, strands from the dull flickering of a kerosene lamp showed through one window, marking vague outlines of a crowd jammed around the entryway. She spoke to the figures on the fringe, and along whispered commands, a gap opened just wide enough for her to push through, then closed. From the doorway she could see that Sylvanus was stretched out on the lower bed of one of the pipe-framed double-bunks that crowded the room. Someone at the foot of the bed held a lantern at shoulder height, but its glare blocked view of the holder's face while it spread light against Ryan bending over the boy. Another someone held another lantern on the other side of the bunk, and she could see George and the boys' dean. She went around to stand by George. "Is he . . .?" She whispered.

George shook his head. "Doc's tried CPR."

Just then Ryan slipped the stethoscope from his ears and let it drop down around his neck. "Get some fellows to ask the night nurse to send a stretcher from the hospital." He had stepped back to speak around the end of the bed to the dean then he addressed himself toward George. "And send someone for the pastor and the Bible teacher. You'll need them."

A pall of silence lay over the crowd at the door. Kate stared down at the boy, his dark features quiet and his lanky body still against the lumpy navy surface of the bamboo-leaf-filled mattress tick. The collar of his uniform shirt with the school crest stamped on its pocket lay open at his neck, but blotches of mud marred the shirt's whiteness, and more patches of the same red-brown were caked along a leg of his trousers as if the boy had fallen. Kate took an involuntary step backward. Just that morning Sylvanus had been in her classroom, a serious, methodical boy. Promising. The previous weekend he'd taught the lesson in one of the children's story-hour groups. The day before he'd been at their house. Now, he lay there, looking as peaceful and relaxed as if he were in a deep sleep. Her eyes began to sting, and she felt a choking in her throat. She took a deep breath and tensed her throat muscles and sensed, more than saw, that a diffused pale cream momentarily reflected against the windowpane and cast shadows along the bunks that blocked her vision into the rest of the room. The glow faded, and some moments later there was a muffled growling of thunder. The rain had stopped, but a new noise, rhythmic and haunting, pulsed through the night. A boy disengaged himself from the others, broke past Kate, and flung himself across the still form on the bed. "Tu-tu, tu-tu." His cries wove into a sing-song, a solo standing out against the sobbing wails of those outside the door. "Big Brother, don't leave us. Tu-tu. Big Brother. We need you."

The men stood where they were, letting the youngster cry out, letting him call to his older brother, letting his words will his brother to return from the unknown where his life had gone. Kate watched. And in her silence her heart cried out its own hurt, its own agony, but her words were mute, unable to put themselves into sounds that could blend with the loud, compulsive outbursts that now filled the room. More boys pushed in, their cries growing until the walls seemed to vibrate with the wails that come in the presence of death and are exacted of those who mourn. She became conscious of a warm dampness on her own cheeks.

"Come."

She felt George's hand on her arm, and her legs mechanically moved in steps to match his as he led her through the wailing crowd and out the open door.

The evening was fresh, as it always is immediately after a storm, and the drops of water that released themselves and clung to her arm as she brushed against a stand of the tall grasses were simply just there. She did not bother to wipe them off. She moved one foot ahead of the other. The suddenness. The shock. "Life. Death. One instant. Only one instant apart."

She remembered a weekend visit at Rolling Hills Mission years earlier. They had sat on the very last bench during the church service. Suddenly a flash reflected along the windows. Kate was not aware of having heard any sound of thunder, but in that same instant she felt her feet seize to the floor. George pitched forward from where he'd been leaning against the back wall, and her body wrenched from the jolt that seared in through her shoulder which was touching him and out through her other side. The congregation sat stunned, silent. No one was hurt, but her mind turned over and over with the sober realization that her own life, the lives of all she loved, could end like that, in one strike, without forewarning, in a moment so quick, so sudden, that it could not be measured. And now. Sylvanus. And only six weeks had passed since she'd received the telegram.

"Telegram."

The word mocked the eight days the message had taken to reach them. Will, her youngest brother on his way to work, had been hit head-on by a drunk driver careening the wrong way along the Interstate. Just like that. Instantly. Suddenly. One moment he was a living, breathing young man, in the pickup he'd customized himself. The next, dead. Gone. Forever taken from their lives. Leaving Giselle only eight months before their June wedding that now could never be. There'd been no goodbyes. None.

"He was a good kid." She'd almost forgotten why she was walking—by George who was holding her arm—along the rain-soaked path—under the dark African sky—spatters of rain still dropping on them.

"Sylvanus?"

"Will," she replied.

49

After the first shock of the telegram, then the letters that marvel-ously had arrived within two weeks carrying the details, she and George had hardly mentioned the accident. She didn't want to. They were so far away. So cut off from the family. Without telephone, without di-rect communication. The kids had gone to the funeral. All three of them. All wrote. So had Giselle.

"Your letter arrived just three days before," she said. "Will showed it to me. I know he would want me to tell you this, because, as he said, it was one of those special letters that arrive so seldom in a life-time. He always looked up to you, you know. We talked about things, and he said that he wanted our marriage to be like yours, solid, with God as a partner."

"Like ours?" Kate's steps still matched George's, but the light from his flashlight had become nothing but a faint blur, and she let him guide her along the path its beam traced.

Will had been one of those tagalongs who didn't arrive till she was in college. She'd not really known him as a kid, but they'd always kept in touch, and when he finished college and was setting up his own business, she'd blocked aside at least one day during furloughs just for him. Especially after the death of their mother. They wrote, though not often, and then one evening for no particular rea-son that she could think of, she had a compulsion to write, to share some big-sisterly thoughts with him.

"It's very easy to get so wrapped up in everyone else's needs," she remembered telling him, "that we can forget our own. Here the sick, the hungry, the near-naked, even our students who have so little and need so much, the ones of the 'inasmuch' can keep us too busy. Doing good deeds, being a helpful neighbor down the street, even being a missionary doesn't give anyone a special pass to heaven—each one of us must invest personal time in getting to know God, to really know Him, and that's the secret of how to become like Him." Then she'd talked about the time that she hoped they could spend together dur-ing their next furlough. Now she still had to adjust to the idea that he wouldn't be there when she arrived home.

"Careful. Here's the turn for our path."

George's voice broke into her thoughts.

"I'm afraid this is going to be a long night." He slipped his arm around her waist. "The uncle over in Lubombo probably already knows. I can drive him, the younger brother, the pastor, and other family members to Loma. Lloyd can come with the body in his pickup." He spoke of his immediate duties, organizing details in his mind as he talked. "I'll probably not be back till after midnight. Then tomorrow we'll use the mission truck to take a choir and friends and relatives to the service."

Sylvanus's home village of Loma was some thirty-two kilometers away by road.

"I can tell the parents that you'll be there for the service tomorrow?" George was asking.

"Yes. Are you and Lloyd going to try to fix the generator before you go?" Her mind began to clear and to deal with the duties that lay before them. "It'd help."

"We'll give it a quick look. I'll take the pickup now and stop by for Lloyd. If the pastor or Doc come by, tell them we've gone to the shop. They can count on us to drive to Loma." About fifteen minutes later the lights flicked back on; then after another twenty minutes George was back. "All arranged," he announced. "This is terrible."

In the light of the house, Kate could see the creases of worry on his forehead, and her own feelings widened and reached out to include him, the director in charge of a boarding school in which a student had just been killed.

"An oldest son. Killed by lightning. The shock of that, plus . . ."

The choppiness of his speech, the way he looked at her, warned that the complications of local superstition were at work. She reached toward him. "People are already talking?"

He nodded and took her hands and pulled her toward him. "They're saying the guilty person is within the family—an aunt, an older sister of the father. Her son failed and had to drop out of school last year. Sylvanus has been doing too well—besides, he's been getting scholarship assistance so he could stay in the dorm."

Whenever anyone died, even among many of the families who attended church, there were always undercurrents of talk. Nothing ever just happened—not sickness, not bad luck, not accidents, not death. Everything was always caused by someone—someone either living or dead. When lightning struck, it was taken for granted that someone had paid for it to be called down by a lightning lancer, a witch doctor with powers to direct the strike at a particular individual.

"Are the parents Christian?" she asked.

"Only the uncle who lives here. The father and mother belong to an indigenous African group who follow a self-styled prophet with the gift of healing, they say. Saw him once—dressed in a long white robe with heavy red embroidery."

"Will our pastors be able to conduct the service?"

"Likely. The boy was our student, and the uncle here is older brother to the father, so he'll be very influential in what's done."

"But lightning struck our school and killed him. What are people going to think about the power of our God when He didn't protect the boy?"

"Oh! That's right. You didn't come till later. The boy was outside—without permission—on his way to get something from a friend who lives over in the nurses' quarters. From what we could see, lightning hit the olive tree across from the dormitory, and a side flash struck the corner of the dorm, knocking off some bricks and breaking a couple of windows. The boy was by the tree— the others found him when they ran outside to escape when sparks shot out of the electrical outlets. If he'd been in the dorm . . ."

Kate nodded. Neither life nor death followed a predictable course. And she thought of the tree standing beside the church at Rolling Hills. It also was struck by lightning and had died and needed to be removed. None of the local woodcutters, though, could be persuaded by the missionaries to cut it down.

"Too dangerous," one of the African pastors had finally explained. "It they touch it, the spirits of the lightning will come to get them."

CHAPTER

A parade of large cumulus rode above the mission, vivid against the sky's clean, bright blue, growing larger as they bobbed along, their billows stretching upward and outward like huge balloons being blown up by some invisible giant. Many had clean, sharp edges; others had begun fraying, the snatches of vapor stretching away like so many bits of cotton being pulled loose to drift on their own. Kate watched from the cane chair on their front porch, and she felt herself beginning to relax. The sun filtered down and around the clouds, hot, yet not as oppressive as it had been the previous week, and its brightness highlighted the mango trees. She liked the big trees. Wide and well-leaved, they locked branches into a shady arch along much of Pioneer Way—the road that cut straight in from the mission's main entrance—where they'd been planted by one of the first missionaries. They again hung heavy with the oblong fruit that was just coming into season.

When she and George had first arrived in Mbinda, neither of them could stand the taste of the juicy, orange-fleshed, somewhat perfume-flavored fruit. Now she couldn't imagine a Christmas season without mangoes. "Maybe it won't be easy," she told herself, wondering how she would react if or when the time came for them to pull themselves away from Mbinda and go home and fit back into the life they'd once known.

Attending Sylvanus's funeral the day before had in a strange way served briefly as a focal point for bringing together the two worlds that were now hers. Instead of having to slip between the part of herself which belonged so strongly to the ways of the home they'd left behind and the part that had begun to assimilate aspects of the culture in which they now lived, she found the pieces overlapping, blending. She'd sat on the perimeters of the little adobe village sanctuary, uncomfortable on one of the flat-seated, straight-backed wooden chairs that had been brought in and positioned along the side wall at the front for the teachers and other visitors of rank from the mission, and found herself not only looking in on but being a part of the ritual. The hard, sharp-angled seat and the single narrow crosspiece of the chair's back caused her to cast envious glances toward those who pushed together on the more-comfortable, backless, mat-covered rows of plastered-over bricks that formed the church pews. Squeezed in among the women on one of those benches, the physical closeness would have helped her to express a oneness not only in grief but in the understanding of the hardships of life. But because of her position, she was expected to sit apart. Even had she been one of them, her position at the school would have exacted that. And now the sharp edges of the chair's crosspiece cut into her back, and inwardly she squirmed with discomfort, though her only outward manifestation was to turn slightly and lean so that her shoulder braced against the wall, and the coolness of the porous mud bricks soaked through the double fabric of the African dress she wore. It felt good.

A subtle fetidness, the odor of too many living bodies packed into too small a space, filled the church, and the dark faces of all those who couldn't find a place inside were pushing into the naked window openings in the adobe walls, blocking what circulation there might have been. This made her glad for the nearness of the door, opening into the little cubicle that served as an elder's room.

Across on the other side of the church on another set of built-in brick benches that paralleled the side walls sat the school choir—the group in which Sylvanus had sung. Only now, instead of sitting with his group of singers, he lay on a reed mat supported by the hospital stretcher that earlier in the morning had been moved from his home and placed in the open area between where she sat and where the choir sang. His still body was covered with a sheet as was the custom in this economy that made wood for building a coffin unaffordable. Kate recognized the sheet. The solid letters stamped in the bottom corner identified it as one from the medical center in the States that had donated several cartons full of old but still usable linens to them when they were on furlough. Most of the dormitory students had no coverings of any kind for their beds, and she'd seen that each received a pair of sheets.

The boy's mother crouched against the stretcher, head in hands. Her blouse hung from her shoulders, which from time to time heaved with silent sobs, and her mismatched skirt cloths of the double wraparound, which all the women wore, were wrinkled and faded. Another woman sat on the floor beside her, perhaps an aunt of the boy. A brother from the extended family hunched at the end of the first of the low benches, guarding a small, knotted cloth bundle between his feet—Sylvanus's earthly belongings.

Kate felt someone touch her arm and heard the low, coarse voice of the old pastor sitting beside her. "Look!" he whispered. "The belly!" He pointed, and her eyes followed the indication of his bony finger, and she felt her own stomach tighten. "It's bloating."

As if to emphasize the truth of what the pastor said, the sheet gave a series of quick twitches, and she saw that it seemed to raise a little higher.

"I hope they hurry before it bursts."

The sheet hitched again, then settled. Across from her the members of the choir seemed to gasp a collective breath in their song and then pitch into the high lead note of the next phrase. In her ears, their harmony splintered into a near dozen individual thready tones then glided into a collective moan. She swallowed hard. The pastor beside her had a lifetime of experience in villages with more than their share of death, where tropical temperatures and lack of mortuary facilities impelled a quick, even a same-day interment. Though she had attended some funerals in the mission church, this for her was a new experience, and she forced her eyes to focus on the small bundle caught between the feet of the brother and avoided looking back at the sheet-covered body on the stretcher. She swallowed again and willed herself to properly hear the melody the choir sang. Then a sudden stir over the audience did cause her to look around, and she saw that those taking part in the service were filing onto the platform. George, as well as the school pastor, would speak.

In the mute light filtering into the thatched building, George appeared unusually pale, that paleness being accentuated by the black suit he wore and the stark white shirt and the dark tie. The roundness of his normally firm cheeks seemed to sag, and he looked tired, very tired. Among the confusion of her other feelings, Kate found compassion. Never before had her husband officiated at a funeral. In fact, as he had confided to her years before, it was his abhorrence at having to deal with death and the dying and mourners that had caused him long ago to abandon his boyhood dream of becoming a pastor and decide instead to devote his life to education and school administration. A good choice, she'd always thought, admiring his talents in dealing with both his students and his teachers. But now that very choice had put him behind the dusty-brown adobe-brick pulpit that looked down on the bier of one of his own students. He stood and laid his Bible on the slanted, mat-covered surface of the pulpit, and Kate felt her hands tense. He looked around the congregation. Then he spoke. And the strength, yet gentleness, of his voice surprised her, and she let her thoughts be carried along as he talked of faith and hope and the resurrection and heaven. The kindness of his words touched her own hurt, and a reality she'd been avoiding did battle with the persisting idea in her mind that Will was still alive and waiting for her to come home. A burning sensation forced behind her eyes as she realized she had to make herself say her goodbyes to those ideas. She had to accept that her little brother was gone, that she must wait, that someday, at the resurrection . . .

When the pastor touched her arm again, she didn't want to let her eyes follow his quiet gesture toward the body. But she did. And she saw that the sheet moved. But this time she did not feel the revulsion that she had felt at first. This was death. And she stared at it and accepted it and was sad. A hollow, lonely, empty sad. And tears burned behind her eyes.

Then they were following the four young men who bore the stretcher toward the cemetery. The entire village population, it seemed, and all the students and teachers, trailed along the unused and overgrown ruts marking the way that vehicles back in more prosperous times had once traveled. Everyone gathered around the open grave—in keeping with their customs the grave diggers had hollowed out a small room to the side of the grave shaft, and after the pastor's few words of final committal, two of the bearers jumped down onto a ledge in the grave to receive the body on its mat. Carefully, quietly, they slid it into the burial room. The brother handed down the cloth bundle he carried and that, too, they placed inside, beside Sylvanus. Then they set a series of poles against the doorway and flattened a mat against them so the earth would not crush in around the body.

57

"Madame." A sudden voice to Kate's right almost made her jump. "He was in your class?"

She nodded.

"And you helped him—with things." A young man she'd seen somewhere before was speaking.

"Some." She looked at her questioner for a moment then added. "He was a good boy. A Christian. We'll see him again when Jesus comes."

"If we believe," the voice said.

Again Kate nodded. "That's something we each must decide for ourselves."

Loma was the largest village in the entire area, the center the paramount hereditary chief used as his headquarters but where Christianity lagged and where the church had the smallest membership of any village in the mission district.

"On the third day they will announce the one responsible," the boy beside her volunteered. "Already the chief has been approached to find which of the lightning lancers did this and to have him imprisoned."

Witch doctors, among them those adept at calling down lightning—for a price, of course—and sorcerers and diviners openly plied their trades in Loma, openly for the villagers, that is. For the missionaries, though, especially those who had not lived in the area for enough years and had not yet earned trust for their understanding, these people blended into the general population in such a way that they were not easily seen.

"One of the village men is now in the prison in town. Madame. It is pitiable. Absolutely pitiable. He has to stay maybe a year or more. In the meantime, his family." And the young man who said his name was Andre spread his hands in the gesture so often repeated to show the hopelessness of a situation. "It is for something in which he had no fault—a fire that he is accused to have set."

58 The villagers were still hunters, though the elephants and larger cats had vanished years before from their hunting territory, and the antelope and other smaller game such as the serval cats and wild boars were becoming more scarce each year. During the long six-month dry season, the men continued to set hunting fires as they always had, and frequently the fires swept out of control, racing across the savanna grasslands, devouring crops in cultivated fields and sometimes sweeping into villages. Evidently the prisoner the boy spoke about had been accused of setting a fire that destroyed the cassava field of someone from a neighboring village.

"He will be held in prison until the price of the field is paid."

Kate's immediate thought was that if he was held in prison where he could not work or even tend his own crops, how could he possibly raise the money to pay for the field, but she had long since learned to hold such questions from her African acquaintances. They had other ways of doing things, and in such a case one in the extended family would be expected to either pay or to find someone who could, and then the prisoner would be freed.

"But just until now, there is no one to help him, and his wife and his children are suffering extremely. A pitiable situation, Madame, very pitiable. I am endeavoring to find some means to help them."

Kate had merely nodded when the story was finished.

CHAPTER

10

"Join us. Food's gone, but we still have chairs."

Kate raised an eyebrow at George, but he ignored its significance and used his foot to push a chair away from the table for their neighbor, Lloyd Parmer, the school's teacher training supervisor.

"Thanks, Prof." Lloyd settled his tall frame on the chair at the end of the table—he and the other missionaries familiarly called George *Prof.* "After such a rough week, are you up to taking a carload out to the village tomorrow afternoon?" He addressed his question to Kate.

"If they're prepared to go?" Kate regularly drove a carload of students into one of the neighboring villages to hold programs for the children.

"They say so."

Their eyes met and both laughed. Kate found herself again being surprised at the clarity of Lloyd's brown eyes and the smooth regularity of his features. So much good looks, poise, and natural good sense in one person continued to amaze her, and having him and his wife, Carole, was, she often thought, one of the greatest assets to their work at Mbinda, especially with the given that mission compounds are notorious for personality conflicts. Missionaries typically are independent and strong-minded—but she and this young French-African were staunch allies in an on-going battle against the ingrained concept that children's programs were unimportant. The notion seemed inherent to all their teacher training students, and, indeed, one common factor among churches of all denominations seemed to be the general lack of children's classes and apparent disinterest in maintaining them if they were instituted. Because of this, they both tried to lead the future teachers under their guidance to an understanding of the importance of child evangelism.

Who's a better example of what children can be taught than Lloyd himself? Kate often thought.

"Tomorrow'll be the test to see if they've caught the idea of planning their own program around a theme." Lloyd's voice, though cheerful, held a hint of skepticism. "Marie's about the only one who's ideas were spot on at our last planning meeting. A bright girl. Says she's working for you now."

"Seems the money she arrived with paid for everything—but food," Kate replied.

"You'll drive then?"

Kate nodded.

"Imagine!" she exclaimed after Lloyd had gone. "Left on a missionary doorstep when he was a baby. I wonder . . ." She looked at George as if he might have the answer. "Do you think it ever bothers him not to know who he really is?"

"Lloyd? No problem."

Kate pushed on with her ideas. "What I mean is . . . well, family and clan and tribe are so important here." She searched for the words to phrase her thoughts. "His folks were stationed so close to the border at that time they can't even be sure of what country he's from. And because of his complexion and features, there's talk that his father may have been Arab—even European."

"What difference does that make?"

"None—I guess. It's just that, well, each person likes to know who he is and where his family comes from. You always hear about adopted kids who've gone in search of their roots. You know, trying to find their real parents."

"Well, Lloyd Parmer certainly knows that he's a child who was well-loved, and I say praise the Lord for missionaries like the senior Parmers—there aren't many families like them out here these days."

"There simply aren't that many missionary families anymore." Kate interjected. "We've got enough houses sitting empty here on our own mission."

"You know what I mean."

Their eyes met, and again Kate felt a rush of confusion.

"That's a family whose service counted for something, who made a real difference by being here."

"Do you think anyone'll ever be able to say that about us— that we'll ever deserve to have it said?" The question was out before Kate realized what she was saying and she rushed on to add, "The Parmer's have given us Lloyd, and I'm so glad he and Carole are here."

Immediately after lunch the next afternoon, Kate eased their pickup out of the garage. George held weekly Bible-study classes for teachers who were recent converts or whose church background was weak, so he was seldom free to go on these village trips. She drove slowly a few hundred meters along Pioneer Way and let the vehicle roll to a stop beside the monument— a stubby stone obelisk that had been designed and built, or so she'd heard, by the first missionary to return to Mbinda after the independence wars of the early 1960s. A school director who, they said, preferred stone masonry to teaching, he'd had the mission drive widened in front of the church and set in the sizable cement pedestal that frequently doubled as bench. Large stones formed the monument itself. Rough, irregular pieces, from an outcropping in the hills south of the mission, fit into a patterning of vibrant rust, shaded with pale creams and browns and silver grays. A cement inset on each side, grayed and weathered by the years, contained this inscription:

IN MEMORY OF OUR PIONEERS
MBINDA MISSION
Est 1923

The sparseness of the words included Africans as well as Europeans because the first missionary had come with three helpers, graduates of the earliest mission training school in the far north of the country.

"We're ready, Madame!"

Marie and five others waited at the monument and wasted no time in arranging themselves in the vehicle—Marie and her friend Jeanne in front, the four boys in back. Lubombo village, only about a seven-kilometer drive from the mission, was also home to Pastor Silas, one of the early church workers. As they approached the village, Kate slowed the pickup sharply, shifted down into second, and swung the wheel this way and that in an attempt to dodge the worst of a series of large mudholes. Then, easing one wheel up onto the roadside bank and the other onto a precariously narrow strip of high center, she tried to straddle a deep, water-filled rut. The ledge crumbled under the left front wheel. With a heavy thud the vehicle hit bottom, then bounced up again, and mud-brown water splashed higher than the hood. Kate held speed, wrenching the wheel hard to the right. The strong back tires cleated in and pushed. With almost more sideways than forward motion, the front wheel dozed its way through the soupy rut then finally climbed onto the dry bank. Kate stopped in the shade of the avocado tree by the chief's house, where the vehicle would be under the watch of trusted eyes.

After greeting the chief and his wife, the students scattered to call the children. Kate, though, backtracked the way they'd come. Mud-brown huts lined the road on either side, their thatched roofs, trimmed smartly around the edges, pitched up into peaks where the weathered-gray grass was stitched into what reminded her of widths of short, off-color broom straws. Some yards held clumps of bananas or mango trees, some had dovecotes, those miniature thatch houses

63

on stilts for the gentle little birds that many of the families kept. Others had similar shelters for chickens.

Some weeks earlier she'd promised to visit Pastor Silas and would do that before joining the students for the main part of their program. As she angled along the path that curved back to a second row of huts, she saw the old pastor, long retired, sitting on a low stool beside his house in the shade. She couldn't help noticing his shoes—their wide cracks, their lack of laces, the way they gaped at the ankles of his sockless feet. He pushed himself stiffly up with his walking stick and then clutching it under his arm reached his hands toward her and silently clapped them together in the gesture of greeting. He called for his daughter, already an old woman herself, who lived next door, and she brought one of those straight-backed wooden chairs that Kate, in her mind, called "company best" and detested because they were so uncomfortable. The daughter placed it by the banana clump at the corner of the house and invited Kate to sit. While they visited, frayed strands of sunlight chased across her lap in constantly changing patterns of sun and shadow as a breeze stirred the tattered outer leaves of the plants.

"It was their singing," Pastor Silas explained, when Kate asked him how the earliest missionaries had gained their first converts. "I was a boy then, maybe seven, maybe nine, anyway of the age to be useful to my parents for watching our goats and also to the missionaries, because I was not too young and not too old to learn to sit in their school."

He told how it had happened that he first heard the singing. "The village elders had been talking in the evening about the man and the woman with pale skin who had come to the flat place above the river, which is near the place of the spirit trees—the place where many years before three large trees had sprung up in a little hollow where water came from the ground. No one went near there, for it was known to be the gathering place of spirits. Anyway, these two white people had come with three Africans, and I remember the hunter who first reported seeing them.

" 'The other three look as normal people should look,' he told us. 'They have dark skin and hair that grows as real hair should grow. But when they open their mouths.' He stopped and spat on the ground as people did then when they wished to have good luck. 'They make sounds that have no real meaning.'

"Others reported that the Paramount Chief had told the pale people and the three normal black people who could not speak properly that they could have that stretch of land at the edge of our village territory for building a school.

" 'Be careful of the white man and his schools,' one very old man warned. 'I know of their schools. They steal the children and give them poison so they forget the ways of their fathers and can follow only the white man's God. Those ways are very dangerous. Be careful that our children are not poisoned.'

"The next morning I convinced my friends that we should take our goats to graze on a flat near there. It was a long walk, and the goats were impatient with our dragging them on their cords so far. We kept well away from the place of the spirit trees, but finally we came to that small rise across from where the hospital is today.

" 'Stake the goats,' I told the other boys. That was something we almost never did. We always just let them go when we were beyond the place of the gardens. Then we crawled up the hill, keeping in the cover of the bushes so no one would see us. Suddenly, from over the hill, I heard sounds such as I had never heard before. In our village, we often sang the old songs of our people that are sung at our feasts and during the night dancing when the moon is big. I loved to sing, and my uncle had already shown me how to make music with the finger piano.

"It was beautiful, that singing. The sounds made no sense, but the melody was like no song I'd ever heard. We hid in the bushes at the top of the hill, and we could see the white man and his wife, and their amazing pale hair that hung like strings from their head, and the three Africans sitting together. After they sang, one of them stood and held something we had never seen before but that we thought might be one of those book things the elders had talked about. And the white man looked at it and made strange word sounds. When he did that, my friends crawled back to where we had left the goats, unstaked them, and hurried away. But I stayed and listened.

"After that, every day that I dared, I would leave my goats with my friends and slip away to hide in the bushes and listen to the music and to the sounds of reading. 'If you tell anyone about this,' I warned my friends, 'I will touch you with the powerful stone my uncle has given me.' My uncle was the strongest witch doctor in our village. 'And your tongue will become dry, and it will fall out, and you will never be able to talk again. And then no girl will ever want to marry you.'

"The threat had its effect. My friends never told. Some days they would even come with me when they saw that what I heard did not harm me. As far as I know, the missionaries never knew we boys were watching, and we kept going back and back for many weeks. In that time, they had begun making some buildings and had found some-one to teach them our language. Then our elders called us together again and said these people were going to begin a school to teach children and that the white man, whose name was Missionary, was going to come and choose children to go to that school.

66

"Well, that created much discussion. Some sided with the old man who had earlier declared that all white men's teaching was dangerous poison. Others thought it might be good if a few of the stronger boys went to the school. Others claimed that the white man had powerful medicine and could cast a spell on the children he wanted and then they could not resist going to his school. Many decided to send their children far away to hide with relatives in distant villages so the missionary would not find them.

"When I heard all that they were saying, I was very happy be-cause I wanted to go and learn how to sing their songs. Already by listening, I had learned some, but I could only sing them inside my mind, for if anyone were to hear me. . . . I had no idea of what might happen, but it could not be good. That night after the people had gone, I went to my father. 'Do you suppose I will be one of the boys chosen for the missionary's school?' I asked. 'I am already very strong and can run very fast, and you know that I have strong protection that our uncle has given us so that I will be in no danger of being poisoned by ideas of their gods.'

" 'Do you wish to go?' he asked.

" 'I think it would be of an advantage to know what they teach,' I said. 'If I am to follow in the work of our uncle, it is good to know about everything that touches the place where we live.'

" 'Aaaaahh, those are wise words for one who has not yet been initiated in the ceremonies for becoming a man. If you wish, you may stay so you will be here on the day they choose boys for their school.' And so it was that I and one of the other herd boys were in the first class of the first Mbinda training school. I told our missionary that I was in school because of the songs, and on the day of my baptism he gave me my new name, Silas, for Paul and Silas sang in prison. And he gave my friend the name of Paul. And he gave me the text in Psalm 40:3 as the promise for my Christian life."

The old man's voice became stronger as he quoted in Swahili: "He has put a new song in my mouth—praise to our God; many will see it and fear, and will trust in the Lord."

From where she sat, Kate could see into the neighboring yards—in most of them, chickens picked for insects or at stray kernels of corn lying on the bare dirt; in one, a dog, its ribs hard against its dull yellow hide and its stomach hollow, lay under a broken cane chair; straw outhouses stood their distance behind several of the huts; ashes and bits of charcoal marked the previous night's cooking fire by the pastor's daughter's house; and a toddler, barefooted and bare bottomed, sat in the dust in front of the hut across the path and chewed on an empty corn cob. A mother and her two daughters walked along the path, straight-sided tin buckets balanced on their heads. All water came from the river on the heads of mothers and their daughters, and, unboiled, served for drinking as well as washing.

I wonder. . . . Kate mused to herself as she listened. *How much has really changed since he was a boy?*

"That new song, the story of how Jesus died for us and is making a home for us in heaven—that gives a hope that our people never before had. Being a Christian . . ." Pastor Silas paused and leaned forward and fixed his eyes on Kate's face. "Being a Christian is having hope."

Kate was thoughtful as she walked back to the meeting tree where more than a hundred children sat on the hard-packed earth, eyes toward the boy telling the story of Jesus feeding the five thousand. Afterward, when they were loading their things back into the pickup, someone touched Kate's arm.

"Do you remember me?"

The voice, the manner, seemed familiar, and then she noticed the bright green shoelaces against impossibly clean white sport shoes.

"Me, Andre. I talked to you at Loma before yesterday. I have received another letter from my friend in prison. I would like to show it to you." And before Kate could reply, he added, "I will come to your house at the mission on tomorrow."

68

CHAPTER

11

Kate paused in the doorway of the study and glanced around the room. "Nice," she complimented herself. She liked the change and wanted to sink down into her corner chair and enjoy the new arrangement and forget about the rest of the world.

"Give to him who asks" (Matthew 5:42).

The command stepped from her conscience, slipping from among the texts with key ideas that years earlier had been forced into her memory, and marched across her thoughts. In reflex, she sucked her bottom lip in and over her bottom teeth and bit down firmly as though a twinge of pain might blot out what she'd told Andre just minutes before:

"I'm sorry, but I can't."

He'd persisted. "But, Madame. He's suffering. You yourself have seen that in his letter." As Andre presented his arguments, Kate had stood before him on the porch, listening, still holding the letter which, as he had promised the day before at Lubombo, he had brought for her to read. The handwriting, the name, both were totally unfamiliar. The story, though, reiterated what he'd recounted on the day of the funeral.

"And you know how prisoners are treated," he continued. "Beatings. No food. Conditions so terrible that even the words needed to describe them are difficult to speak."

Andre's insistence caused Kate to hesitate. George, as usual on a Sunday afternoon, was in some distant part of the mission with Lloyd, checking, repairing, planning—she wasn't sure which or what, for those two never lacked a project to occupy any of what might have been their free time. Mbayo had just left, taking a basket of bananas to the children's ward. Families, as in most African hospitals, had to provide the basic patient care and food, and, according to Ryan, hunger was an underlying cause of most of the medical problems. So she'd sent the bananas with Mbayo. Even Jonas had the afternoon off.

"Madame, if the money isn't paid tomorrow, who can know what might be done to him? He must have help. Now!"

When they had first arrived at Mbinda, the pastor and the woman in charge of the church ladies' group had come to them. "Don't believe all the stories people bring to you," they'd counseled. "Many will come asking for help because they know that missionaries have money. Some will have real needs; others simply know how to tell good stories about terrible things that are not so." Kate and George had at the beginning referred all doubtful cases to one or another of the Africans, but as they became more acquainted with their surroundings and with the people themselves, they began to rely more and more on their own judgment.

"There's no one else who can help." Andre's voice filled with desperation. "When I see how his wife has nothing for the children. And I myself saw last week how he is at the prison. Madame . . ." He paused in a manner that aided comprehension of the results that could not be spoken in plain words. "You are our only hope. You must have pity."

The plea reached into Kate's sense of duty toward her fellow beings. Usually she did what she could to relieve suffering, for, if at all possible, she wished to escape any responsibility before God that could become hers by refusing the help that might aid one of His human children.

"Madame. You are the only one who can help."

The words were forceful this time, and Kate responded by handing back the letter. "No." She shook her head firmly. "I'm not the only one."

Andre slipped the paper under his arm and held out his hands, again, in that eloquent gesture of total lack that many others who had stood before her on the porch had used when coming to beg for her compassion. "Then what can I tell my friend?"

"Tell him that I can't." She turned and put her hand on the door handle to indicate that their discussion had come to its end.

"But Madame . . ."

"I'm sorry; I can't." She'd spoken with finality, and now as she crossed the room to her favorite chair, she could still see the strange look that had crossed his face and how he'd stuffed the letter into his pocket and said a weak "goodbye" and had turned and scuffed his way along the walk. She sat down and tried to focus her attention on the woodcarver's chairs they'd just brought in that morning. The mask faces carved at the top of the wooden backs stared back at her with their blank eyes, and somehow the idea came to her that what she had done was neither right—nor was it wrong.

When he comes back, I'll ask the pastor. She didn't speak aloud, and she didn't tell herself "if he comes," for she was sure that Andre would be back, and then she put aside thoughts of his visit and let herself enjoy the new arrangement of the room.

The chairs belonged, just as she had hoped they would. They were definitely African. Solidly African in the way a museum piece speaks of its origins. Yet they were comfortable in a way that reinforced the atmosphere of the room and made it what she wanted it to be—an oasis where she could temporarily isolate herself from the jungle of mission problems, from that struggle for survival that permeated the waking and disturbed the sleeping hours of those who lived in every direction, from the troubles of those who, like Andre, traversed their porch and endeavored to become a part of their lives. And with thoughts of him she was reminded of how a parasite pushes in and lives from its host, feeding and being nurtured and sapping away the life force of the one who is doing the nurturing, and she did not like the analogy.

Earlier, when they were newly-arrived, she had followed the paths away from the mission and into what she thought would be the isolation of the tall savanna grasses where she could find respite and rest from the constant people demands that crowded to them because they were what they were—missionaries. But the people were everywhere— on the paths and in the fields—and with her pale skin and lack of facility in the tongue of their birth, she could neither blend and be one of them in the small nothings that bring relief from the burdens of the day nor could she slip away to be alone. The Africans, it seemed, found their personhood in being together, and they could not understand the need of any person, especially a woman, to be by herself. So she had created this room with her books and selected pieces of furniture, making it her sanctum, a place to have her quiet times in the early morning hours, a place to work at her school preparations in the afternoons when she needed freedom from disturbance, a place to share with George in the evenings, and on those rare occasions when someone arrived who viewed life from a perspective that complimented and fit comfortably with hers, a place to invite that person to come and sit and enjoy.

72

Hippo, her choice piece of African art, now stood between the chairs. The dark wood-grain tracings flowed smoothly over the lighter brown of his rotund body, and his legs were frozen in stride. His mouth closed benignly around his long, bulging snout and was drawn into a mischievous grin, and his tiny, upright ears perched atop his head as if they'd been hurriedly attached for a temporary make-do by the creator when he couldn't find any proper-sized ears for a beast of such proportion. For her, it'd been love at first sight when she'd seen the grinning, chubby-framed sculpting at the woodcarvers' place. That had been the April they'd looped by Victoria Falls during an Easter-break purchasing trip for the mission.

They'd spent a refreshing day hiking, getting soaked in the spray of

Main Falls, then standing close to the edge high on Danger Point and gazing down at the Zambezi River surging through the narrow gorge, and being amazed at the immeasurable volumes of water falling and falling. Like real tourists, they'd taken each other's pictures at the base of David Livingstone's statue. The giant likeness of the pioneer missionary-explorer, thought to be the first white man to see the falls, stands on the Zimbabwe side. Another tourist, looking from where Livingstone stood, had snapped a photo of them together. She'd had it enlarged, and it now hung on the wall adjacent to the chairs. The rainbow arching over their heads in the picture was vibrant against the billowing clouds of spray thrown up by the falls.

That day was one of those occasions that have few parallels in a lifetime. Later that afternoon when they arrived at the craft village, she'd felt almost like the proverbial schoolgirl strolling along the midway at the fair with her best beau, when she'd seen the big hippo and they'd spontaneously stopped and George bought it and lifted it into her arms. Its solid wood proportions, though, did not cuddle against her as had the big blue shaggy dog he'd won for her the summer before they were married, but it did add a friendliness to the room now, and its natural-wood color blended with the chairs.

Only one other time since their arrival in Africa stood out as being more special than the visit to Victoria Falls, and that was a wintery June day in Johannesburg. Snugging their windbreakers about them, she and George had strolled along the bustling streets. Each time they had visited there, they found themselves amazed that such a clean, prosperous city bursting with high technology could be on the same continent and such a few air hours away from their mission. Early the same morning a MAF charter plane had picked them up at Mbinda's air strip and taken them directly to the international airport where they'd connected south. Since their flight on to Europe wasn't leaving until late evening, they'd come into the city for the day.

"Oh, look!" Kate pointed at the window of a tiny jeweler's shop tucked away in an alcove. "One of those would be just the thing for your mother's collection." She indicated a grouping of souvenir spoons.

73

One row in George's mother's spoon collection traced the history of stops they'd made on their travels since they'd become overseas missionaries. "We've never taken her one from Jo'burg." Then she noticed the sign leaning against an easel at the corner of the display. "Wedding sets, 40% off," she read. She looked up at George.

"Come." He spoke quickly, reaching for her hand. "Let's go in and look. Maybe this is the time . . ."

The jeweler brought out a large tray of rings. "All Johannesburg gold," he assured them. "What sizes are you looking for?"

"Uhhh . . ." Kate looked down at her hand, and suddenly it had seemed very pale and weathered and naked. In this country where couples were not considered married unless they had their rings, how could she explain? Besides, she had herself never completely understood the ban their North American church had traditionally enforced on wedding rings because they were jewelry, one of those items of *outward adorning* that should never be worn. "Maybe we should measure," she finally said.

"I like these." George pointed to a set sitting apart from the others. The exquisitely worked matching patterns caught the light, scattering it into fragments and giving them the appearance of being set with diamonds. "My wife deserves nothing but the best."

74

Kate smiled up at him, and then shook her head. "For traveling, I think something plain would be much more appropriate."

They finally agreed on a very plain set. "And one of the souvenir spoons," George added, producing his credit card. When they left the store he suggested they get a sandwich and have lunch in the nearby park.

They found a quiet corner in the park. He took the box from his pocket, opened it, and slipped the smaller of the two rings onto Kate's finger. "Happy twenty-fourth anniversary to the woman of my dreams." He stood, bowed before her, then brought her hand to his lips. "It's the least I can do to show my love and devotion." His words were very quiet.

Chapter eleven

Kate reached for the other ring. "And this," she said, "is to show the world that you are the most wonderful husband any woman could have." And she worked the band onto his finger. "Such strong hands," she murmured. "Strong. And these will be a symbol of our strength." She tipped her head up and their eyes met, saying speeches they could never commit to voice, and she felt him grasp her hands and draw her to her feet and cradle her close against his body. Emotion raced through her being, and she let herself melt into his embrace.

"Lucky we have this corner to ourselves," George whispered into her ear.

Just then a loud outburst of laughter caused them to tense and pull apart. A bevy of teenagers raced toward a picnic table not far from where they stood.

"Not so alone after all." George leaned forward and brushed her cheek with a quick kiss, then they settled at the table, sitting as close as any pair of young lovers, giving the impression they might be a couple of trysting middle-agers—he somewhat paunchy and balding and she plain of dress and feature.

Kate spread out their simple lunch then laid her hand on George's. Automatically, both bowed their heads. When George had finished grace, Kate let her eyes rest on the rings. "After all these years . . ."

Her sentence drifted into that area of what they had many months earlier agreed was not to be spoken of further. When she looked up, George reached a finger across her lips. "We're free now, and the past . . ." He shook his head as if by that gesture whatever had happened was gone and had no bearing on the todays of their existence. "Let's make these rings symbolize the two new people we've become, people who're one in their love for each other and in their love for their God."

The ring had felt strange on her finger, and she twisted at it. "It's just that . . . that I've wanted to be able to do this for so long . . ." Silence covered their thoughts again for another long moment. "Thank you, honey. Thank you so much for making me so happy."

George slipped his arm around her, and for a while they ate in silence, enjoying their togetherness, and yet each was lost in separate thoughts. Certain emotions that twisted through Kate's mind, though, had to be spoken. "But when we get home and visit the churches . . . Can't you just picture dear little Aunt Harriet and her awful horror if she'd see us—you and me—wearing rings?"

George laughed his quick, short laugh. "She's such a saint."

Kate nodded. "That's just the problem. She's always so careful to do what's right and pleasing to the Lord. These modern times must be very difficult for her. Remember the last time we were there—the furor because one of the youth teachers had dared to wear her wedding ring while teaching the lesson—and dear Aunt Harriet was strong in the middle of all the discussion, insisting that no baptized member of the church be allowed so much as to step onto the platform while wearing a ring. How would she react? Her very own niece! Her only kin in flesh and blood who's become a bona fide missionary of the church—an ambassador of God, as she loves to say. Can't you just see her? Sitting on the front row, hair swept up and under the navy pillbox hat that she must still wear, posture-perfect and as proud as punch of her missionary kin who've come to tell the brethren how the work of the Lord is moving forward among the heathen in their African field of labor. Then can't you just see her mouth drop and her eyes rivet on their hands as they step into the pulpit—both of them wearing wedding rings!"

George laughed again. "How'll she ever be able to enter through the *pearly* gates and walk the streets of *gold*?"

"George!"

"All right." He ducked his head in mock humility. "There's more truth than humor in what you're trying to say."

"I've found so much freedom now . . . now that we're learning how to believe. And now . . . I want to be able to share the joy that I'm finding."

George squeezed his arm more tightly around his wife. "I hear what you're saying," he said. "We must be careful. The African believ-

76

ers are used to seeing missionaries who come from different backgrounds and who have different customs. In some countries the "sinner" is the one who doesn't wear a ring. But I'm afraid that in our part of down-home America—even if the church has officially accepted wedding rings for those whose culture or convictions require one—we'll still find those who'd be blinded by a little band of gold circling our fingers. So . . ." He paused thoughtfully. "How about when our plane lands in Seattle that these go off until we're back in safe territory?"

"But don't you think that's being hypocritical?"

George shook his head. "I think it's doing things Paul's way by not doing anything that will cause our brother—or our aunt—to fall."

Sitting, now, in the haven of the study, Kate lifted her hand and looked at the ring she still wore—it had become such a part of her that she was seldom conscious of it. Yet, as time went on, it had in its own way begun to remind her of the very things that they had promised each other to forget. Rather than dwell on that, though, she thought of Margaret and of her recent letter with an invitation to stop on their way home and to spend a few days with her. A smile played across Kate's lips as she remembered how they'd met as seatmates during the long flight to Seattle from London's Heathrow Airport.

"We've had ever such a lovely chat together," Margaret had remarked when approach to the airport was announced. "I'm so fascinated by the good work you've described, and I'd be ever so happy to have you give me your address so we can be in touch after you're back at your mission."

Just then George took the little ring box out of his briefcase.

"Certainly," Kate replied as she began to twist the ring off her finger. "I'd love to correspond with you. There's so much we can share." Then when she handed her ring to George, she suddenly became aware of how her new friend was watching them. "Oh!" Realization of the implications of what they were doing suddenly registered. "Please . . ." She patted the older woman's arm. "Don't get the wrong idea. We really are missionaries.

And we really are married. It's . . ." She searched for quick, easy words to explain the complicated situation. "It's a long story," she finally said, "but the gist of it is that we're members of a rather conservative church and an elderly aunt is meeting us at the airport with my brother. She's so proud of us being missionaries; at the same time she's strongly convicted that anyone wearing jewelry—and to her wedding bands are jewelry—well, that person has lost the way with the Lord. She's such a dear that we wouldn't think of doing anything that she would find upsetting."

Margaret was shaking her head. "I believe you," she said. "No one would bother to make up a story like that. And, please, do give me your address—I admire anyone who does a work such as you describe . . . and who also has such concern for an elderly aunt's feelings."

CHAPTER
12

"No!" A tightening of dread squeezed around Kate's chest and stomach. "No!"

Rene had arrived, dropped off the mail at the house, and then had rushed away to get George and Lloyd to go with him to his projects. Jonas worked in the garden. Mbayo sat at the ironing board in the workroom. Her ability to produce undamaged, crisply-pressed items continually amazed Kate. That ability also relieved Kate from the necessity of having to master the art of piloting one of the bulky, charcoal-burning devices that were widely used for ironing in nonelectrified Africa and the risk of letting embers drop out and eat their way into clothing. Now, standing by the table, she lost awareness of Mbayo's presence around the corner and stared at the letter she'd just pulled from the stack of mail and so expectantly had ripped open.

"Oh, Mom and Dad," The words sprawled on the paper in Karla's large, round writing. "I'm writing from the hospital. It's my fourth day here, and I'm still quite weak. Our baby—it was a little boy—is gone."

"Gone!" Kate's mind didn't want to accept the word. "Karla's baby?"

A few weeks before they'd received the telegram about Will, Karla had shared the first news about the baby. "Yep. We're pregnant!" Jamie, in typical Jamie fashion, had added in his own note at the end of the letter. "And we hope you're as excited about becoming Grandpa and Grandma as we are about being the first to give you that privileged status!"

"Grandma!" George had grabbed Kate exuberantly and swung her around when she told him the news. "A little grandbaby—of our own—to play with!" They'd counted off the time and found that the baby would be nearly four months old by the time they arrived on furlough.

"Kimmie's been with me," Karla's letter continued.

Kate felt some relief at that. The two girls, only sixteen months apart and inseparable as children, were still best friends. Karla had a flair for the domestic. She loved cooking and decorating, and it had been no surprise when she'd double-majored in home economics and early childhood education. She and Jamie had married the week after her graduation and had bought a new home on the edge of the city, an easy fifteen minutes in one direction to the plant where he was a research chemist and about twenty minutes in the other to where Karla taught home arts at the church's junior secondary school. Kimmie, on the other hand, had been the artist, the child poet, and they'd rather expected her to go into teaching too. To their surprise, though, she developed a deep interest in biology and computers during her senior year and had announced that she was going into nursing—not the ordinary floor-walking kind of hospital nursing but the kind that would fit her to be a member of a team working in some field of developing medicine—maybe in transplants. She finished her RN and her bachelor's and now was earning credits toward her master's in Nursing Science while working in the intensive care trauma unit of the university hospital. She'd taken an apartment on the same side of the city where Jamie and Karla lived, and the two girls often got together and drove the two hours to the college where Kenny was already a junior religion major. Kate was pleased with the way the three of them stuck together, and knowing they kept in frequent contact and looked out for each other helped to ease the pain of being so far away from them.

"You don't know how hard it is for us to have you way out there," Karla had written during Kate and George's first year at Mbinda.

They'd left just after Kimmie graduated from secondary school. Karla had already finished a year in the local junior college and the two sisters went away to the same college that fall. Kenny had lived at Mbinda with them for the first two years, doing his schooling by correspondence.

"When things come up, all the other kids can just pick up the phone and talk to their parents," Karla had lamented in that letter. "For Kimmie and me, though, it's like we don't have parents. Like you've just walked out and left us. And there's no one. Just Grandma. And you know how she is . . ."

Kate had cried when she read that letter.

When they were making their overseas plans, she hadn't realized just how isolated they were going to be. On the information sheet describing the mission, the nearest telephone was listed as 100 kilometers away. What hadn't been said was that the telephone system had fallen into disrepair and that no one had the finances to reestablish its links with even the provincial capital. She'd never been able to talk to her girls from Mbinda. In fact, the only time they'd been able to phone from Africa was the first year after they'd left Kenny behind in boarding school in the States. They had driven the two days to the city for Christmas, and she and George had used a large chunk of the money they'd saved for their holidays to talk to the kids. The lines had buzzed and crackled, and the connection had been so weak that even when they'd hollered into the receiver, they still had to repeat and re-repeat themselves so many times that by the time they'd shouted a Merry Christmas to each of the youngsters, the operator had announced that their allotted ten minutes—at $15 each—was finished and had cut their line.

Kate re-read the letter she still held and sensed the pain that it had cost the girl to put what had happened into written words. And she felt tears coming. "A telephone—even a telephone." Her wish became an agony of prayer. "Some way. To talk. To just be able to talk."

The envelope bore a November 5 date stamp. Almost four weeks had gone by since it had been mailed.

"Oh, my poor baby." Kate's throat tightened, and still holding the letter, she took long, striding steps down the hall into the haven of her room and threw herself on her knees, burying her face in the overstuffed comfort of her chair. The seclusion of the room held her in its quietness, and tears flowed until her eyes began to ache with that dry ache that comes when there have been too many tears, and her sobs gapped out with wispy gasps. She felt weak, drained, but her mind continued to struggle with the news and begged to know the whys of what had happened. Mechanically she pushed herself upright and forced herself to her feet and to go back to the table in the living room where the other letters lay and retrieve the envelope she'd recognized as coming from Kimmie and one from Kenny.

"Karla's going to be OK." Kate had brought the letters back to read in the security of the study and felt encouraged by the message in Kimmie's printing that marched in neat, optimistic letters across the page. "The doctors aren't sure what brought on a miscarriage at this time—she's already into her second trimester—but they're suggesting she won't have problems with future pregnancies. Just the same, they're cautioning them to wait before trying again. Poor Karla and Jamie. They were so happy about this baby. Karla had already begun fixing up the nursery. And this, so soon after Uncle Willie's funeral."

Tears blurred Kate's eyes again. "Willie. Karla's baby." She could no longer read. "Oh, God." She looked toward the ceiling. The greatest sacrifice of going to the mission field was having to be so far from her babies. That's what they were to her—Karla, Kimmie, Kenny— still her babies. "God. Hold them close." Her body tensed, and unconsciously she doubled her hands into fists until her nails and fingertips dug into the letters she held. "Couldn't You at least have given us a telephone?" Her words burned with accusation. "Most missionaries these days have at least that. To tie them to their homes and families. But us. Our children. They need to talk to us. They need us. Don't You understand? Don't You know that we need to talk to them?"

And again she let her head drop against the wing of the overstuffed chair. And again she sobbed.

"Kate?"

She hadn't heard anyone come in.

"Kate? Darling? What is it?"

She looked up at George and her mouth seem to freeze. She couldn't open it. And put what had happened into words. Not yet. Instead, she held the letters up to him.

He took them. "Is there something with the kids?" He dropped onto the wide arm of the chair and slipped his arm around her shoulders, and she pushed her head against him and let him hold her. "Oh, George." She rocked her head back and forth and then let it rest again against the comforting softness of his side. "The baby. Karla's lost the baby."

She felt him slump back.

"The baby!"

And she heard pain in his voice, and she reached her free arm around him, and she could feel his chest contract as he drew his breath in. And they sat there, holding each other, each with private pain filling their individual beings.

"A month ago." She spoke at last. "And we didn't even know until now." She continued to hold her head against his side, and she became aware that something warm and moist was dropping onto the arm she held around his chest. "And we can't even talk to them. Oh, George. We can't even talk to them."

CHAPTER

13

"Anyone born in October, raise your hand!" Lloyd's cheerful request rode somewhere to Kate's right as she moved among the mingling of missionaries and African leaders in their living room. Woody Elliot nodded to her.

"Nice idea, Kate."

She felt her cheeks flush. "Thanks," she managed.

"Certainly is." Luanne spoke from behind her.

Kate turned, hoping Woody hadn't noticed her blush.

The person-to-person scavenger hunt idea did seem to be working—people were mixing and obviously enjoying themselves. After mission headquarters had assured them that extra help would be brought in, she'd agreed to hostessing the committees at Mbinda, and she and Carole had organized a get-acquainted party for the first evening. She drifted from group to group, chatting, until she noticed Jared Mason, a student volunteer who taught the missionary children at Rolling Hills. He sat in the corner, head bent over his paper.

"How are you doing?" she asked, stopping beside his chair, but even as she spoke she saw that his paper was blank.

"OK, I guess." He spoke toward the floor.

"Mmmmm." She pulled one of the wooden dining chairs around

to face him and sat down. "Somehow I get the impression that everything isn't exactly all that OK."

He shook his head.

"It can be really lonely in a crowd, can't it. I sometimes feel so," she took an exaggerated deep breath, "so alone . . ." The dogeared corners of an envelope showed above the edge of his shirt pocket. "Especially when I'm with a bunch of folk I don't really know and I get to thinking of all the family and friends I've left behind. And wishing for mail and news from the really special folk." She watched his face as she talked, hoping for some hint that she was getting on the right track.

He nodded. "Yeah." The one word sounded flat and unenthusiastic, and he didn't seem at all like the energetic, creative young fellow the Rolling Hills folks bragged about. "It gets really lonely."

"Did you have letters from home in the mail they brought from the city this morning?"

He nodded.

The crowd behind her continued to weave a pattern of laughing and talking. "Good news?"

He shook his head.

"Do you want to talk about it."

He continued to stare at the floor. "Jenny sent me a 'Dear John.' "

"Oh no!" The shock and concern in Kate's voice was real. She'd also heard about Jenny, the girl Jared had left back home. "You must feel terrible."

He nodded again. Then he looked up at Kate, and she could read the hurt in his eyes. "If there were just some way I could talk to her, a phone, something. If we could just talk this thing out . . ."

As she reached out and put her hand on his arm, Kate felt again the hopelessness of her own wishing to be able to talk, to be able to hear from Karla's own lips that she really was doing all right. The weeks were easing the pain, but . . .

"She wrote this letter three weeks ago." Jared spoke again. "Three weeks. I may as well not even write back. But how can I not write? I thought . . ." He reached up and started to pull the envelope from his pocket then let his hand drop. "I thought we had something going that would last."

"She's a very special person, isn't she?"

An almost smile curved onto his face. "Very special," he repeated. "And the nice way she says things—even in this letter—about how she needs her freedom now, while I'm gone, and that maybe, someday, after I'm back and when we're a little farther along in school, if it's the Lord's will . . ."

"And what about you?"

"I think she's the most wonderful person . . . and I'm going to miss her letters. Miss her. Miss . . . oh, I don't know what to think."

"For now, Jared, don't think."

The misery in his eyes told her that he considered that an impossible idea.

"I want you to take this piece of paper and go out there and make yourself ask people these questions. Jared, I'm a mom, almost a grandmom," and again she felt the ache in her own heart, knowing that statement was no longer true as it had been just a few weeks earlier, "and a teacher, and I'm telling you, make yourself get out there and be part of this group."

He stared at her.

"I mean it." She stood up and reached for his hand. "Up." She pulled, and he responded. "And out. And good luck. You're going to have to work quickly if you want to be in on the prizes." She let go of his hand and pointed him toward the nearest group. "Do I remember someone mentioning that you had a birthday a few weeks ago?"

"Yeah."

"I think Lloyd's birthday's in October too. He's the handsome black fellow just over there. Check with him."

And she felt a sense of satisfaction when he strode over and slapped Lloyd on the back. "Did I hear that your birthday's in . . ." His forced jovialness sounded almost real.

"Kate."

At the sound of someone speaking her name, she turned and found herself again looking up into the face of the handsome director of Rolling Hills Mission. And again there was that fluster of emotion. "Do you need help with a question?" She hoped she sounded sensible.

He nodded but said nothing.

"Well . . ."

"The confusion's getting a bit much in here." There was a kind of confidentiality in his tone. "Could you come outside with me so we can talk?"

The tone of his voice and the way he looked at her just then. . . . She didn't want to put a name to what she felt.

No! Not now! The refusal flashed through Kate's thoughts almost as clearly as if the words had been spoken, and in her mind she clearly saw what she'd written in her journal only two days earlier. "I don't know what it is . . . Karla, Sylvanus, Will, Marie, her people, the hunger, the thefts, the rumors of trouble, the problem between . . ." She left the ellipses this time because she didn't want to write "George and me." And then she went on with "Being here, no phone, no communication to the outside world, especially now . . ." She'd not finished that sentence. "God. I don't want anything to separate me from You. Not . . ." Again ellipses. God could fill in the blanks and read between the lines. He could see into her heart and understand it better even than she did herself. And then suddenly she'd been angry again. "Still! Angry!" She pressed the words hard into the paper. "Please. If ever I do anything similar to . . ." Again the avoiding of details. "Knock me down. Anything."

The brashness of the last remark hadn't registered at the time.

"Just for a few minutes." Woody spoke again, and his simple request brushed aside the caution that had flashed through her thoughts.

"Sure." And she followed him out through her front door, across the front porch, and into the night.

In reputation, Sherwood "Woody" Elliot stood tall among missionaries and Africans alike. He was a missionary's missionary—a good leader, a no-nonsense administrator, and active in evangelism as well.

He maintained a good working relationship with most of the Africans and was respected by the other missionaries. Besides that, he had looks and a restrained dignity and a startling sense of humor that everyone, including Kate, found charming.

"Come around here. Careful." He reached out and touched her arm as if to help her.

The warmth of his hand on her arm gave her a thrill of expectation.

"Let's go and sit in the swing I saw over there." He guided her toward the mango trees where George had hung the old lawn swing they'd brought from their home in the States. "I saw you talking with Jared. I don't know what you said—but whatever it was . . ."

"Poor kid," she broke in.

"He's a good boy. Has the makings of a fine missionary. Thanks for taking time for him. You have a talent for that, a special way with words and people, and right now I need the help your words can give, that you can give."

Woody Elliot wants my help!

Now Kate was glad for the darkness that hid the flush of pleasure she again felt on her cheeks, yet when he let his hand slide down her arm to take her hand, she knew she should pull it back. Instead, she let herself be led toward the old double lawn swing. And she liked it.

"I . . ."

Just as she started to speak in reply, she felt something catch under the inside edge of her right heel. Her foot snapped sideways, and she pitched forward, her hand slipping free. She flailed out with both arms, struggling to keep her balance, and her legs swung into long, stumbling steps. She willed her body to lift itself back into the realm of equilibrium, but its momentum served only to carry her into top-heavy lurches that dropped her lower and lower until her body thudded to a stop on the ground.

"Kate! Are you all right?" Woody spoke in alarm.

She pushed herself up into a sitting position. "I . . . I stepped on something." In her embarrassment, it was the only thing she could think of to say, and she laughed shakily. "Nothing unusual for me."

In the vague light coming from the living-room windows, she saw him reach both his hands toward her. "Can you still stand?"

"Sure." She held her own hands up and let him pull her back to her feet. "See. I can stand." She pulled her hands free of his and swiped them over the skirt of her dress to brush away telltale stragglings of grass. Where her right foot should be, though, she felt only a numb vagueness blocking between her leg and the ground, but she forced it to lift and to move ahead in practice steps. "I'm sure glad it didn't rain today and that I at least chose to land on the grass." She rattled on, forcing a lightness to her voice to cover the awkwardness she felt as she continued to test her foot. "I'll be fine." And she began a slow circle around the palm tree that stood in the corner formed by their front walk and the house.

"Where are you going?" Woody swung into stride to keep pace with her.

"Just limbering up my foot so it doesn't go stiff." The words sounded overbright and overoptimistic, even to herself, and she began her second loop around the palm. "Keep walking," she told herself. "Keep walk . . ." Just then a pain seared from the outside of her foot through her ankle. She gave a quick cry and stopped, resting full weight on her good foot. Testily she slid the other forward.

"Here."

Kate tensed when Woody touched her arm.

"Let me help you to the porch."

She tried to shift weight for another step. "I'm fi-I-ine!" A scorching pain pushed the word into a near scream.

"Kate! Let me help you!" It was a command, not a request, and grasping her hand, Woody bent forward, ducked his head under her arm and scooped her into his arms.

"Woody! Put me down!" She spoke stubbornly.

"I will. On the porch."

"Get George!" Her voice was sharp with determination.

"I will."

And then she was remembering again the prayer about being knocked down. She began to laugh. Shakily. At the same time, she felt Woody settling her into one of their cane porch chairs. "Are you OK?"

She started to nod then shook her head, and the compulsion to laugh subsided.

Woody stood in front of her, shadowy light from the windows falling across his handsomely chiseled features. "Just stay right there, and I'll get George. And Ryan."

"Just George. Please. For now."

"What happened?" Alarm edged George's question.

"Stepped on a stick—or something—that rolled. And my foot snapped when I went down—and I can't walk."

"I'd better get Ryan."

"I don't need a doctor. I just need to put ice on it."

"Kate. Be sensible. Of course you need a doctor."

"I—Oh . . ." She dropped her head into her hands. "It hurts."

"I'm getting Ryan."

"OK. But don't tell anyone else. Except Carole. She's going to have to carry on."

"We'd better take her down for an X-ray." Ryan spoke quickly to George. "Bring your pickup around so we don't have to carry her so far."

"But . . ."

"Hush up, young lady, or I'll have the night crew come with a stretcher and tell everyone to come out and watch you go."

Kate hushed.

"Well, George, you may as well go back and take care of your party." Ryan sounded resigned when they had Kate at the hospital and ready for the X-rays. "I'll be a while getting this picture developed. Then I'll get this young lady of yours patched up and bring her home myself. But whyever-in-the-world she chose a time like tonight to do something like this, I'll never understand, because, for once, I was beginning to enjoy a party."

Although the X-rays showed nothing broken, Ryan insisted that the foot be wrapped to the knee. "If this were at my clinic back in Toronto, I'd slap you in plaster to your hip."

By the tone of his voice, Kate couldn't tell whether he was joking or whether he was simply being cantankerous.

"You've stretched and torn things in there that are going to need time to heal, and you're going to have to keep that foot up. Not an ounce of weight on it for a week," he warned. "If you promise to stay down tomorrow and keep your foot up, I'll let you take a pair of crutches now."

"But, Ryan. All these people. I'm in charge."

"All you have to do is to give orders. Your M . . . whatever her name is, she can deliver whatever messages need to be delivered."

"But Charlie Clendon's come all the way from the States to have that workshop for us missionaries. I . . . Don't you think I could go to that?"

"All right. I'll give you a wheelchair. But use it—and keep that foot up. Do you understand?"

Kate would like to have said that she understood—that she'd understood for a long time that he didn't have the ability either to feel sorry for his patients or to talk to them as though they might be feeling individuals. Rather, it obviously suited him better to boss them around as if they were simply things—items and objects that conveniently developed conditions for him to operate on or who expediently hurt themselves so he could dress their wounds and show his incomparable knowledge. "Of course I understand," she said. "Now. May I please go home?"

Instead of answering, Ryan sent the duty nurse to the pharmacy with a written order. "Before the night's over, you're going to be wishing for something for the pain. So, before you leave this hospital, I'm going to see that you take something. And when we get you home. Remember—NO weight on that foot for ONE WEEK."

"That's ridiculous." Kate barked back. "You've taped it. By morning I should be able to walk."

"All right. You want to be stubborn. Do things your way. But I promise you, it'll take much longer to heal—if it heals at all." He called for the duty nurse to bring a wheelchair on her way back from the pharmacy and wheel Kate out to the pickup. Everyone had gone by the time they were back at the house, and the generator had been shut down for the evening. "Make sure she keeps her weight off this foot," Ryan insisted to George. "She's too hardheaded for her own good. Whatever she was gallivanting around outside for and stepping on things she had no business to step on, I never want to know. Regardless, I've brought a wheelchair and a pair of crutches. She has pain killers, so don't let her be complaining about how bad that foot hurts and how it's keeping her awake." He made little effort to hide his irritation.

"Sure, Doc. I'll see she behaves herself. And thanks. Sorry you had to miss the last of the party. Carole did a great job, and folks said all sorts of appreciative things when they left. They asked me to pass on their regrets and best wishes about your foot too." The last part was addressed to Kate.

"This couldn't have happened at a worse time." Kate looked up at George. "After all my complaining about committees coming to Mbinda . . ."

"What were you doing out there with Woody?" George asked when they were finally in bed.

"He wanted to talk—about Jared, I think."

"Jared?"

"I think so. I fell before I could find out."

George moved closer to her and slipped his arm over her shoulder. "I'm sorry." He pushed his face against her neck. "About your foot."

"I love you."

"I know. I'll get someone to cover your classes tomorrow."

Kate reached up and slipped her hand into his. The hardness of the ring that circled his finger pressed against the back of her hand. "Remember the day we bought our rings."

"Mmmm-huh."

"That still means an awful lot to me." Her words dragged with drowsiness, and she felt herself drifting.

CHAPTER
14

"You're all alike. None of you show any respect for the black man." Footsteps and loud voices arrived on the front porch at the same time, and from where she sat, her leg blocked up on a stool, Kate very clearly recognized the voice of the mission president.

"But pastor." George interjected in smooth contrast.

"Not one. I've been here since before yesterday, and how many of you have come to welcome me or my wife?"

Kate had never before heard their African leader raise his voice, but then she'd met him only on a handful of occasions. He'd always impressed her as a dignified gentleman, who, though rather quiet and noncommittal, and not as progressive as she would have liked, let it be understood that he was chief, the one in charge.

"Your doctor. Your director from Rolling Hills."

At the reference to Woody, Kate tensed.

"You missionaries are all alike. You're just here to get what you can."

"I've no idea which missionaries have or haven't already been to where you're staying, pastor, but the steady stream of villagers going to see you worries me—I'm concerned that you haven't had any time to rest." Kate admired George's calmness when just overhearing made her blood pump more quickly—she'd always thought their African leader liked them, particularly George. "Why don't you sit here for a few minutes, and I'll see if Mbayo can get us something cool to drink." The scraping of chair legs against cement indicated that George's offer was accepted. "As you know, my wife is rather off her feet as a result of her little accident last night. Excuse me."

Kate waved to George as he came into the living room then put her finger to her lips and shook her head when he started to speak. Instead, she motioned him closer. "There's juice in the fridge." Her voice was very low. "Mbayo's over helping the others prepare lunch for the guests, and I've had no choice but to overhear your entire conversation."

"Sorry, pet," George whispered. "I'm hoping a spot of something cool will have a calming effect."

When George took the juice to the president, he immediately began telling about the student evangelistic groups Lloyd had organized. "They have seven people ready for baptism during the service you'll be conducting this weekend, pastor. Next month a group starts going to Loma. You heard about our student who was killed by lightning." George gave the president no room to reply. "Well, he's from Loma. When we went for the funeral, we found that the church there hasn't been doing too well. Through the service and the personal contact of those who went out, interest has been revived, and some of us . . ." Kate noticed how George hesitated then hurried on without mentioning the word missionaries. "We've worked out a plan to take a group of teachers and students out there every week."

94

"Yes. Yes," said the president. "That's good."

"Whew!" George let out a breath of relief when he came in about fifteen minutes later after the president had gone, and he leaned against the closed door.

"Whatever happened?"

"Ryan. Woody. Frustrations."

Kate feigned no notice of his mention of Woody's name.

"Money vanishing. People placed in positions because they're family. Hospital supplies 'walking' away."

She nodded. "And expensive books disappearing from school then 'miraculously' appearing in homes of pastors who've had children here."

"I stayed out of this one, Pet. The poor president. Africans like handling things privately and taking time, as much as is needed, to let matters arrange themselves. While we want action—and NOW. I agree that sin must be called by its right name, but, Katie, that doesn't mean we have to shout at the sinners! And this morning Ryan—well—he waxed extremely eloquent. On his latest visit to the new health center, he found ALL the mattresses, ALL the sheets, ALL the blankets Rene brought for the beds—every one of them gone and the patients sleeping on bamboo mats. Being Ryan, he visited the homes of the clinic director and the two nurses and insisted on seeing where and how the families slept. Well, the short of it is that he found clinic mattresses and bedding in all three houses. And, of course, he pointed out the family connections between the clinic director and certain church administrators. Then Woody told his story—a good one but poor timing. Though he mentioned neither names nor relationships, everyone knew that the pastor he was talking about is the president's nephew." George pushed into details without pausing. "It seems this particular pastor had a deal going with a deacon—half of the offerings they collected went to the church and the other half was split between the two of them. No one would have known about the pastor's cut if it hadn't been for the deacon's mother."

"His mother?"

George laughed. "He'd told her the money was his salary. When the board became suspicious and replaced the deacon, she filed suit against the church, demanding separation pay for her son's loss of income. During investigations, the pastor's involvement came to light. Of course, he's being transferred—and that's another thing that helped elevate our good doctor's temper. The pastor's being assigned to stewardship. He'll be the one who's to go from church to church to encourage fidelity in giving. I'm so glad our general representative was chairing. He's African and one of the most understanding and tactful men I've seen. Otherwise . . . Whoa!"

"So that's what not showing respect is about?"

"Well, what triggered it, anyway. There're undercurrents, too many

95

of them, against missionaries. Our status, our incomes from the home-land, the deference we're given, causes jealousies. Some like us; others don't. With the push for democracy, our enemies are freer to fight us. At the same time, African leaders know what we know—that as long as we're here, more help comes in from the outside world. Then there's the way we sometimes get so focused on the work of doing good, of helping, that we forget the people themselves, their way of looking at life, their values, their code of politeness, and what they view as civilized behavior." George paused and shook his head. "We're players in an interesting drama, and it's becoming more important than ever for us to pay attention to our cues."

Kate had slumped down so that her head was resting in her hand. "And I'm not too sure how much longer I want to be involved on this stage."

"Where's your spirit, Katie?"

"Certainly not in my leg. And certainly not in my foot. And certainly not encouraged by all the rot we have to deal with."

"Rot? Now-now."

"Those guys you were just talking about. They . . ." Kate paused to give herself time to take a deep breath. "They, and their parents. They're all products of our mission schools."

96 "Despite what I've just said, I think that's part of why we're still needed, to help maintain a broader outlook, to help show that religion's not only a matter of black and white and right and wrong but of getting to know God. Of discovering truth."

"Of truth . . . ?" Kate's question was interrupted by a tapping on the door.

"Yes?" George called out, but at Kate's look he got up and went to the door. "Well," he exclaimed, and he pulled the door open wide.

"Madame?"

"Come in! Come in!"

"I hope it is all right that I came now after my classes, but I learned that you have hurt yourself bad, so I picked these flowers for you. My mother . . ." Marie paused. "My mother told me that white ladies like to have flowers in their houses, especially when they are sick."

"What your mother said is absolutely right." Kate held out her hands for the bouquet of bougainvillaea that Marie held, flowers that obviously had come from the hedge behind the girls' dormitory, and she took the bunch loosely, letting the leaves cushion her hands against the long, woody thorns. "How is it your mother was so wise?"

"When she was a girl at school, she worked for a missionary; and when I was little, she used to say that she wished for me to go to a school where I, too, might one day be able to work for a missionary." Marie smiled. "And here I am. Maybe it is that God has remembered my mother's wishes for me."

"I'm sure He has some very special plans for you," Kate replied.

"Should I come to work again on Tuesday?"

"Yes. Come."

"Is there maybe something I can do now?" The girl seemed eager to be of help. "Mbayo, I know, is very busy with all the visitors who have come."

"Yes. One little thing. We'll ask Mr. Director to find a vase, and you can arrange these flowers in some water. Then, if we need your help on another afternoon, Mbayo will send for you."

"And, Madame?"

"Yes?"

"Would it be all right for me to pray with you—like the pastor has been teaching us to do in our Bible class?"

"I'd like that very much."

The three of them closed their eyes while Marie asked the "Great God of the Heavens" to help Madame's leg to be better soon. When the girl left, her bouquet stood centered on a doily in the middle of the coffee table—the rich pinks, the whites, the red accents of the triangular (three-petaled) blossoms, the healthy green of the leaves, cheerful against the dark wood.

"There goes one good reason why our work is still important."

Kate didn't respond immediately to George's comment but sat absorbed in her thoughts.

CHAPTER
15

When George wheeled Kate into the school's largest classroom the next afternoon about a quarter of an hour before the workshop was to begin, several missionaries were gathered around Rene. "In villages the people at least have gardens," he was saying. "In the city . . . even top wage earners in government offices . . . mostly everyone eats only once a day; some once every two days, or three. Others . . ." He stopped and shook his head. "I was in a home before I came. Husband. Wife. Eight kids. Nothing for a whole week but tea made from avocado leaves."

"Good for flu." George grinned. He liked herb remedies. Banana stem juice to remove warts; green papaya to calm toothache; chopped comfrey in lieu of vaccinations for day-old chicks. "But for hungry kids . . . !"

"Yeah." Rene's voiced sounded distant. "A whole week. They were just sitting, no energy to play, nothing."

"What can we do?" Jared's sudden question echoed what Kate so often asked herself. "Grow more food?"

Rene nodded. "That's our goal." During his years of work in development, he'd added a large measure of practicality to his enthusiastic optimism, and he went on to describe the ever-present challenges caused by the unavailability of transport, the impossible roads, the lack of seeds. "We need more village training centers to offer short courses in gardening and nutrition and health, places where the people can learn appropriate ways of making better lives for themselves." As he talked, Kate looked at the handful of people in the classroom. Their mission made only the tiniest of dots on the map, and she wondered how they could put even a little dent in the enormity of the need.

"You know that where we have schools and agriculture projects the people aren't only eating better but the church is growing—fast."

"I'd like to affirm what Rene's saying."

At the sound of Woody's voice close to where she sat, Kate turned. She hadn't noticed him come in and stand by the door, and now she smiled and dipped her head in silent greeting.

Woody nodded back then continued. "Two years ago Rene suggested we start a project near Rolling Hills. About the same time, the chief of one of the villages came to see me. He'd had a dream and wanted to know if I could interpret it for him. Well . . ." And he paused and smiled, and Kate felt particularly included in that smile. "I always tell these folk when they come to me with their dreams that I don't have the gift of interpretation, but I hear them out. And the chief told how in his dream he'd seen a Bible passage written on a wall—some verses from Isaiah 65 about building houses and planting vineyards. And he quoted me these words: 'My chosen ones will long enjoy the works of their hands. They will be a people blessed by the Lord.'

"When the chief learned that his village was the one Rene had suggested for a project, his dream made perfect sense to him. He went home and inspired his people. They cultivated fields and made bricks, and things started happening. Today those people brag that they can eat three times a day every day. They can afford to buy better clothes, and they have a school for their children and a health center. They've also built a new church—and it has the largest attendance of any church in the area. When people are eating and they're healthier, then ideas of God and heaven . . . well, God does need us here."

Kate had the sensation of being a stranger looking in—a stranger who knew too much. *How can he . . . ?* The question broke off in her mind. She started to correct the *he* to *we* but instead found herself comparing this apparently committed-to-God missionary with the person who had called her outside that evening. They were the same person—and yet they weren't. She remembered the shock that had rocketed around the missionary community some years earlier. Two families from the neighboring country had suddenly packed up their goods and returned home. Like that. Kate continued to watch Woody, and her thoughts shrunk away from making further comparisons.

"Culture shock," the more generous had suggested back then when the news first broke that the husband of one family had become too involved with the wife of the other. Explanations followed of how living in a foreign culture can trigger out-of-character behavior in the best of people and can easily be manifested in extramarital relationships. Kate, herself, had at the time considered that as a rather convenient way of explaining away inappropriate behavior as something less than it really is—sin. She now continued to watch Woody, and she knew a warmth and pleasure that could only be attributed to the fact that the two of them were together in the same room. And again she tempted herself with surmisings of what it was that he had wanted of her the evening before.

Just then Charlie Clendon, the workshop speaker, came in. His greeting included everyone, and as he went to the table that served as teacher's desk, Kate's attention swerved toward it. The table's warped surface suddenly stood out, and she saw too clearly how very old and very unsightly it had become. *Wonder what he thinks?* she asked herself. *Fresh from America and at a bush station.* And her gaze wandered to the faded mud stains, narrow and somewhat squiggled, that angled up the face of the peeling pale green walls where the students, during their assigned work periods, had scraped away termite traces. A hole gaped into the attic where a long-missing ceiling board should have been. The right replacement had never been found, and she remembered a class the previous year and the girl writing an exam at the table under the hole and the lizard that fell and the boy who'd collected it from in front of the screaming girl and carried it outside.

"God's Spirit touching hearts with truth." Charlie's voice brought her to the present. "What is the truth that you know?" He looked around the room in a way that seemed to draw each individual into his confidence. "Is your truth fact? Is it reality? Is it simply belief? Or is it a relationship?

"When I was a little fellow," he continued, "I looked forward to the day when I would be a missionary . . ." And he told of his dream to go to some steamy jungle in a faraway country and bring the truth of Jesus to darkened heathen people. "The Lord had other ideas, though, so now when I was asked to hold a series of workshops across Africa—well, being here is a dream come true. I'm seeing that mission service, though, isn't always as glamorous as I'd pictured it, and I know that you folk know truths about day-to-day life out here that I, as an outsider, can never fully comprehend."

"Brother, life here is often beyond comprehension. Even for those who've been out here for years," Woody interjected.

Many heads nodded, and Kate struggled to keep her thoughts focused on the direction of Charlie's ideas.

"Isn't that how many feel about God—that His ways and His workings are beyond our understanding?" Charlie responded, picking up on the observation. "So let's open to that beautiful Hebrew acrostic poem, the longest chapter in the Bible— Psalm 119—and make the eighteenth verse our prayer for this week: 'Open my eyes so I may see the wonderful truths in your law.' And since we're in school, we'll start with a quickie test—open Bible." He explained how he wanted them to skim the chapter and find and copy at least five phrases that contain ideas key to knowing truth and to living it. "Ten minutes," he said. He pulled an old, white kitchen timer from his pocket, wound it, and set it on the desk. "Ready. Write."

Kate flipped through the four pages the psalm covered in her Bible and noted down a couple of phrases. Beside her, George was busy with his own writing, and she glanced over to see that his big scrawl already covered many lines. When she looked back at her Bible, her finger pointed to verse 133. She smiled to herself and quickly copied it. When the timer sounded, she had already completed her five ideas.

"As you've noticed," Charlie said, "this psalm deals with the law—the torah, which in Hebrew means teaching, direction, instruction, or all the revealed will of God. Now before you share what you've written, think of the story Jesus told about the rich young ruler. Remember that the young man asked Jesus 'What GOOD thing must I do to have eternal life?' (Matthew 19:15). How many of you have the same question? Do you wonder what GOOD things you must do in order to impress God?"

Everyone's eyes focused on Charlie.

"Keep that question in mind. Now, let's go back to the notes you made from the psalm. Who would like to share?"

"I like the way it begins in the Good News version," Ryan said. " 'Happy are those whose lives are faultless.' " Several others added phrases, most from the first sections of the psalm.

"Did any of you get to the later verses?" Charlie spoke from the corner of the table where he had perched himself.

Kate shifted in the wheelchair and carefully adjusted her bandaged leg on the foot rest; then she raised her hand.

"Yes?"

"Well, personally, I found verse 133 rather appealing."

He nodded for her to continue.

"Keep me from falling."

Kate let her gaze turn toward the table across the aisle where Woody sat. He was laughing with the others.

CHAPTER
16

"We have it all organized, Madame. My sister Brigette-Therese will come, and she and Jonas and Maurice and his sister will serve." Mbayo sounded confident. "Mbinda is highly honored to have guests from America and so many other places, and we'll do our best so they will know we're happy to have them."

"I'm sure you'll make this evening's banquet a time to remember." Kate stood in the kitchen doorway, balanced on the crutches Ryan had given her—despite her impatience with his orders. She found that even though four full days had passed since her accident, the foot would not, could not, yet support her weight.

"We'll do our very best," Mbayo promised again. "My sister and Jonas have been practicing to carry things properly and to say the right words. Shall I take your plates and serving dishes to Doctor Ryan's now?"

Kate nodded. "And the soup tureen—you know, the large white soup bowl. I promised Mademoiselle Luanne I'd send it. Ask Jonas to help you."

That evening when she limped on her crutches into Ryan's living room, Kate caught her breath. The candles, the flowers, the white-covered tables, the atmosphere. Maurice came to show her and George to their places. His dark suit and ruffled shirt accented a charm she'd not noticed before in the hospital's young laboratory technician. But then, she seldom saw him without his white lab coat. *No wonder certain of the younger women are attracted to him*, she thought, and she wondered about the careful linking of his name with Luanne's by one of the national nurses. Such musings, though, were cut short in the shuffle of everyone being seated, and the welcomes, and grace. Then the servers came in.

"Can you believe that!" Kate touched George's arm and pointed his attention toward the waiter balancing a tray of plates filled with soup. "Mbayo said she's been making them practice." She smiled and nodded to the young gentleman in white shirt, black trousers, and black bow tie.

"I always told you Jonas has potential," George responded.

"Amazing!" Kate watched, admiring the confident bearing of the young man. "I never realized that he could be so . . . so poised." In her mind she'd never seen him as anything other than simply the boy who worked for them—the one who lumbered about their yard in baggy coveralls and bare feet, working to his own rhythm and leaving his tools where they dropped.

104 Jonas came and went with several trays of filled soup plates, and Brigette-Therese quietly set them in front of the guests. And, watching them, Kate wondered if in the homes of the servers themselves they ever used the tools so deftly handled that evening. Or if they had knives and forks or even spoons for their family meals. In the homes she had visited, nshima, the favorite local food, a stiff porridge made with the coarse, starchy flour the women pounded from dried cassava—sometimes called tapioca root—was served in large pans. The men and large boys gathered around one, and the women and children ate to the side from the other, all of them breaking off small pieces of nshima with thumb and forefingers of their right hands and rolling them into small balls that they dipped into the side dish of sauce and then popped into their mouths to be swallowed whole. The sauce was usually made with palm oil and cassava leaves or other greens and seasoned with tomatoes or onions or peanuts or other products from their gardens, according to the time of year. Sometimes, when it was available, they added fish. The more affluent, the pastors and teachers and nurses and merchants, had houses with eating rooms and owned tables and plates and spoons and forks and knives. Others used round, open-sided, sun shelters they had built in their yards. The village peasants, though, ate beside their houses, sitting on low homemade stools or on mats or animal skins or on the ground itself. During times of plenty, their menus might be stretched to include separate pots of yams or potatoes or rice, sometimes beans or even meat.

At church one weekend a group of youngsters presented a play that included a meal scene complete with real food—beans. Kate remembered that part well. The single dish had been carried to the table by a servant who supplied each actor with a spoon, and they all ate from the common dish. At school, the dormitory students were required to supply their own dishes and tableware—and the cafeteria strictly enforced the rule that a student who did not come with an eating utensil as well as a bowl would not be served. Now, as she looked down the long table under its snowy white cloths—who would guess they were sheets borrowed from hospital stocks— set with china and silver and crystal—borrowed from the missionaries—she felt a sense of near-pride that such a beautiful atmosphere could be created from their meager resources. Small vases holding red flowers from their yards—alternating bouquets of dahlias and roses—provided attractive accents between the candles.

A few minutes after everyone had been served, Mbayo came to consult Kate. "The cooks have had a little problem," she explained. "The main course is not yet quite ready, but there is lots of soup. Do you think we should serve more?"

"Certainly. Tell the servers to bring it in the large tureen and go to those whose plates are empty."

Mbayo kept her eyes toward the floor. "Yes, Madame," she replied.

Kate's back was toward the door leading to the kitchen, and she leaned forward to speak to the mission president, who sat at an angle across from her. She sensed a sudden change in the table conversation. She looked to the side. Jonas and Brigette-Therese stood behind Rene. Jonas held the beautiful, big silver tray their children had given them for their twenty-fifth anniversary. On it sat . . .

"Georgie!"

Ryan's voice cut above the other table sounds. He raised his hand and pointed toward Jonas.

Kate dropped her hands to her lap and suddenly became very interested in twisting the corner of her napkin into a very tight and very tiny wad. At the same time, she saw Ryan lean forward. He spoke along the table toward George.

"I didn't realize that's what they called you." His voice sounded unusually cheerful and very loud.

George shook his head and looked down.

"What. . .?"

The next question was never completed, for in that instant Kate found her tongue. "It's never been used before. I can assure you of that, because George and I . . ." She bit off what she started to say and changed it to "because it has always been kept in our storeroom, and I certainly don't know how it happens to be here now or why it's being used to serve." Her words rushed out and they, too, were too loud.

By then everyone was staring at Jonas. He and Brigette-Therese looked at each other. It was plain to see they understood that something was not just as it should be. At the same time, it was also plain that they were not exactly sure just what it was. Then both of them stared at Kate. For what seemed a very long moment, no one said another word.

"I hope you will not be angry with us, Madame." Speaking in her most careful school French, Brigette-Therese endeavored to fill the silence. "My elder sister says that you would not allow us to serve soup at the dining table from the kettle in which it was cooked. And since your other soup bowl slipped and happened to become broken when it fell to the floor, and when the accident happened we knew that you had hurt yourself and we did not want to trouble you any more, she went to find this other soup bowl that my sister knew you had in your storeroom, and we washed it very well as my sister says we must do with all things that come new from the stock before they are used."

All the dinner guests seemed uniquely interested in her run-together explanation.

"A soup pot, you say?"

Kate recognized Charlie's voice and looked toward the far end of the table where he sat. Brigette-Therese and Jonas also turned to look in his direction.

"They told me, before I came, that I might encounter some interesting experiences, that folk in Africa sometimes do things differently."

Brigette-Therese stood quietly beside Jonas, who had by now become statuelike with the silver platter immobile in his hands.

"GEORGIE!" Charlie read the name again.

George flushed. "That . . ." He pointed at the pot on the platter and burst into a series of giggles. He forced a deep breath and rushed the rest of his words—"wasagoingawaypresent." At that moment, the beauty of the stark-white ceramic glaze against the polished silver registered in Kate's mind. If it weren't for the bold crimson letters . . .

"The staff—" And a series of giggles humphed out again. "Of my last—ha-humph—school—" George managed to say. "They thought that—ha-humph—personalized facilities . . ."

Charlie stood and moved around the table to Brigette-Therese and Jonas. "Please," he said, lifting the large, antique-styled container from the tray. "Used to be a cafeteria host back in my school days." He held it shoulder level with his left hand in traditional butler fashion, then moved his right hand in a graceful sweep to draw attention to the large handle and full contours. "Isn't it beautiful?" he asked. "A going away present, you say?" He looked at George. "A personalized chamber pot?"

Kate laughed with the others.

Two mornings later she watched from the doorway of their house, still supporting herself with crutches, as Woody helped his wife, Marion, into their pickup. He turned and lifted his hand in a final wave, and Kate felt a pang of the emptiness that comes when leave-takings happen too soon. Even after he had climbed in and shut the door and had driven out of sight, Kate still stood there. Then she looked down at the white envelope she held.

"To read after we're gone," Woody had said when he'd dashed up to the house just minutes before and handed it to her. "Take very good care of yourself." And before Kate could think of a sensible thing to reply, he had turned and sprinted down their walk and onto the road to where the pickup waited. She turned, and leaning her weight onto the crutches, swung across the now very empty living room and along the hall to the study. There, she eased herself into her corner chair and opened the envelope. The single fold of paper held only a few lines of writing.

"I can't begin to repeat how sorry I am about your being hurt— and I blame myself for what happened. Please, do follow orders and let your leg heal as it should, for I'm hoping to find you well and strong and happy when I pass through Mbinda again in about six weeks' time. Looking forward to seeing you then. With wishes and prayers—Woody."

Kate refolded the paper, put it back into its envelope, slipped the envelope into a book she'd been reading that morning, and then she sat and stared across at the room, thinking many thoughts. The empty eyes in the mask faces in the backs of the wooden chairs stared back, and again she had the recurring sense that there was something she should be reading into those blank stares, but she didn't know what it was.

CHAPTER 17

Kate pushed herself up from the chair and limped slowly across to the other side of the room. The week was up and her foot, true to the calendar Ryan had set, was carrying her weight for short distances. She reached up and tugged at the edge of the curtain to pull it closed over the corner window.

"George—EEEEEEEE!"

George crossed the room in long, quick strides.

Kate flicked her hand. "Kill it!" she screamed, pointing to the floor.

George pivoted and brought the heel of his shoe down—hard. "Are you OK?"

Kate shivered and slumped back against the wall.

George lifted his foot and looked down. "It's . . ." He bent closer to get a better look. "It's . . ." He straightened and stepped back and slipped his arm comfortingly around Kate's waist, and she allowed her eyes to look at the thing that now lay in a tight S, still and unmoving.

"Sweetheart . . ." George began in a soothing voice and squeezed her. Then, abruptly, his words broke with a "ha-humph!"

Kate tensed. "Not funny!"

"But Katie, I just—ha-humph!-humph! . . .

She pulled against his arm.

"I killed—a—humph—A TAIL!" A full giggle snorted out. "Katie, I killed a gecko's TAIL!"

Kate stood stiffly by her husband. She did not laugh. She did not say anything more. She simply opened and closed her hand, and as she did so, her skin prickled into goose bumps, and shudders raced between her shoulders, and then she fisted both hands and pressed them up against her chin, wishing the rubbery wriggly crawly feeling would go away.

George pointed at a spot on the wall above the window. "Ha-humph!" he snorted again, and his arm flailed free from her waist, and he doubled into a series of giggles.

Kate dared her eyes to turn upward to look in the direction he had pointed, and her skin prickled again when she saw a sickly-beige body, its cold, rubbery texture angled motionless on its spindly-toed, suction-cup feet at a spot about four inches above the midpoint of the curtain rod. Its head was arched up, away from the wall, and two cold eyes stared back at her.

A gecko. And its body had no tail.

Her skin crawled. Only moments before, that same rubbery body had been in her hand. Her very hand! When she had grasped the curtain. It had pulled free. But its tail had stayed. Squirming! In HER HAND!

110

Only by sheer determination had she learned to live in the same house with those little pale bodies. Even though they'd stuffed lengths of foam into the cracks where the high ceilings had in places shrunk away from the walls of the old house and had tacked protective stripping along the bottoms of the doors, the geckos and other even less-wanted visitors continually found ways of slipping in. There'd been the hand-sized, hairy spider crouched by her bed stand one evening. That had inspired a leap from floor to center bed. Then there were the scorpions, dull, brick-red fellows, not more than a couple inches long, who occasionally appeared, just like that, sitting in a corner, stingers arched over their backs. One morning she'd stubbed into a solid clay mound, bigger than a football, on the floor in the middle of the hall—the overnight creation of termites. Not only were the geckos less objectionable than those, they ate termites and other lesser-sized invaders.

Frederick J Cat, their gray tiger-striped mouser who bore his name as the result of having arrived while Kenny was with them, was fascinated by the little lizards. She and George had watched one day when Frederick J cornered one. He swatted at it. The gecko scooted, out of control, across a brick. Frederick J leapt after it, swatting again. Kate was about to call the cat off when, suddenly, the gecko flipped to its feet and raced full tilt toward the wall of the house. Frederick J seemed not to notice that his prey was escaping. Instead he sat, head turned and lowered, staring. He swatted again—this time at the tail which its owner, true to the protective habit of its kind, had left behind to distract its pursuer.

Kate had laughed then.

Later that evening, someone tapped at the door. "May I speak with Madame?" Kate heard Marie asking George.

"I'm sorry to disturb you, Madame," the girl said when she came in, "but I have news that can change the plans we've made."

"Why don't you sit down and tell me about it."

"I have received a letter from my home village written by someone for the mother with whom I lived. The news is only a little good."

"Only a little good?"

"That's right, Madame. Only a little good."

"Did you bring the letter?"

Marie nodded.

"Do you suppose I should read it?" By experience, Kate knew the quickest way to get to the crux of the problem would be to read for herself.

Marie nodded again. "Yes, Madame, I think you should read it, and that's why I brought it with me." She paged through the notebook she carried and found a rumpled airmail envelope. An olive-gray stain spread over much of its lower half. Diesel fuel. Drums of diesel—for refueling—were as perennial on the overloaded trucks that provided the area's only public transport as were the people and goats and chickens and goods piled high on the open backs. Everything invariably arrived in less than perfect condition. Marie lifted the flap, drew out a folded sheet, its edges ragged from having been torn from a school notebook, and handed it to Kate.

Kate scanned the first few lines carrying the usual declaration that the writer was very happy to have the occasion to take "this little piece of paper and my poor pen" to share with you "my news" and to tell you that "all is going well except . . ." The "except" is what interested her.

"The mother with whom you were living," the writer continued, "has asked me to write these words to you and to tell you that during one night after you had left and while the chief was away the bandits returned and attacked the homes of Papa Enos and Papa Justin. They came while everyone was sleeping, breaking down the doors and chasing the families from their beds. By the time any of the others realized what was happening, the bandits had left, taking all the clothes and belongings from the houses and leaving the thatch on the roofs burning. Both families are gone and we have heard that they are in the city where it is safer for them. For this reason," the letter continued, "we are telling you that it is better to stay where you are during the Christmas vacation and to not come here. It is too dangerous for you to be here now but possibly you can come after the school year has ended. Everyone sends their greetings and we are waiting to hear your news."

Kate folded the letter and handed it back to Marie. "That means you won't be able to go to harvest your field."

"No. But I will write a letter to ask the mother to do that and to send me a sack of cassava with a truck so I can have it to eat and some money so I can pay for my next school fees."

"That's a good idea," Kate encouraged, though she considered the possibility extremely remote that either food or money would arrive. "And since you must stay, perhaps you would like to have some extra work?" she suggested.

"Yes, I would like that."

"Pastor Rene has contract work for some students in the new garden project he is starting. Mr. Lloyd's in charge. If you'd like, I can talk to him."

"I would like that very much, Madame. I like garden work."

"Then I'll let you know tomorrow."

"Oh, thank you, Madame. Then I can go now?"

"Just one question."

"Yes, Madame."

"You've told me that your chief sent you here because this is a mission of his church, yet you've said that we have no church in your village. How is that?"

"I don't know exactly, but it seems that when the chief was a young man, some missionaries visited our village, and afterward they sent some teachers. The people say that what was being taught was very interesting, that it made good sense. Several, including the chief, were baptized. But then the teachers left, and no one else came, and the people had no pastor to teach them anymore, and the church got old, and it fell down in the rains."

113

Kate had heard similar stories from other villages. Adobe buildings lasted only a few years. With no leaders, the people also lost interest.

"The chief told me, though, that in his heart his church still lives, and he asked me to learn all I can so when I return to the village I can teach him and the others.

"And are you learning things to teach them?"

"Oh yes. I didn't know before that the Bible has so many interesting and good things. I like my Bible classes more than any of the other classes. And the pastor has said that I can be in the class that will study for the baptism and that maybe when there is another baptism by the end of the year, I can be baptized. There is one thing, though, Madame." Marie hesitated. "The chief asked me if I couldn't please buy him a Bible. But . . . I had to give all the money I had to the school."

"Doesn't he have a Bible?"

Marie shook her head. "No, Madame. Almost no one has a Bible in our village."

When the girl was gone, Kate sat, head back, regarding the upper edge of the wall across from her, looking but not seeing. "George." Her voice had the sound of being very far away. "Are there any more Bibles and study books left?"

"Maybe a couple. Why?"

"For Marie's chief. I did some asking around during committees. The Africans tell me there's been nothing out in that part of the province for over twenty years, that for all practical purposes our mission does not exist for those people. And that . . ." She searched for something emphatic enough to say. "That's a sin!"

On Sunday afternoon Kate called Marie to the house and gave her a well-wrapped package containing five Bibles and five study books in her local language. "One set for the family of your adopted mother, one for the chief, the other three for families which the chief chooses," Kate instructed. "In your letter, tell them to study together at least twice a week—and to pray. And let them know that we're praying for them too."

114

"Oh, Madame, they'll be happy, very, very happy." The girl held the package reverently in her two hands, and for a moment Kate thought she was going to lift it to her lips and kiss it.

"And more good news," Kate continued. "Mr. Lloyd says you should be at the farm shop at seven-thirty Tuesday morning so he can show you your new work."

"Emergency, Pet." George strode into the house about an hour later. "Could you help me throw a few things together in case I have to spend the night."

"Spend the night where?"

"In town. The hospital's main microscope vanished. I've been with

Doc since they discovered it's gone. A tile's lifted from the ceiling over the microscope table to make it look like thieves crawled in through the attic—but it's a mystery how anybody could get into the attic from outside. We suspect an inside job. Regardless, we've got to report to the authorities—ask them to do a search. By the time we get to town on these roads, we probably won't find anyone to report to till tomorrow."

Kate shook her head. "I hear what you're saying—not that I like it."

"Sorry. But I can't let Doc go alone. Anyway. The deans have everything organized for the kids to leave tomorrow morning on the trucks we've hired. Otherwise . . ." He shrugged. "School's out. There's nothing particular that has to be done."

Kate stood and hobbled toward the kitchen. "I'll make you a few sandwiches. And there's plenty of water in the fridge." Boiling drinking water was another of Mbayo's daily tasks, and she kept a huge pot of water sitting at the back of the old kitchen range almost perpetually, ready to take advantage of the fire as soon as it was lighted to begin the midday meal. With the wood supply near the mission dwindling, they tried to make-do with one hot meal a day, eating mainly fruit and bread in the morning and just snacking in the evening. "Do you think you can find something for lunch in town tomorrow?"

"I'm sure the pastor's wife'll make us rice and beans. We should be back in the afternoon." George went to find his sleeping bag, "not that it's cool enough now to need one," he called back to Kate, "but it makes a good mattress to ease over the hard places."

So it was that Kate was alone that evening. She went to the study and settled herself at the desk with her notebook journal. "December 21, Monday. Mbinda Mission," she wrote, and then added the bit of question she'd borrowed from Charlie's workshop, "What good thing?" She sat, pen stuck between her fingers, chin cupped against her palm, elbow braced on desk, staring into space, and somehow she found herself thinking about Woody and remembering how he'd said her

115

name that evening and how good it had felt when his hand had closed around hers. "Six weeks."

The voices of her mind drifted dreamily.

"Kate Shayne!"

The warning of her own voice jarred through her imaginings. She locked her fingers together and twisted her hands and felt the hardness of her ring. And George's words on that day in Johannesburg stood against her other thoughts. "Let's make these rings symbolize the two new people we've become . . ."

"New people?"

Suddenly she was hearing that other voice, an innocent, casual voice. "When Mr. Director stops in that town he always goes to the pastor's house." She'd tried to bury that information where it wouldn't trouble her. But it kept resurfacing. Abruptly she pushed against the desk, and the chair rolled back, and she stood and began to stride back and forth across the study.

"Lying. He's lying." She slid her hands into the deep pockets of her skirt. "I want to go home." She was no longer thinking of the children. Or of being near them. Or of telephones. "I want to get away—to get him away—from her."

116

She continued to stride back and forth, considering places to go, to live, to work. Again the realization penetrated that they had no home, no place to go. They'd sold their house before leaving for overseas. They had no property. If they went, they'd be at the whims of where a job for George might be. But what job? In education? Administration? Now? After their years overseas?

In frustration she stamped her right foot down—hard—and the pain arched across it and upward through her ankle and into her leg. Startled, she stood where she was until the pain eased and she could limp back to the desk, where she dropped into the chair and let herself slump forward so her head rested on the notebook where she had been writing.

CHAPTER 18

"Luanne!" Kate stepped back in surprise the next day and swung the door open. The Australian nurse's spotlessly white uniform was as pressed and prim as always, but her tawny hair, normally drawn back and fastened securely into a bun, straggled over her ears, and her firmly molded lips moved as if they were testing words and then not wanting to speak them. "What is it?" Luanne usually was so rushed when she stopped by that Kate considered it inappropriate to invite her in. Now she motioned toward a chair.

"When will the doctor and your husband come?" Luanne's words came in a twanged rhythm as she lowered herself into the chair.

"Possibly toward evening. Why?"

"No one's told you?"

"Told me what?"

"About the accident?"

"Accident?"

"The pickup taking students to Loma. A runner came, and I've just asked Lloyd to take two nurses and stretchers in his vehicle. I . . ." Luanne's voice faltered.

"Are some of our kids hurt?"

Luanne nodded. "Somewhere in the hills on the other side of the river. They must have hit a bad patch of mud and slid out of control and slammed into a bank." Now that she had started talking, she seemed unable to put the matter into quick words. "Your student Daniel, from what the messenger said, was sitting on top of the framework—like they always do but like they're always told not to do—and his leg got crushed between the truck and the bank."

"Daniel? Is it bad?"

Luanne nodded. "It sounds like it. And one of the younger boys, from what they describe, a broken arm likely. And . . ." She paused and her hazel eyes grew rounder and larger, and a rim of moisture formed around them. "Maurice had gone with them. He wanted to see his brother."

Kate listened, not speaking, waiting for Luanne to say what she needed to say.

"The truck carried a barrel of fuel. Somehow Maurice fell between the barrel and the frame, and it clamped him across the chest. They say he can hardly breathe. That there's blood. I sent our best nurses. Oh, Kate. I wanted to go. To be with him. But . . . there's no one else to get things ready to receive them. To prepare the operating room. And the doctor's not here. And . . . what are we going to do?"

The details Luanne was pouring out tried to order themselves in Kate's mind. Local folk had been dropping hints about Maurice, the handsome hospital laboratory technician whose poise had made him such a good host the night of the banquet, and their missionary nurse. Kate, though, had never previously heard Luanne bring his name into conversation. She glanced across at the clock. "George did tell me to be at the radio at four," she said. "That's in about twenty minutes."

"Do you think they'll come today?"

Kate nodded. "We'll find out when." Then she turned the conversation back to Luanne. "Maurice is quite a capable person, isn't he?"

Luanne was studying the floor. "I really haven't talked to anyone before," she admitted. "The doctor has no patience for missionaries 'fraternizing' with locals. But . . . why are we here? And Maurice? He and I. Well. You know he did his laboratory specialty in South Africa. He's not like the other fellows who've never been out of the country and don't know anything other than their village way of life."

Kate went to stand by the younger woman and laid a hand on her shoulder. "He's become very special to you, hasn't he?"

Luanne started to shake her head, then lifted her hands and let her face drop into them. "We've been talking . . ." Her voice was muffled. "I don't know. People say an African only wants a white woman so he can use her to get out of the country. To go overseas. To get further education. But . . . Maurice . . . I . . . we . . ."

Kate sat on the edge of the big chair and slid her arm around Luanne's shoulders. "You're worried?" she asked and felt her neighbor's head nod against her side.

"Oh, Kate, from what the runner said—he's hurt worse than bad. I wanted to go, but I was afraid. Afraid I couldn't help him. Afraid of how I might react. Afraid."

Pity. Kinship in feeling. Kate's emotions stretched out in support of Luanne, and she squeezed her again.

"He needs to have the doctor here."

Kate again looked at the clock. "We'll go to the radio now." She slipped her arm free, stood, then reached her hand to Luanne. "I'm still going pretty slow with this strapped foot of mine. Pray, Luanne. Pray that someone comes on. That even if they haven't finished their business, that we can get the message to them to come—immediately."

"I have been praying, Kate. In my heart I'm praying."

For the first few moments at the radio, they heard nothing but a rumbling of static and a few louder snaps caused, possibly, by a distant storm. Then a faint "Sixty-Eight. Sixty-Eight."

Kate quickly held the microphone up. "Sixty-Eight is by." She almost shouted the words, willing the operator on the other end to hear. "Is that you Seven-Nine?"

"Roger. Roger." The reply was faint.

"Are Doctor Bellington and Mr. Shayne still there?"

"Negative. They . . ." and the voice disappeared under a loud stuttering of static.

"Please repeat. Please repeat."

"Doctor Bellington and Mr. Shayne left . . ." And again the words faded.

Kate looked at Luanne then hollered into the mike. "What time did they leave? What time?"

A burst of static was the only reply.

Kate drew a deep breath and forcefully repeated the question. A distant voice seemed to reply, but she could not be sure. "Repeat. Please Repeat."

"They left . . ." The voice flared clearer. "Fourteen hours."

"You say they left at fourteen hours. At two o'clock?"

"Affirmative."

About forty-five minutes later Kate heard their pickup coming up Pioneer Way. Then in another ten minutes, even before George came into the house, she heard a second vehicle. "Lloyd?" She shook her head in amazement and looked upward.

When George did come in, he was not alone. "Lloyd just came with the fellows hurt in the accident," he reported. "Luanne had already met us. Said you knew. Her friend's hurt bad. And Daniel. Doc's going straight to surgery. And . . ."

Kate heard what he was saying, but she was staring past him at the rotund person who stood behind him.

"Sorry, Pet." He stepped forward and kissed her on the cheek. "I'm not sure if you've met my friend. Arno Steveny. You've probably seen him in town. He's the big chief at the brewery."

Big for sure! Kate thought as she acknowledged his "Pleased to meet you" and invited them both in. "Are you going to be spending some time with us?" she asked.

"Not sure." The large man lowered himself carefully onto the couch.

120

"We found him stranded just a few Ks the other side of the junction," George explained. "He'd already sent a messenger on for parts."

"Alternator," Arno inserted. "That monster's always needing a new alternator. Should travel with at least two spares."

"Anyway, Doc and I invited him to the mission—he'll be staying over in the guest room—so he left some guards with the truck, and here we are. I told him I was sure you could find something in the fridge for us to eat and drink."

"I'll get some juice for both of you right now. You must be thirsty." The words came automatically.

When she came back with the juice, Arno accepted his with a "Thanks! This looks very good." He took a sip and smacked his lips appreciatively. "I knew I couldn't expect to find anything from my plant at your place—you missionaries usually don't give me much business—so I had the boys toss a couple cases into the back of your pickup." He turned to George. "Do you have a fellow who can bring them in?"

When George went to the door to call for Jonas, Kate felt her face blanch. Not only were they not drinkers; alcoholic beverages were strictly forbidden on the mission grounds. "Uh . . ." She searched for the right words, words that would gently explain that it would be better not to bring any beer into the house.

"You might want to share it around with the other families," Arno continued happily.

"Bring two in and put them in the pantry," George was telling Jonas. "Deliver the others to Parmers and the Doctor and Mademoiselle Luanne." Kate could not believe what she was hearing. Then Jonas came in through the door almost hidden behind the two red cases he carried.

"I know you folk don't even care for Coke," Arno bubbled on. "So I had my boys put in some of our new lemonade soda and the old favorite, orange."

"My!" exclaimed Kate, "That certainly is very thoughtful. And . . . a real . . . ." She started to say "surprise" but instead said, "treat."

"You know Arno's wife goes to our church in town?"

"Yes. Yes," agreed Arno almost before George had finished the question. "Since that time the doctor took care of her—she had an operation out here at the hospital a few years back—she was so impressed with the way she was treated, and with the doctor. She never expected to recover when she fell sick, you know. There'd been some problems between her family and me, and she was sure one of them had put a spell on her and that she'd never live to come home again."

Kate had heard that he was married to a local woman and that their children were studying in France.

"Well, when she recovered so quickly and felt so much better than she'd felt in ages, she decided that was all because of you folks' church. She's been going every since. And she keeps after me to come with her. Yeah. I might . . . But, how can I? A brewer? Get involved with your church?" Arno laughed as if that were the greatest joke. Then he began to cough. "The doctor said I should 'ave a visit wi' 'im in 'is office while I'm 'ere." His words came out mostly in halves on a series of wheezes. "That 'e might be able to 'elp wi' this."

Much later, after they'd gone to bed, Kate finally had a chance to ask George about the microscope and the trip to town.

122

"Well. It seems Maurice had slipped Doc a very quiet tip about a group who're operating out of Loma and who've got inside contacts here on the mission. Who, though, is the puzzle that has yet to be solved. So Doc badgered the chief of justice until he promised to send out an inspector. Not just about the microscope but for the diesel fuel, the thefts from fields and gardens—which includes your pineapple—and the medicines disappearing from the hospital pharmacy."

"By this time the microscope's probably already in the back room of one of the scores of little clinics in the city."

"Or, maybe under a heap of clothes at the bottom of a basket in a back room of one of our own mission houses," George suggested. "Wherever. We need help to find it—and they're sending a detective."

"Detective?" Kate laughed as though there were something

funny about the word.

George ignored her reaction. "What's this about Luanne and Maurice?"

"Seems there's truth to the rumors we've heard. Luanne talked some today—and I get the idea that she wants someone to help her think this through."

"Well, Pet, if there's anyone here who can help her think . . . I don't know how you do it, but you've got some charisma that attracts others to confide in you."

"Charisma." Kate laughed again, but this time her thoughts spun off in another direction. *Help others when I can't even help myself?* Aloud she said, "I certainly don't have any great wealth of wisdom to share, but a listening ear does sometimes allow others to hear themselves think out loud so they can find their own solutions."

"Then listen carefully, Pet," and George reached out and pulled her close to him. "I love you. I love the new you I'm seeing lately. The way you do your hair. The way. Oh, I just love you. And every time I hear myself tell you that, I believe it more and more."

"I love you too."

The profound tropical night with its moonless darkness was broken only by the occasional *chu-umph* of a tree bat, the chirps and murmurs of the insects, and the soft trill of some night bird. They said nothing more, but Kate lay there sorting through thoughts and wondering how she could, or even if she should, share them with George.

A lone lamp stood on the battered metal stand beside the bed in the far corner of the ward, its pale flame glimmering just enough to highlight the whiteness of a nurse's uniform.

"Luanne."

The nurse took the hand that reached toward her. "Don't try to talk," she whispered. For a few moments the only break in the silence was the raspy coughing from three beds over and the night sounds coming through the open window. Then she spoke again. "I'm proud of you. Hurt so bad yet still able to tell the others what to do until Lloyd got there with the nurses." She could tell that Maurice smiled, and she smiled in return and squeezed his hand and enjoyed that feeling of relief that comes when a doctor has told you that someone you care about very much is going to be all right.

"Daniel?"

His question was one she didn't want to answer completely right then. The doctor was worried, too worried, about the boy. "Resting," she said, and left it at that.

CHAPTER 19

Kate slipped out of bed early the next morning—predawn was the coolest and quietest time of the day—and hurried to the study to be alone to write. Soon the glow from the twelve-volt fluorescent fixture fell comfortably over her desk, but the strength of its light did not reach the corner where the two dark wood chairs, the hippo, and the basket stood. In the shadowy half-light, the tiny mouth in the mask face on one of the chairs looked pensive, as if it were about to speak. "Nothing ever just happens." She could almost hear it wisely repeating that premise so basic to the everyday life of the people around her. The idea formed the context of local logic, for in traditional philosophy, everything—good or evil—is caused by someone, and that someone could be either living or dead.

"Don't talk to me about germs," a young hunter had argued to Ryan when he arrived with a grossly infected leg wound. "My aunt is angry with me because I hunt and find game while that lazy son of hers stays at home and sits in the shade."

"Is that so?" Ryan asked as he examined the leg.

"It is the truth," his patient responded gravely. "She's the one who made the gun misfire and caused the wound to become as it is."

"Did she go hunting with you?" Ryan feigned innocence.

"Aah-ahh. Her." The answer might have been spoken in disdain, but the words continued in an almost respectful tone. "She's been dead now for many years. Maybe even ten. When I awoke from my sleep that day before going hunting, I had a sharp pain in my leg. I should have paid attention to the warning and stayed at home."

Pains, the twitching of an eye, the spasm of a particular muscle— all these were taken as warnings that something bad was about to happen. "Superstitions." Kate shook her head in a way that could have been taken as belittling. Suddenly she remembered something she'd heard many times during her growing years. "God orders and controls all events of our everyday lives." Some Christians even claimed that a particular thing happening was sure evidence that God had sanctioned it. "Then Woody?" The question rushed in. "If the two of us are brought together . . . then it must be good—and right?" She clutched after the hope that this might be true. "If he comes and . . ." She lapsed into dreamy speculations. "But how can God approve of something He's specifically forbidden?" With the shock of cold water, the new question smacked across her daydreams. "Things happen. Guns misfire because of mechanical defects, because of carelessness, because of other reasons, not because of dead aunts. Wounds became infected because of neglect. People . . ."

"Find excuses to do what they want." That's what George had said when . . .

Kate gasped. A gray blur sailed across her line of vision. And landed on a chair cushion. "Frederick J!" Her voice almost shook. The cat lifted his feline head, stretched his mouth into an exaggerated yawn, then arranged himself into a comfortable curl.

Masks and other ceremonial objects belonging to the traditions of local tribes intrigued Kate, but she'd never seen them used except at commercial dances for tourists. A few times they'd spent the night in one or another of the more distant villages and had sat with the family at the evening fires and joined in their talk. Other than that, her meeting ground with the people was almost exclusively at school or at church or at her own home. And she felt cheated. Cheated because the work they were obliged to do sheltered them from getting to know the very people they'd come to help and from an understanding of their way of thinking about life and death and the conditions that controlled both.

"If God created Lucifer, who became Satan, and if He knew Lucifer would sin, then, really, God is responsible for our sin, isn't He?"

The first time one of the boys had posed the question, she brushed it aside as mere rhetoric to prove the asker's superior intellectual powers. Now when she heard it, she took the question more seriously. In the traditions of ancestor worship, religion controlled every aspect of life, and all events were manipulated by the spirits of dead ancestors. Sometimes the spirits worked alone, sometimes they worked in cooperation with the living. Regardless—no matter what happened—there was always someone else to blame for any bad outcome.

"But Lucifer didn't have to sin." She heard herself repeating what had become her standard answer. "Lucifer and the other heavenly beings, as well as people—we're all created with the freedom to choose. We ourselves are responsible for the choices we make."

Woody?

Her own words spoke against what she wanted. She, herself, was responsible for what she chose to do. She thought again of his upcoming visit. "At committee time I prayed for help. I fell and hurt my leg. And that's where it should end." She spoke firmly.

Light had by then erased the shadowy effects of the room. Sunrise happened so quickly at their latitude that at times the sun seemed literally to jump into the sky. The seasonal mists, though, had again veiled its progress, and were now filtering its light through their opaque curtaining, dulling it, and pulling the mission into an enigmatic hush. She pushed her chair away from her desk and went over to the window. She found the mists intriguing, and in some ways almost an extension of her own thoughts. Usually they drifted in fragmented streamers, mostly tracing the wandering path of the river, innocent bits that accented the morning's freshness. But then there were the other times, such as this morning, when they blanketed the entire mission, gathering it into a nebulous, ill-defined sphere, wrapping it with a brooding, melancholy atmosphere. And she stared out into the filmy, indistinct distance and saw in it the vagueness of her own earlier resolutions.

"That's where it must end," she told herself firmly now.

In the background she heard George talking to someone, and with a start remembered that Arno was coming for breakfast. She left her desk as it was and headed for the kitchen. Then from the hall she plainly recognized Ryan's voice.

"Someone should go for them."

"What's happening?" she asked when George joined her in the kitchen.

"Daniel. Doc thinks we should get the parents."

"Is it that bad?"

George nodded.

"Who's with him now?"

"One of his school friends.

"How far's their home?"

"About 120 Ks past Loma. And if you think the road between here and Loma is bad . . ." George shook his head. "Can't travel the other side without a four-by-four." He sounded tired. "So it's between Lloyd and me. Lloyd's the only one who can supervise the contract kids, so . . ."

"Here, would you set this on the table?" Kate heard what he was saying, but instead of encouraging or even speaking to the idea, she handed him a plate stacked with several slices of bread and a pot of her homemade mango jam. "In honor of Arno I'm going to light the propane stove and whip up some oatmeal with mashed banana. Another stalk's just come ripe—if you're going over to the hospital, take some down for Daniel and his friend. And for Maurice, if he can have anything." Her comments hurried from one item to the next. "Have Luanne give the rest out in the kids' ward. How is Maurice?"

"Pretty miserable, Doc says, with all those broken ribs. But he'll be fine."

128

Just then Arno came.

"The pastor's boy, is it?" he asked, on learning about Daniel's condition. "Look," he said. "I know the boy's village. I know the roads. I have all day with nothing to do. Let me take a vehicle and fetch them."

Kate looked at George. "That's a super offer!" he exclaimed. "Let me say Yes before you can change your mind."

"I'm serious. Maybe I could use the opportunity to be locked in a vehicle with a preacher."

"Something's on your friend's mind," Kate remarked after Arno had left.

George nodded. "The Africans with his truck were saying his wife had a dream—about a road that led to the mission and that if someone came and offered to take him along that road, he should not refuse." Dreams frequently played a prominent part in stories the school staff and other mission workers recounted when telling what had influenced their decisions for Christ. "Well, he's here."

It was late afternoon by the time Arno returned. He left Daniel's parents at the hospital then brought the pickup back and parked it in the garage. "Quite a road, and quite a day," he commented when he brought the keys to Kate. "Mind if I have a drink?"

129

"Fanta?"

"I'd prefer some of your good juice, if there's any more to be had."

"Sure is." Arno had already settled into a living-room chair. "We'll be having supper in about an hour—so, why don't you just stay?" she invited. "George should be home soon. In the meantime, there are several of our newer"—she emphasized the word newer—"magazines in the rack by your chair." She needed a pineapple for her fruit salad—the ones remaining since the theft had just started ripening—and when she returned from the garden, George was talking with Arno.

"Our Daniel's pretty low," she heard him say. "I was just at the hospital, and the parents are praising the Lord you brought them today."

"Happy to do it," Arno responded.

"Daniel's is an interesting story," George continued. "In August his father and I both were at mission committee meetings in the city. He told me that since Daniel was beginning his final year at school, it was time for him to be baptized, and would I please see that he be baptized in the next baptism. I asked if that's what Daniel wanted and his father said, 'Well, it is a good time. He knows all the church doctrine and is a good boy. Since I'm a pastor, I'd like him to be baptized.' Our church, of course, teaches that baptism is an individual matter, so the best I could do was to promise to talk to the boy.

" 'Your father wants you to be baptized,' I said. 'Is this what you're planning?'

"Daniel didn't answer me directly but instead said, 'You know that I'm expecting to enter the government university next year.' He wants to study medicine. 'Then you'd like to be baptized before you go,' I suggested, and he replied that he thought he should wait until he'd finished medicine and was ready to go to work. This didn't exactly add up to what his father wanted, so I pushed him further. 'Don't you want to be a Christian?' I asked.

"He said he definitely did, that he believes in God and in the Bible, and that having grown up in a pastor's home he can't be **130** anything other than a Christian. Then he explained that certain university classes and examinations are held on the Sabbath. And he told how some older friends who were already at the university had asked to have them on another day. In some cases the request was granted; in others it wasn't. Those who didn't write their exams were failed and dismissed from school.

" 'If I'm baptized, that shows I'll do everything the church teaches,' he told me. Then he said 'What if next year in my first year at university, when I'm having to prove myself as a student—what if I have to choose between writing an examination on the Sabbath day or of being dismissed from school? What if I'm not strong? What if I choose to take my exam? I can't be baptized now and make myself a liar.' "

"Now that's a man!"

The force of Arno's interjection surprised Kate.

"That's the sort of fellow I'd like to have working with me in my office—one I can trust."

"Why do you say that?" George asked.

"Well, as I understand it, the Sabbath is supposed to be some sort of sign between the person and God." Arno paused and cleared his throat. "Don't worry, since my wife got converted, she's been talking and quoting texts and telling me to get down on my knees and repent. Well, I've always thought religion was good for women and kids. My folks sent me to Sunday school in the Cathedral when we lived in the city—Dad was a regional officer in the colonial service, and I was born out here." He paused again, then began in a softer voice. "Sometimes a man has to make hard choices, and one of them has to be about God. All my wife's talking got me started reading the Bible, and I see in the Old Testament that Sabbath keeping is a sign of someone who worships God."

Kate was astounded by what she heard coming from the brewer's mouth.

"It's not something you do to prove anything to anyone, not even to God. It's something special between you and God." Arno laughed apologetically. "Well, I'm not a preacher, so I don't explain things with the right words, but I see being Christian as following Jesus Christ's example, and the Sabbath's part of that package deal— a sign of who you are, not of what you do. That's why I like what that young man told you. He's honest and not about to take a vow that he's not sure he can keep."

"Doc's pretty worried about him." George's voice sounded grave. "The injury itself is bad enough. Now he finds the spleen's damaged by a chronic malaria, and he's not sure the boy's strong enough to cope with all the mending his body needs."

There was no significant change in Daniel's condition that day or the next. Then it was Christmas Eve. Arno was still at the mission, and as usual he was at the breakfast table precisely at seven. "Don't you folk do anything special for Christmas?" he asked.

"Believe it or not, Christmas is our biggest family tradition. But . . ." Kate let her words trail away—it wasn't comfortable to explain the lonesomeness or the pain of the news about Karla's baby. She didn't want any reminders. "Well," she finally said, "putting up decorations and baking special goodies just makes me miss our children all the more."

"Don't you have any kids here?"

"Hundreds of them." Her reply was automatic.

"I've always thought that you Americans knew how to make a real Christmas."

Arno's comments rode with Kate. "Do you think we should do something?" she finally asked George. "Maybe invite the others over?"

"Wouldn't hurt."

Before midmorning she had Jonas carry notes around to Carole, Ryan, and Luanne, asking if they were free to come for the evening. Lloyd and Carole had already invited some of the African teachers to their place. Ryan had been at the hospital nearly around the clock for the last three days and was looking forward to getting to bed early. Luanne's reply was simply that, "Maurice needs me this evening."

Primed for a party, Kate called Jonas. "Bring me those two big boxes that are stored on the top shelf in the garage," she instructed. "Then I have another message for you to deliver."

CHAPTER
20

A rosy glow backgrounded the three tall palms in Ryan's side yard. "Perfect!" Kate let herself relax into the sunset's quiet beauty. The day had been hot, too hot, and most of it had found her in the kitchen with Mbayo. Fresh from the shower now, she stood on their wide porch enjoying the more comfortable evening temperature. As she watched, the glow began to fade—darkness always rushed in to cut short their sunsets—and the intensely silhouetted palms changed to a flat gray. Voices approached. She turned to greet the forms that trailed toward her along the walk. Then they were in the living room.

"Merry Christmas!"

Six heads turned and stared at the huge figure that swayed through the doorway.

"Ho! Ho! Ho! Merry Christmas!"

Arno's voice was unmistakable, but his ample chins were now hidden under a long cotton beard. A large mustache poufed out, curling up at either side of his face. A red Santa suit hugged around him, straining at its buttons. A big lumpy sack drooped over his left shoulder.

The six youngsters continued to stare.

George appeared. He dragged a tree toward them. "Come!" He

stopped in the middle of the room and smiled.

The youngsters sat where they were.

Arno let his sack drop to the floor and nodded and motioned to them. "It's time to trim the tree."

Marie and Jeanne and the four boys got up from their places and took pieces from the boxes Kate brought and put them on the tree as they were told. Kate waited for the excitement, that special Christmas Eve feeling to fill the room. The youngsters worked mechanically. Even when the tree stood smothered in colorful ornaments and tinsel and garlands, the six youngsters regarded it with a matter-of-fact noninterest and went back and sat in their places.

Kate felt disappointed. *It's not working*, she thought. *They don't understand.*

George slid the tree toward the wall then bent to do something as Arno reached back and flipped the light switch. Momentary darkness fell, then a gasp echoed along the couch where the boys sat.

"That's . . . That's . . ." Job's voice groped for words.

"Beautiful!" Marie spoke reverently. "I've never seen anything so beautiful."

"Like real silver and gold."

"Like stars, all clustered together."

134

Young Luke hunched forward as if to better examine the lighted tree. Jeanne sat close to Marie in the chair they shared, silent, statuelike.

"Isn't that more magnificent than anything you've ever seen?" Marie's question hung momentarily unanswered.

"I . . ."

The single syllable aspirated into silence, and for a few moments no one spoke, no one moved.

"I think that must be what heaven's like." Jeanne's awed voice broke the silence.

"Maybe like the glory of the angels who came down to sing for the shepherds." Arno spoke now and struggled to his feet and went to stand close to the tree. The multicolored glow softened the heavy red of the suit he wore and rested on the pages of the open Bible he held. Soon his rich baritone made Luke's story of the first Christmas come alive. When he finished reading, the room was quiet until Marie's clear soprano spontaneously pitched a note. The others joined.

"Silent night, holy night."

Kate opened her mouth to sing with them, but the words faded on her lips. Her eyes rested on the faces of her young guests, but all she could see was a confusion of mud huts and a Bethlehem stable and youngsters who lived with nothing more than stars and evening fires to light their nights.

Their evening ended after they ate and opened the gifts that were in Arno's bag—flashlights and books and packages of cookies—and George drove the six students home to Kato village. Arno went back to his apartment. Kate sat alone, enjoying the still lighted tree, feeling good about the evening and remembering other happy times past. The insects sang their usual evening songs, the warm darkness rested solidly around the house, and she felt the contentment of Christmas. A knock startled her. She got up and went to the door.

"Luanne!"

"Excuse me for coming now, but . . ."

"Come in!" Kate exclaimed. "Have some Christmas cook-ies and juice. George has just taken the kids home, and . . ."

Luanne had already settled herself in a chair and was shaking her head. "Your tree's beautiful, but I can't eat."

The tone of her voice stopped Kate from insisting that she have something. "Have you just come from the hospital?" she asked.

Luanne nodded.

"How's Maurice?"

"Healing very nicely."

"You were able to spend an uninterrupted evening with him?" The glow from the Christmas tree lights had a softening effect on Luanne's square features.

"Mostly. But . . . have you heard that Sylvanus's mother is being accused of causing Maurice's accident, of putting a curse on him?"

"Sylvanus?" Luanne's question caught Kate like a sudden whirlwind. "The boy who was killed by lightning? His mother? But whateverfor?"

"Because of the microscope."

The details hit Kate's mind in a disjointed jumble. "I don't follow."

"Well, as Maurice often says, the people here complicate things that aren't complicated. But this time it's getting too complicated."

Kate studied Luanne's face as she rushed into her story.

"Maurice's aunt came in this evening—a very wise little lady who's been a Christian for years. She told us what the villagers are saying—that Maurice has accused Sylvanus's uncle, the mother's brother, to the doctor as being the head of a band of thieves who are stealing from the mission and that they're responsible for taking the microscope."

As Luanne talked, Andre's name came to Kate's mind, but she had no idea why it did.

"One of the young men from the village—they call him 'Douze'—claims to have overheard two people talking, one telling the other that Maurice had told the doctor that the uncle was the ringleader of the thieves. Douze . . . that's French for *twelve*, you know."

Kate nodded.

136

"Well, Douze—Twelve—claims to have thirteen witnesses who heard him telling this to the chief. Since he has all those witnesses who heard him say what he said, he claims that what he said has to be true." Luanne paused and shook her head. "His logics best me, but what I do know is that since Maurice's aunt says that since Maurice is accused by Douze of telling this to the doctor, Sylvanus's mother went to the strongest witch doctor in the village and asked him to fix a curse so that Maurice would be killed in an accident on the way home."

"How did they know he was traveling?"

"Simple. All the villages around know everything that goes on in the mission. Their ankle express gets news out faster than we can travel by car."

The story Luanne was telling resembled many others Kate had heard. "What are they saying now that Maurice survived and is going to be OK?" she asked.

"That he has a stronger power."

"You mean, the fact that he's Christian?"

Luanne shook her head, and again Kate was struck with the idea that the younger woman could actually be pretty if she'd soften her hairstyle and get some blouses in roses or reds that would bring out the color in her face. "Then what?" she asked.

"Charms, Kate. Charms." Luanne leaned forward. "Something fell out of Maurice's pocket when the accident happened—a small black object—and they're saying it gave him strong magical powers. Kate, the truth is that Maurice did lose something. When I visited Victoria Falls, I had a craftsman make a tiny ebony picture case. I gave it to him with my picture in it. He had it in his pocket before the accident—and now it's gone."

"Your picture? A magic charm?"

Luanne nodded.

"What does Maurice's aunt say?"

"That the God of heaven is stronger that any *knickknacks*." Luanne used a word that local folk use when they want to avoid saying the real word when referring to charms that come from the world of dark arts. "That God protected Maurice and prevented him from being hurt worse."

"And Maurice?"

"The same thing he always says—that people talk because of their need to destroy someone who they think has something better than they have. Actually, the morning before the accident he told me he woke up with a sharp pain in his side, and he asked me then if I thought he should travel. Of course, I told him to go. That pains aren't warnings from the spirits, that they usually have logical scientific explanations."

Just then the lights blinked, warning them that in five minutes the generator would be shut down for the night. "Stay right where you are," Kate told Luanne. "I'll bring in a solar light." As she went to get it, she was remembering what George had said about Maurice having given a tip to Ryan about the village theft ring. For the present, though, she decided to leave that fact unmentioned.

"All this now." Luanne slid forward on the chair. "Like I said the other day, I've been thinking about my relationship with Maurice. Seriously thinking. He seems to have the idea that I plan to take him to Australia on my next furlough to meet my parents so we can become officially engaged. Of course, he asked me to be his fiancée long ago.

"I like him—I love him—a lot. He has a depth of personality I've never known in any of the boys I went out with back home. But when I get married—if I get married," she corrected. "I'm almost thirty, and at my age I need to have a husband who understands my way of thinking. Who'll agree with me on how our children will be raised. Who . . .won't be mixed in the hairy-scary of village sorcery and be accused of carrying my picture as a charm against evil spells. Who . . ."

Luanne's hurried recital lagged abruptly, and in the shallow glow of the fluorescent light Kate could see her squeeze her eyes shut. In the next instant a sob broke her restraint.

138 "Cry." The single word Kate spoke conveyed assurance rather than permission. And Luanne sobbed. By some instinct Kate understood that she preferred to cry alone. Later, maybe, she would need the comfort of a hug. While she waited, she heard the door open and then George's solid footsteps came into the room. She looked around and their eyes met, and without faltering he continued down the hall and on into the study.

"I'm . . . I'm sorry." Luanne forced the words between scattered sobs that had all but settled into quietness. She fumbled in her uniform pocket then brought out a folded tissue and dabbed it at her eyes and blew her nose. "Everything has become so—so complicated." After saying the word, she looked up and there was the faintness of an almost smile. "I can't tell Maurice—not now—not until he's better—but I can't take him home with me. Not now. Not ever. This time when I go, I've decided that I won't be coming back."

"Not ever?" Kate could not hold back her surprise. Luanne was a career sort of person who she'd assumed would stay in the mission field for a lifetime.

"Never. I got the forms during committees and have already started filling them in."

"When?"

"I'm due for furlough in May. But the way I feel tonight—I wish it were tomorrow."

"I'm sorry. I mean, I never expected. I mean . . . are you sure that's what you want?"

"There's a job waiting for me in my old hospital."

"I know that Ryan relies on you ever so much here."

"That doesn't make it easier." Luanne spoke slowly. "The Lord's had me here these four years for a purpose, I'm sure. Now . . . it's the time to leave."

"I wish I didn't have to say that I understand. But I do. Even though I don't want you to leave." Luanne had become such a dependable part of the mission that Kate simply never considered the possibility of her deciding to go home to stay, but with the givens she'd just outlined . . .

"In lots of ways I don't want to leave. Like they say, the mission field is a good teacher. I haven't enjoyed all the lessons. Some are almost too hard."

Kate nodded. "I guess we all have our own hard lessons." In some ways she spoke the words as mere fillers into the conversation; in another way they formed a cover for happenings in her own life that she could never share. Not with anyone. "I get the idea sometimes that God sends them so He can get our attention."

Luanne nodded, and their conversation lapsed into bits of trivial chat. Finally Luanne stood as if she were intending to go. Kate also got up and held out her arms, and Luanne let herself be pulled into them. "Thanks, Kate," she said. "Thanks. The Lord has been so good in having you here for me."

CHAPTER
21

"It's not an easy matter to find something of this sort." Bondo's squat body perched on the edge of one of George's office chairs, and his feet were planted in a position that could launch him into hurried flight, should the need arise. "It could be hidden in many places."

Kate looked up from the reports she was filing for George and watched the detective as he talked. That was easy. His eyes never met their faces, but, instead, roved from place to place, seldom stopping to regard any one item for any measurable length of time except for the brief periods when he fixed them low and to the side. His service-green shirt and khaki pants gave the impression they were intended as a uniform, even though the rumpled shirt gaped, leaving the bottom button to bulge over his belt, which seemed to have no purpose except to sag with his trousers and to make room for a naked expanse of round tummy. He spoke from the side of his mouth, and the way he tipped his head before he began each new thought, his eyes darting to the window then to the door that stood ajar, reminded her of a robin cocking its head to find worms on a spring lawn. It also gave the impression that he was watching for anyone who might overhear and carry away anything he might say. He kept his tone low and confidential.

Chapter twenty-one

"I need fuel for my motorcycle and something for lodging."

He glanced over his shoulder toward the door again, and involuntarily Kate's eyes followed in the same direction. She saw no one.

"It will take many days. Maybe even a week."

"But I thought you said the microscope was taken by someone in Loma?"

"Aaaah. Yes. Taken. That is what my sources of information say." Only the left side of Bondo's lips moved as he spoke. "But from someone else I have heard that a dealer in a distant village has approached a pharmacist with a microscope for sale. One that seems to resemble very much the description that your doctor has given."

"I see."

To Kate's discerning ear, George's voice did not sound very convinced. "It will take time. And there will be the matter of lodging."

Cued by the way George shifted in his chair, Kate expected a reply that would serve to terminate the discussion.

"Since this concerns the hospital," he said, "you need to discuss fuel and lodging with the doctor."

"But, sir." Instead of looking at George, Bondo's eyes found the window. "The doctor is not an easy man to deal with."

"The doctor is a fine gentleman, honest and fair," George replied. "All the arrangements for finding the microscope will have to be made with him."

141

Bondo forced the conversation into a few more detours around the same subject before he finally excused himself, got up, and with a weak handshake to each, left "to see the doctor."

"He's already seen Doc," George grinned. "This was just a courtesy call—and a shot at trying to double the take."

That afternoon the long tail of bluish smoke that followed a red motorcycle down Pioneer Way and around the corner onto the main road toward Loma was the last token any member of the mission administration saw of Detective Bondo. That was Monday, a week after Ryan and George had reported the missing microscope. On Thursday, Christmas Day, Arno left.

Something more than a week later, a note did come from Bondo, hand-carried by a Loma man. He'd been put on a false trail, the note explained, since the microscope reported was much smaller than the microscope taken from the hospital. But, he continued, the doctor shouldn't give up hope, because another suspicious microscope had been seen in a village far to the east. He would gladly pursue it, but that would mean many days, and there was the matter of fuel and . . .

"We've paid for enough of Detective Bondo's many days!" Ryan spoke forcefully. "That microscope's sitting right here on this mission, I'm sure, in the back room of . . ." He clipped his words before he cited any names.

George, as he told Kate later, had tied what Ryan was saying with New Year's Eve. On the day of New Year's Eve, the mission truck driver had brought, as had been the custom for many years, three freshly slaughtered carcasses from a beef ranch some ninety kilometers away. One was to be divided among the mission workers as their New Year's gift. The other two were to be sold at a reduced price. That evening, Zamu, the same guard who'd been on duty the night the pineapples had disappeared from George and Kate's garden, stood at the shop gate checking purchasers in and out. When the generator went off at nine, as usual, a crowd still waited around the table where Esther, the cashier, was taking payment and writing receipts. Lloyd quickly connected the solar light he'd hung in a tree branch above the table. After a few minutes that light blacked out.

People laughed and talked and milled around while Lloyd traced the cord with the beam of his pocket light, found and fixed a loose connection. "I'm sure I heard the gate close just when I got the light back on," Lloyd told the others afterward. And I know I saw folks walking away carrying stuff, but Zamu was standing there, as businesslike as always. Afterward Esther's receipts tallied with the kilos listed as having been sold, but the kilos sold were only half of the meat weighed out to sell.

"The hospital doesn't have money for that kind of carryingons!"

Ryan exploded. "Tradition or no tradition, as long as I'm here, there'll be no more beef for anybody's New Year. If the workers want meat, let them send their wives out to get it and carry it home on their heads. Better yet, if they're such great hunters, let them go out and find the antelope that still should be roaming these plains." Later he spoke to George. "What do you know about this fellow, Zamu?" he asked.

"Not much, except that he's the driver's brother and their clan belongs to Loma village."

When school started the following week, Kate had all but forgotten Bondo and the microscope and the missing meat. Ryan had taken the bandaging off her leg, and she could walk to the school and back without discomfort. Maurice had been discharged from the hospital shortly after New Year's Day—but an outbreak of dysentery in outlying villages had kept the nurses occupied with the flood of patients being brought in, and she hadn't had a chance to visit with Luanne since Christmas Eve. Daniel still hovered. Some days he was awake, alert, and starting to feel better. Then there'd be a relapse.

"Penny for you thoughts." George had slipped into her classroom during their brief midmorning break.

"Nothing. And everything. Is something new at the office?" George seldom visited her classroom.

"Lloyd just stopped by. We think this weekend is a good time to start taking student groups out to Loma."

"Sounds good."

"What I really want to know is, is your foot up to handling driving out there?"

"Sure. But I thought you planned to come with us."

"Yeah. I'd like to. But my teachers still need me. With so many young Christians on staff, and them being the ones who teach Bible to the kids . . ."

Kate nodded. "There's so much. So much that needs to be done."

Just then a whistle's shrill cut the morning. They went to the door and stood and watched as the students quickly formed lines in the courtyard and stood at attention, awaiting the signal from the chief of discipline that would allow them to march back to their classrooms. The uniform white of the shirts and blouses and the navy of their skirts and trousers gave them the appearance of a businesslike group of scholars. At a nod from the chief who stood in front of them, the prefects at the head of the ten lines stepped forward, and the others followed, the navy-and-white lines peeling away from each other and streaming toward the open doors of their classrooms—the two longest groups to the two lowest classes, then four to the pedagogy block and four to the scientific building.

"See you at lunch." George lifted his hand in a quick wave and turned along the covered walk that skirted the edge of the block and reached across the gap and then stretched along the other classroom building to the administrative offices at the end. Kate stepped back into the room where Marie's class again filled all the tables. She looked over the crowd of youngsters who at the end of two more years of schooling would qualify not only for their secondary diplomas but for their primary school–teaching certificates. Before the end of the current term they would have assigned observation in the mission school, and some would begin their practice in classroom teaching.

Marie sat in her place at the front table. "A different girl." Kate was pleased with her smiling alertness. "A good student. A good kid. With a good future."

144

Other than the usual process of having to settle the students back into the routine of school, the week passed without incident except that a senior boy from the city brought mail. George and Kate spent the evening together in the study reading their letters. Three had come from Karla.

"I'm mending," she'd written in the first. "Physically, emotionally—and spiritually." Then in another she'd added, "I want to thank both of you for being the kind of parents you are, for having helped us grow up with faith in God. Thanks, Mom. Thanks, Dad. Thanks to both of you. And some day, maybe after a year or so, Jamie and I do hope to make you grandparents. Kimmie's and Kenny's letters backed up what Karla said about getting back on her feet; then the bulk of

Kimmie's dwelt on Ron, the general surgery resident who's name she mentioned more and more frequently. "He's a good doctor, well-liked," she wrote, "with a very promising future. He'll be finishing his residency in April. And . . ."

Kate tried to fit this information with details from Kimmie's earlier letters. Divorced after a brief try at marriage in his early college days, Ron had settled seriously to his studies, had completed medicine with outstanding grades, and had been taken as a resident at the university hospital. "Tall, dark, and handsome" was the way Kimmie described him. "Extremely intelligent, a fine sense of humor, kind, gentle . . ." Obviously Kimmie, with her romantic bent, was convinced she'd found the perfect man. "And with every prospect of becoming an outstanding surgeon—and very rich!"

Something nagged Kate and would not allow her to relax into the contentment that should be natural when her daughter had such apparently excellent prospects for a happy and prosperous future. Kimmie hadn't specifically said anything about Ron's religious affiliation, and she hadn't elaborated many details of his family background except that he'd been born overseas—his father had been a career officer in the army—but had grown up in the States.

"His mother's parents live in Thailand," she'd written this time. "He doesn't remember ever seeing them. And his dad's family are all in the east, but his folks plan on coming out so you can meet them while you're here on furlough. You'll just love Ron with his dark wavy hair, his brown eyes, and his tanned complexion. He's an absolute doll!"

Kate looked at George for help. "Do you think that she's trying to sell us on a marriage? To a fellow of whom we might not necessarily approve?"

"Do you mean because of a previous divorce, mixed parentage, and possibly not being a church member?"

"That's how it sounds to me."

George nodded. "She's an adult, going on twenty-four, professional, with a good head on her shoulders and well able to care for herself."

"Practical, capable, and self-sufficient. Yes, I agree. But she's still our baby—one with a hopelessly romantic streak running through all her good sense."

"Our parents gave us free reign." George winked.

"They probably knew better than trying to interfere too much."

"Well. . .?"

"But it would still be nice to be there to share some of the wisdom we've gained before it's too late."

"I'm afraid the best wisdom and advice we can give at this point is to open our arms wide and accept this young man as the one she's chosen and to support them and love them and—if their ears are tuned—to counsel when appropriate."

"George." Kate's voice carried mock sharpness. "You have too much good advice for your own good. Wherever did you get all of it?"

And the look he gave her cut deep into her heart.

CHAPTER 22

Kate sat on a stool in the shade and watched. The Loma children, more than a hundred fifty of them, crowded together on the ground, cross-legged, dark faces intent against the dull, tattered, and almost mud-colored clothing that hung over their bodies. Hard syllables and clipped vowels filled the air. Kate understood some of the words—she had mastered greetings and a few simple questions in the local language—but for the most part she relied on the translator who sat beside her. A boy, maybe eight or maybe twelve, it was hard for her to judge the age of these village children, stood to recite the day's verse. His legs were even more spindly, if possible, than those of the other children, and his knee joints knobbed under dusty skin. His thin arms hugged the jagged bits of cloth intended as a shirt, holding them together as he crossed his arms over his chest in the posture children must assume when they stand to recite their lessons. His maroon polyester shorts, knotted at the waist to make up for the elastic that had given up its duty, bared patches of his brown bottom. His short hair looked rusty and brittle, and it kinked into sparse knots around a large, scaly, fungus patch. Yet he stood with assurance, and when he spoke his words were clear. When he finished, a chorus of loud amens from the other children applauded his efforts.

"Who is that boy?" Kate asked after the program, pointing toward the skinny youngster in the worn maroon shorts. He was called over, and Kate's questions were translated to him.

"He says his name is God's Gift and that he is brother to the same Sylvanus who was killed by lightning," her student translator replied.

"Same father and same mother?" Kate found that question tedious, but of necessity she asked because in the African way of counting family, the term *brother* might mean someone who has the same father or grandfather, or it could be stretched to include any distant male relative.

"Same father," came back the reply, "but he had another mother, and that mother is now dead, so he has no one to look after him." An explanation followed, which informed her that Sylvanus had been the child of the father's head wife.

"Does he go to school?"

"He did attend the village school, but when he was in the third class, his mother died."

"Is he going to school now?"

"He says not, that his grandparents, who care for him and his younger sister, haven't the possibility to send him."

148 Kate was beginning to piece the story together. "Where does he live?" she continued.

Several of the older village boys stood at the back of the group of children that now ringed them. "He lives with the mother of his father," replied one, and a quick discussion ran back and forth among the other boys. "They are saying that the mother's family accused the father's mother of causing the death of their daughter, who is this boy's mother, and so they sent the children to that old woman saying that since she is responsible for the death of the mother, she must now care for them."

When the translation had finally run the gauntlet of the family relationships and accusations, Kate wasn't exactly sure who had done what. "Then the children are with their paternal grandmother?" she asked. "As punishment because she's the one accused of being responsible for the mother's death?"

"That is what they say," the interpreter replied.

"How old are you?" She now spoke directly to God's Gift in one of the questions she herself could phrase.

"Eleven."

She noted his wasted frame, and she felt something she'd felt before, and she knew that her heart was leading her to become involved in another life, and she was afraid if she followed her heart that she would be led in a way that would carry her beyond what she was capable of doing.

"George," she called when she arrived home. "Are you here?"

"In the study."

She found him on the floor with several Bibles and commentaries and other books spread around him. "Looks like they've been asking more tough questions."

"Yep. These guys keep me studying. How was Loma?"

"Had an excellent turnout. More kids than I could count. George. Is Rene taking applications for more Kids for Kids projects?"

"Think so." George looked up from the floor where he still sat among his books, and Kate could see the little furrows beginning to pucker his forehead.

149

"I learned today that the Loma school hasn't got enough space for even a quarter of the area kids—even with running double shifts. I took a quick look at their buildings. They're too typical. Small, dark classrooms. The thatch leaks. No benches or seats of any kind—kids sit on bricks or rocks or on stools they bring from home. Among the kids themselves there are signs of too much malnutrition, especially for being so close to our mission. And . . .

"George, I met this little fellow who's name is God's Gift."

CHAPTER 23

"Kate, can you talk some sense into this man?" Ryan met her in the hospital's wide entrance hall and rushed into his request. "You're the one person around here he might listen to." He pointed toward a thin man hanging back in the shadows beyond the last window.

Something about the way the man stood seemed familiar. Old khaki trousers drooped around his bare feet, a long hole slit the side of the tee shirt that may once have been white. "What's the problem?" Her voice sounded tired. She was tired. It'd been a long morning at school, and she was in a rush to get home, to get at the grades she needed to compute and hand in to the registrar yet that afternoon.

"He's brought a youngster from Loma—bitten on the hand by a snake—probably puff adder—a couple weeks or more ago. The hand's essentially rotting away, and if the boy's to survive, his lower arm must be amputated. The father refuses. Some nonsense about if his boy must go to the world of the spirits, he must go as a whole man. Despite appearances and in spite of his obviously heathen beliefs, the man speaks a comprehensible French. So does the boy. That's why I sent for you."

Kate wanted to say that she wished Ryan would deal with his own patients, but she bit back her words and looked toward the solitary man and nodded and went to him. "Papa," she began, "I understand your boy is not well."

The man looked at the floor.

"What is the problem?"

"His hand is very bad and the medicine of the village healer did not help, and therefore the boy has asked that I bring him here to the hospital of Mama Kate."

"Hospital of Mama Kate!" The phrase caught her by surprise, and with a sudden understanding of why she'd been called, she looked down the hall to see the trim figure of their unpredictable doctor striding toward his office.

"The boy says that the God you tell about can make him well."

"That is true," she replied. "The God of heaven has all power. And the boy, he has been seen by the doctor?"

"Yes, Mama."

"Then let's go see the boy," she suggested. "What's his name?"

"He is called Little Glory."

The flat springs of the bed in the children's ward where the child lay were covered by a bamboo mat in lieu of a mattress, but an old gray blanket, folded crosswise, lay between him and the mat. The piping of the bed's frame had once been cream, but most of the paint had been barked away. Similar beds jutted out from the wall on each side of the large, hollow room. Other children lay or sat on them, and the adults with them sat on or by the beds or even under—for someone was curled on a mat, sleeping, on the floor beneath one of the far beds. The ward's atmosphere, despite the dingy green of the walls and the bare gray of the cement floors, hung heavy with the strong, clean smell of antiseptic. Little Glory lay still, covered with a lady's worn wraparound cloth, and his hand lay across his chest on top of the cloth. Though the hand had very recently been wrapped in a new bandage, ooze had already begun staining through the thick, white gauze.

"How are you doing?" Kate asked brightly.

"It's going well, a little bit," the boy replied.

"You have done well to ask your father to bring you to the hospital," she said. "With the doctor's help, God can make you well." She smiled and reached out to take the youngster's good left hand. "You are one of those who comes to the children's meetings, aren't you?"

"Yes, Madame. And I also am in the group who has been chosen to work in the garden and to be in the new school that you are going to build. That's why I asked to come here."

"Is that so?"

"Yes, Madame. The teachers who come to talk to us each week tell how the God of heaven can heal those who are sick. I have prayed to Him, as they have taught. And now I have come here to the hospital of the missionaries to be made well."

As the child spoke—his words simple and pure and trusting—Kate's heart twisted, and within herself she wished she could pray with so much faith, so much assurance, and have a similar confidence that she, too, could be made well. "And if you and your father do exactly as the doctor says, you will be made well," she promised aloud. "I'm going to leave you now, but I'll come back to see you this evening, and we'll talk more about this." On her way out she stopped at Ryan's office. "Is amputation the only way to help him?" she asked.

"Nothing's left of the hand." His forthrightness made his words not to be questioned. "I wouldn't even want you to look at it—it's putrid and revolting. Why? Didn't you get through to the father?"

"I haven't really tried yet. I just talked to the boy—a bright little fellow—and he tells me he's prayed to the God in heaven and that he's here because he knows the missionary can make him well."

"He can be made well." Ryan spoke forcefully. "But not if that hand doesn't come off. Look, Kate, an orthopedic friend of mine in Toronto has promised to fit any of my amputees with an artificial limb. With a hook like they can make these days—that kid'll be the envy of the entire area. I—I wish I'd had the chance to do something like that for Daniel."

The expression on his face did not belong to the Ryan that Kate thought she knew. Defeat? Sadness? Compassion? Something other? She couldn't tell what it was. All she knew was that she was seeing a Ryan Bellington she'd never before seen—and that since the pickup accident, he'd been different. Many talked about his battle to save Daniel and how on the night the boy died that Ryan had locked himself in his office. Some claimed he cried. That they had seen his tears. Several weeks had already passed since the funeral.

"Daniel's testimony and his courage touched many people. That boy was such a witness in his death." Kate said.

"I know." Ryan's voice had taken on a softness that earlier she had not thought him capable of expressing. "He had promise. He wanted to be a doctor. Such a waste."

In the silence that fell between the two of them, Kate wondered about the rumor that Ryan had once had a son. Ryan himself never spoke about the past other than to say that he had applied for mission service the year after his wife died and that he'd been at Mbinda since. She was also remembering the first vesper service after Christmas vacation when Daniel's roommate spoke to the students. He told how Daniel had chosen not to be baptized because he was afraid of what might happen at the university. "He sees now that was a mistake," the boy continued, "and he wants you to know that he has opened his heart completely to the Lord. He's asked me to say that if he'd done that earlier, he wouldn't have had to worry because, at each moment when we choose the Lord's way instead of the way we ourselves want to go, there'll be no temptation too big for us." Complete silence filled the church. "Whether he gets well or not, he wants you to know that he has chosen to take God's will as his own. And he has asked me to ask each of you to make the same choice because he wants all of us to be together in heaven."

That week several of the older students came to the school Bible teacher and asked him to put their names on the list of baptismal candidates, and all of them still regularly attended the preparation classes.

"Ryan, Daniel's death was a disappointment and very sad, but we

153

all know that it wasn't a waste."

The doctor nodded and made no effort to argue.

"And I've stopped by to tell you that I've promised the little fellow with the bad hand that I'll be back to see him again tonight. I think it'll be useful to tell both him and his father about the offer of your Toronto friend."

Ryan nodded again. "Thanks" was all he said.

Kate waited for the generator to come on before she went back to the hospital that evening—she wanted the benefit of the lights being on in the wards when she talked to the boy and his father. She carried a plastic bag when she left the house, and both seemed to be waiting for her when she entered the ward. "And how are things going?" she asked, setting the bag on the doorless metal stand that stood by the bed. After acknowledging their replies, she added, "I've brought some bananas and bread and a little milk." The father clapped his hands together in the silent sign of appreciation so much used among the villagers.

"The doctor tells me he can help you become well again." Kate addressed her words to the boy but stood so she could watch both his and his father's faces as she spoke. "He has already talked to your father, hasn't he?" and she turned to face the father squarely. "Have you discussed what the doctor said with the boy?"

The father looked down at his own hands.

"The doctor was telling me about his friend in Canada who can do marvelous things. He can make new legs for those who lose their own legs, and they can walk again. He can make new hands for those who lose theirs, and they can work again. You have seen the ones who have received wooden legs from the Mission of the Helping Hearts, haven't you?"

"But those are no good." The father spoke quickly.

"They work." Kate replied equally as quickly. "They are better than no legs, but compared to what the doctor in Canada can do . . ." She shook her head. "And he has promised to send a new hand here to Mbinda hospital for anyone who needs one." She turned to the boy.

Chapter twenty-three

"Your hand has become very bad, hasn't it, until it's almost no hand at all, but the doctor tells me if he takes away the bad part, the rest of your arm will become like new again. And when it is better, he can get a new hand. It will be different than your old hand, but it will be very strong, and with it you'll be able to do things which no one else can do. It will be very special, and I'm sure you would like to have one of those, wouldn't you?"

The boy looked up at her as she talked, and she wasn't sure that he was comprehending everything. The father, though, seemed to understand. "After tomorrow would be a good day for the doctor to do what needs to be done, wouldn't it?"

"Yes, Madame." The father seemed ready to say something more, but he remained silent.

"Then I should tell the doctor that the next day after tomorrow will be good for the operation."

"It is as you say." The father spoke more to the floor than to her, and Kate realized that it was very difficult for him to say the words. "Now, before I leave," she suggested, "let's pray together and ask the God of heaven to be with both of you, to send His healing, and to bless the doctor in the work that he must do."

The surgery went well, and Ryan sent a message to his friend in Toronto.

CHAPTER
24

Kate slammed the stack of applications against her desktop. "Mbayo!" she yelled in the direction of the door.

A quick shuffling responded along the hall's cement floor as the soles of Mbayo's flip-flops traced her hurry, and almost instantaneously the young woman appeared, dustcloth in hand. "Yes, Madame."

"Who brought this?" Kate clipped her words and held up a large, rumpled, brown envelope with her name printed on it in large, crooked letters.

"That young man who was working for you in Loma."

"Where is he?" Kate forced the words out in sharp staccatos.

"I'm not sure, Madame." Mbayo kept her eyes toward the floor as she added hastily. "But I am sure he can be found."

"Then tell Jonas to find him! Immediately! Tell him he must come to see me—at once!"

"Yes, Madame."

Mbayo disappeared—quickly and quietly except for the scuffing of the flip-flops—and seconds later it seemed Mbayo's lungs had suddenly multiplied their capacity as her mild house voice billowed into a yell that rivaled the loud, harsh speech of any village woman and would be impossible for Jonas to miss. Kate had long since quit being surprised at the incongruity of that voice suddenly proceeding from the soft-mannered girl, just as the girl had learned to handle Kate's sudden outbursts of impatience. Kate continued to sit and to glare at the smudged form that lay on top of the stack of papers. "Wrong! All wrong!" And she clenched her teeth together and squeezed both hands into fists. "And I was sure he'd understood. He repeated the instructions—in detail—pointing out step by step exactly what he was to do. And he promised! Promised!" She brought both fists down—hard—on the stack of papers. "And Rene's expecting these!"

During the development director's last visit they'd finalized plans for a Kids for Kids project in Loma. "It'll be work—lotsa hard work," he'd warned her. "But it's good work. Satisfying. And when you see that new school—gleaming white with a sheet metal roof at the edge of the village—and all those little kids in uniform and the gardens they've planted themselves and when you see how much healthier they've become . . ."

Whenever Rene talked about the village development projects he spearheaded, his eyes lighted, and he literally leaned into what he was saying. "I can tell you, Kate, it will be worth every bit of extra work it's going to cost you. You'll never regret it. Never."

His enthusiasm had swept her along, and the previous week she'd spent all Sunday plus two full afternoons in the village, driving home after dark, working till late each night to be ready for her next morning's classes. Shimba, the young development agent George and Rene had recommended, worked with her, and while she took pictures of the kids—head and shoulders, passport-type poses as required by the organization, he'd made the lists giving name, birth date, sex, and picture number for each child. To be doubly sure there'd be no confusion in matching pictures with the correct application forms, they'd had each child hold a slate for the picture showing his/her name and number. She'd congratulated herself on the foolproofness of that idea and had left Shimba behind in the village so he could complete a Kids for Kids information sheet for each of the children. "Remember," she'd reminded him when she'd left, "every question must be answered for every child. If any information is missing, Kids for Kids will refuse our applications."

"I understand, Madame. Be assured that you can count on me, and I will certainly do the work as you have explained. No problem."

"And when you bring the completed forms, be sure they are arranged in order by their numbers—and don't forget to make a second copy of the master list." At the time Kate had wished she'd thought to bring along carbon paper so she'd have a backup list to take home for herself.

"No problem, Madame," Shimba had repeated. "I'll have everything just as it should be."

"Just as it should be!" Again Kate shuffled through the stack of papers on her desk. "Three hundred application forms! And not one that has all questions answered! And . . ." She shook her head in exasperation. "After living and teaching here this long, I should know better!"

From previous experience she knew she should have been less optimistic, and she knocked the stack of papers into a semblance of an organized pile and shoved them to the side of her desk. The time they'd prepared a mission newsletter for friends back home, she'd given a stack of envelopes, a list of addresses, the school address stamp, and a sheet of postage stamps to one of the more capable senior students. "Like this," she had explained, writing up a sample envelope. "Address here—and be sure the country to which it is going is on the bottom line—school address stamped in the upper left corner—like this," and she pressed the rubber stamp carefully into the corner, "postage stamp pasted in this corner."

The first few envelopes had been neatly and correctly prepared. Then, suddenly, school address and postage stamp swapped corners, and the country of destination entirely disappeared from the remaining addresses that were scrawled in uneven lines across the envelopes. "Maybe I expected too much from someone who's probably never in his life received a letter from the post office," she'd suggested to George then. "But is it too much to expect someone to follow instructions that he obviously understands and to correctly complete a job for which he's being paid?" she asked herself now. "Especially if that someone carries a diploma that shows he has a degree in rural development from an institution of higher learning?" She slapped again at the stack of forms, trying to make it more even. "The high cost of cheap labor!" She grumbled under her breath, repeating the expression that Rene so often used, then got up and walked over to the window that faced the road. Staring out, she forced herself to concentrate on the blue, blue of the sky, the lazy white clouds, the green border the tops of the mango trees pasted along the horizon, to listen to the birds, to admire the simple elegance of the waxy yellow blossoms on the frangipani bush. And the visual impact of her surroundings, the springlike beauty of Mbinda that afternoon, once again worked as a soothing tonic to her frustrations.

A man pedaled a black bicycle slowly along the road and into her range of vision, and she noticed that a goat, head hanging submissively, was strapped to the back carrier—a sight she'd seen so often that she gave it no thought. Three women walked from the opposite direction, and as they walked they frequently readjusted and reknotted the flat yardage of their outer wraparounds. Two balanced large basins on their heads, the other a long rectangular garden basket. All three had hoes hooked over their shoulders, the large cultivating blades balancing them, and from the leaves hanging over the edges and the long tubers protruding above the sides of their containers, she could tell that the women had just come from their cassava fields. The starchy root, almost totally lacking in other nutritional elements, provided the staple food in the local diet. Behind them came two men with their long, hurried strides rapidly closing the distance. One was Jonas—she could tell by the bounce to his loping stride and by the floppy blue coveralls he wore—and when they were nearer, she could see that the other was Shimba. She went to the front porch to wait for him.

"And how was your week at Loma?" she asked after they had finished the required greetings.

159

"Very good, Madame. You have received the envelope with the applications that I have finished and left here for you this morning when I came?" He smiled a smile that indicated he was obviously pleased with himself for having completed and delivered his assigned work.

"Yes. I found it," she replied. "That's why I have called you. Wait here, please." She motioned him to one of the cane chairs that sat on the long, covered porch, and a few minutes later she returned with the stack of forms. "I see that you have completed many of the blanks on each, but where is the master list?" she asked. "The one with all the children's names and numbers that you made when I was with you?

"Ahhh, yes. That." Shimba leaned back into his chair. "That. Yes, I believe that it is somewhere with some of the other papers I brought with me. Yes. I think it probably must be where I left it in the place where I am staying."

"You know that we need it so we can verify the numbers and names on these forms and match them with the photos." With so many children having the same or similar names that belonged equally to boys and to girls, mix-ups happened easily. "And have you made the second copy as you promised?"

"And that. Yes, I was very busy with all the children whom I had to see and for whom I had to get so much information. As you can know, Madame, such work indeed requires a great deal of time, and it is not easy to find the parents of all the children who are the ones who can tell the information that we must have for the questions on the papers."

"Yes," Kate agreed, "I understand that getting all the information requires a good deal of time. That is why I was surprised to learn that you had come back so soon. I didn't expect you until after tomorrow."

"It so happened there was a vehicle coming yesterday in the afternoon, so I decided that I should come with it and not wait for the other one that will be coming after tomorrow."

"And the second copy of the list?" Kate spoke the question a bit more insistently this time.

Chapter twenty-four

"Ah, yes. That I will make for you this afternoon."

"That will be good," she replied, maintaining her calm and pursuing her questions in a way that she hoped might fit with his pattern of logic. "And about the questions on the forms. I see that many blanks still have nothing written in them. In fact, too many blanks were left empty."

"But there are so many children, Madame. It was not possible to find the answers to so many questions in so little time."

"I did not find one form with every question answered," Kate replied. "You remember the rules that we discussed."

"Yes. All the blanks must be filled, but . . ."

"In this case, ALL means ALL." And she held up a form and pointed to each space on the page. "Each of these blanks must have an answer that is both correct and appropriate."

Shimba made no reply.

"And in this blank, where you are to tell something specific about each child's family, I see that you have written the same thing on every form—that the child's family does not have the money to send the child to school because the family is very poor."

"But that is true, Madame."

"I know that it's true." Kate continued to maintain an even voice. "That is why all these children were chosen to be sponsored by the Kids for Kids program—because they are TOO poor. And that is why I told you NOT to write that answer in any of these blanks. You remember. I told you to give details about the child's family."

"Yes, Madame."

"For example." And Kate leafed down three papers. "This form for the boy named God's Gift. In the blanks that ask about his parents, it says that his mother is dead and that his father is a cultivator—which is correct. But it does not say that the boy and his little sister live with their old grandmother who is no longer strong enough to cultivate her fields and that she is the sole person responsible for him and that neither his father nor either of his father's other two wives provide anything for the boy. Nor does it say that he helps his grandmother weave baskets to sell so they can earn a few pennies for food.

"And this one." Kate held up another form. "The form of Little Glory who was here at the hospital so long, the boy who had his hand amputated. It has no mention about the boy's hand." She gave the two forms to Shimba. "Do you understand what I am saying?"

"Yes. I understand now that I should tell something about the children and their families."

"Yes. About each child. And that will mean asking many questions. Do you understand?" she asked again.

"Yes, Madame. I understand. Thank you for showing me my error. I will do better the next time."

"And—the matter of birth dates." Kate had a list of several topics to cover. She hoped when she finished her verbal explanations and gave him the new list of instructions she had written that he would remember and do as he was requested. "Many, many of the forms have no birth date."

"But you know the problem. The parents often don't know which year their children were born."

162

Kate nodded. The problem was very familiar—many of their own students had "imaginary" birth dates, as they called them. Villagers seldom registered a baby's birth, and after the births of many children, it becomes difficult to know which one was born in which year, let alone to remember on which day a particular child may have been born. "But, as we discussed before, the form must have the date that has been determined, for use at school."

As she spoke she was remembering a discussion with a group of mothers who had brought their children to be photographed. A tall girl, already beginning to show the signs of coming womanhood, was registered. She had never before been inside a school, she said, but she wanted more than anything to learn how to read and how to make figures.

"This one, she is six," the mother stated categorically, pointing to the tall girl. "Because she will be in the first class."

"But, Mama," Kate replied, using the title of respectful address. "The girl is very big to be six."

"She is six." The mother asserted and turned to her friends for help.

"Six! Aaahaaah!" And the woman standing closest to her spoke in emphatic agreement.

At that, sharp voices spoke up spontaneously among the other women. "But my Gabriel was born in a year after she was born and my husband had the boy's birth date written on his card, and he is now nearly nine," one declared.

Another waved her right hand, palm out, from side to side in the sign of total disagreement. "She was already a girl the year of the heavy rain that made the river rise and wash away the houses that stood near the bank," said another. "My Bibi was born in that year, and she is already promoted to the second class at school."

"She's also older than mine," claimed another. And another. And as the women compared notes among themselves, they came to the conclusion that the girl must be twelve, maybe thirteen, and since the mother could remember that this girl was born about the time of the planting of the corn, they decided to give her a birthday of November 1.

163

"Shimba." Kate spoke his name almost sternly. "You must take all these forms—every one of them—and go back to Loma with the truck. Do not return to the mission until each one is filled—completely and correctly."

"But Madame."

"Mr. Director and Pastor Rene gave you money so you would have enough to pay for your food and lodging while you work." Kate spoke quickly now, sure of what was coming next and suspecting that the argument may have ties into the real reason for his premature return and unfinished work.

"But I had to pay for the truck when it came."

Kate stared at the young man. Exasperation. Frustration. Futility.

She could not define her exact feeling. "All right!" she exclaimed. "I will advance you enough for three more days of work—and to pay for the truck." Then her speech slowed, and her words became loud and precise. "But you will not receive one bit more until you return with the job completed."

"Very well, Madame." And Shimba's smile was very disarming. "I will see you at the end of the week. With everything as you have said. You can count on me to do exactly as you have asked."

CHAPTER 25

"It is very kind of you to let me come with you." Little Glory's father held himself stiffly on the seat, feet braced, legs angled away from the gear shift, and his words jarred in rhythm with the road. "And you will let me down by the path that goes to Lubombo."

"No problem." Kate maintained a steady grip on the wheel. Big, comfortable drops of rain splatted against the windshield, and distant clouds began organizing themselves into a dark slate-colored sheet that dropped lower toward the earth. She reached for the wiper switch. "Pray that storm misses us!" This she said in English to Luanne who sat on the other side of their passenger. Just then she realized the depth of the puddle ahead, and jamming her foot against the brakes, she wrenched the wheel hard to the left and reached for the gearshift. The vehicle twisted in the new direction, skimming the bathtub-sized hole, then lost footing. Mud-brown water splayed up, and she was forced against the door by the weight of her two passengers. Her body tensed. The vehicle flipped toward its center of equilibrium, and she fought to hold the wheel steady. With a jolt, they bottomed. The front tire churned against the mushy roadbed. The motor growled in a low-pitched grumble that throbbed against her eardrums. She was aware of nothing else except for the wish, a powerful, prayerlike wish, that the vehicle would pull itself out. The wheel continued to churn. Their list sharpened. Then the tire cleated against something solid, throwing a shudder through the metal cab. It pulled itself upward. They straightened. "Whew!" The quick exhaling of her breath expressed both exclamation and commentary.

They continued to twist, bump, and splash along the gutted road until it settled into a gritty, one-lane surface that allowed near-normal speed through a forested flat. Thick-leafed branches, liana-draped, matted into a solid wall of tropical deciduous on either side, blocking them into a lonely corridor. "And Little Glory, how is he?" she asked now that conversation was again possible.

"He's doing well." The father showed every sign of being reconciled to the fact that removal of the boy's hand had been for the best and that he was resigned to the long wait that Ryan had warned him about before even a temporary hook could be procured. "That night. Aaaa-aaah!" And he told about the screams that had awakened them and how he and the mother had rushed into the thatch shelter where their boys slept. Little Glory lay on the far side of the sleeping mat, writhing and moaning. They carried him outside to their bamboo bench. Someone found a stick and lighted it in the coals left by the evening fire. In the wavering light, they found the puncture marks. "The boy cried and cried," the father continued. "At daybreak I went to the home of a healer, but, as you know, his medicine was not good enough."

166

Kate did not pose any direct questions about the treatment. Root doctors, the traditional healers whose practice stayed more within the practical rather than the mystical realm, used a variety of natural substances. For snakebite, some made poultices with bark from a certain tree; others applied what they called a snakestone—a flat, black, rocklike substance prepared with a secret mixture of saps and other extractions. These, they said, drew out the venom from the bites of certain snakes. Science tended to somewhat support their claims. Other healers worked with magical mixtures and incantations.

"With necrosis to this extent—it was a puff adder, no doubt,"

Ryan had said from the first.

Members of the viper family, puff adders account for a large percentage of Africa's serious snake bites. Ryan, always ready with counsel, urged the missionaries to be on the lookout for these snakes and to wear high, sturdy boots when working in the fields or hiking. Though they are night hunters, adders like to bask on the sun-warmed ground along paths where their mottled bodies blend with the dust and the tall grasses. "If something comes along, they won't move till they strike," he cautioned, "and then they throw the entire length of their bodies, stabbing their fangs in deep. Like that! Wham!" He slapped his fist into the palm of his other hand to impress his hearers with the power of a puff adder's strike. "The venom attacks tissue and blood cells, and horrible pain sets in immediately. This young fellow Glory's hand is typical of what can happen—if the venom doesn't kill you right out." He went on to explain that even with a mild dose, and even when gangrene doesn't set in, joints—especially in fingers or toes near a bite—can be left stiff for life.

"What's the best thing to do when someone's bitten?" Kate's question had been almost involuntary.

"Keep the victim quiet and bring 'im to the hospital." They all had laughed at the seeming incompatibility of his suggestions with their roads. "Well, the venom spreads through the lymphatics, and lymph flow is markedly increased by muscle movement—so if you're bitten, don't move any more than absolutely necessary. And, never use a tourniquet!"

Little Glory hadn't been brought to the hospital until two weeks later. When the first healer's medicines failed, the parents went to a diviner, who offered to find the one responsible for the snakebite and to achieve a compromise with the spirits by laying a curse on that person. Then, he promised, the boy wouldn't have to suffer so much. "But he demanded a goat in exchange for his work," the father said. They had already paid two chickens and some money to the first healer. "The boy asked many times for us to bring him to your mission, but how could I when I had always used strong words against Christians?

Yet the boy was only getting worse every day . . ."

The rain became more insistent while the man told how he and the mother were so touched by Little Glory's treatment at the hospital and how that caused them to decide to go to the Loma meetings and how they were soon to be baptized. Then just after they turned onto the main road and had started into the hills, the downpour caught them, narrowing the world into a tiny space that moved with their vehicle. The wipers struggled, pushing against the cascading rain. The effort was useless. Kate let the vehicle creep to a near standstill. "I'm afraid to stop." She had to shout to make Luanne hear.

And then, like that, the downpour stopped. It left swollen, creamed-coffee-colored torrents to cascade along both sides of the road. The atmosphere was still a misty gray, and light was fading. Lloyd had left Loma at least half an hour ahead of them, while, at the request of the village nurse, she'd stayed so Luanne could visit two patients. The nurse had been posted in the village when Rene received funding for a health project as well as the Kids for Kids school, and Kate trailed along as he led them to his patients' homes.

They stopped at a tiny hut. Two fist-sized triangles, cut into the gray mud-bricks, one on either side of the door, peeped out

168

from under the untrimmed thatch, giving the wall the appearance of a face. The nurse called to announce their presence and, sliding his hand under the old cupboard handle door knob, lifted and pushed at the same time. The door scuffed inward, its bottom dragging against the packed earth. A tired voice spoke from somewhere on the floor. When her eyes had adjusted to the dimness Kate saw the woman, thin and wasted, lying under her ragged cloth. Luanne knelt, her knees on the edge of the mat that served as bed, and taking the old woman's hand spoke gently in the local language. "I will leave something for the nurse to give you," Kate understood her saying. "And that will help you to feel stronger."

After they left that house and had visited the other which, if anything, was even poorer, Luanne turned to give instructions to the nurse. "Both of these women need food as much as they need medicine."

"I understand that," he replied. The faded green of the loose-fitting operating room shirt he wore made the gravity of his features appear even more severe. "The costs for their medicines are already on the list for the very poor that Pastor Rene has promised to pay. But they have almost nothing to eat. And their families. You know how it is now in the season after the planting and before the harvest. With food from the last season almost gone, there is no extra even for a poor old mother who hardly eats anything as it is."

Luanne nodded. "And milk. Is there milk to buy at the market?"

"Yes. Some little bit."

"They must have milk," she said.

"But, Mademoiselle, how can they buy milk? Even I, at the prices they have nowadays and the money the way it is, I can't afford to buy even a little for myself."

Luanne was reaching into the pocket of her skirt. "They must have milk," she repeated, handing the nurse a fold of bills. "I'm trusting you to see that they get it and some bananas and perhaps a little sauce made with peanuts. Next week I'll bring you a supply to keep at the dispensary for such cases."

Kate continued to hold the pickup at a steady pace through the hills, and they had already begun the descent toward the Mbinda side. Suddenly they slanted into a slow, sidewards motion. She turned in the direction they were sliding, but the vehicle made no effort to respond. Then, before she could do another thing, the truck dipped sharply to the passenger's side and dropped to a complete stop. She shifted into the low low of four-wheel drive and touched the gas. Mud sprayed up behind the spinning wheels. The truck did not move. She tried again. More mud. The truck seemed to shudder. Kate wrenched her head around in time to see the last of her other four passengers jumping from the back. She also saw that the edge of the canopy leaned into the road bank.

"It appears you are stuck, Madame," Floribert, one of the senior boys, observed, coming around to her window.

"Yes, it does appear so," she agreed.

"We can push you," he offered cheerfully.

"Let's look first." She tried to clear the muck coating the edge of the tilting cab, but her foot slipped, and she felt a cold smear paste itself through the side of her skirt. Her shoes disappeared into a soft ooze. Momentarily she envied the boys' presence of mind as they slushed about, feet bare, pants cuffed to their knees. Kate skidded more than walked to the front of the vehicle and bent forward to look.

"Lo . . . !" Floribert, crouched in the mud beside her, also peered under the vehicle and pursed his lips with concern. "Loooo . . .!" His exclamation drew into a mournful note.

Kate felt her own lips pursing. The frame dug into the road's solid edge; both wheels disappeared into the soupy slush that filled the deep roadside ditch. She shook her head, and her eyes met Floribert's. "We need help." Her three words echoed hopelessly in her own ears. Dusk was settling, and within minutes darkness would be complete.

CHAPTER
26

Luanne and Kate watched the tiny light bob away from them. "If it takes two hours to hike to the mission . . ." Luanne's voice broke the silence.

"By day," interjected Kate. About then the light disappeared, indicating that Little Glory's father and the two boys with him had crested the hill. Darkness was now complete. Floribert and his friend who had stayed as their guards huddled in the back.

"Then by the time Lloyd comes . . . we'll never be home before eleven."

"Were you supposed to work tonight?" Kate asked

"No, but . . ."

"Other plans?"

"I suppose that's what you could say."

"Mmmmm." Kate wished for a sweater. It couldn't be less than sixty-five degrees, but the storm had caused a sudden drop from the almost consistent warmer temperatures to which their bodies were accustomed, and she felt chilly. A dull glow in the sky's lower quadrant indicated where the moon hung behind the thinning clouds. *Charumphs* and whistles and a series of subtle, muted calls indicated that the nocturnal creatures were settling into their evening routines, and the rhythmic metallic twang of what sounded like thousands of frogs soon echoed around them.

"Kate?"

"Yes."

"If you were in my place, what would you do?"

"About Maurice?"

"Yes."

"I thought you had it all worked out."

"I did. But it's not easy."

"Oh." Kate shifted her feet and felt her body threaten to slip along the seat's sharp incline. She grabbed the steering wheel and rebraced her feet.

Luanne seemed not to notice. "When I told him that I wouldn't be coming back and that I wouldn't be bringing him with me, he . . . well, I guess he wasn't expecting that, and . . ."

Kate waited for her to say more, and when there wasn't any further explanation, she asked, "Are you having second thoughts about what you should do?"

Luanne drew a deep breath. "Second thoughts, yes. But I know what I must do." She paused again. "Marriage is God's symbol of His relationship with us. I want a marriage that's good and strong—between two individuals who care deeply for each other and understand and are always looking out for the best for one another. Like you and George."

Kate started to interject that outward appearances can be deceiving, but thought better of it and said nothing.

"I know in my mind what is right and best for both of us," Luanne continued. "I have no doubts about the rightness of my decision—and really, it hasn't anything to do with his being black and my being white, nor with him being African and me being Australian. It's because . . . because we're so different in our way of thinking, in what we expect in our everyday lives, and, therefore, expect of each other. But in my heart . . ." Luanne paused again. "It's difficult. More difficult than anything I've ever done before. Especially seeing him at work every day, living on the same mission. Kate, when these people want something, they do not give up easily."

The clouds had broken and the moon, almost full, hung like a flat disk, bright against the dark heaven. A sprinkling of smaller, lesser luminaries stretched away from it like a scattering of sequins, and the light reflecting down on the section of world in which their vehicle was marooned was dim and sallow and only served to aggravate Kate's impatience with their inability to free themselves from the circumstances that held them where they were. Time dragged. Both women would have liked to get out, to walk, but in the cool, humid night air mud refused to dry quickly as it did during the daylight hours, and their abhorrence of wallowing through it held them back. At last headlight beams pierced the night, and within minutes Lloyd slugged his sturdy four-by-four beside them, and he and George were discussing what to do. George handed in two pairs of boots. "In case you'd like them," he said. "You'll probably find it more comfortable over there, watching," and he waved his hand toward the far side of the road.

After digging down the edge of the road that blocked the wheels, the men attached the cable from the winch on the front of Lloyd's truck, and minutes later the pickup stood on the road where it belonged. It was past midnight when they finally reached the mission.

Monday afternoon when Mbayo called her to the front door, Kate found herself confronted by a rather well-dressed young man who wore startlingly green laces in his white sport shoes. "Remember me?" he asked.

"Well, yes, I know I've met you somewhere," she hedged.

"Andre," he prompted. "I told you about my friend in prison."

"Yes." She recollected their earlier meetings but purposely retained a hesitancy in her speech. "I remember."

"Well, Madame, you will be happy to know that I have found those who have been able to help my friend, and now there's only a small amount left, and he can be set free."

"Oh, is that so?"

"Yes. All that is left now is about . . ." Andre cited a figure equivalent to about ten dollars. "Madame, his suffering has become absolutely extreme . . ."

And again as Andre spoke, dark feelings stabbed into Kate's conscience, and she felt more than thought the idea that if she did nothing to ensure the freeing of that poor prisoner, the eternal consequences of her inaction would be resting against her own salvation.

"Madame, if we don't act this week . . ." He shook his head slowly from side to side to indicate the gravity of what was sure to be the outcome. "If you can help us with that little sum that remains." And he reached both his hands toward her in the gesture of extreme need.

Kate wished George were home so she could ask his opinion. Mbayo worked in the other room, but she hesitated to call her. "Wait a moment." She spoke abruptly, then went to the study. When she came back, she thrust a roll of bills into Andre's hands; and when he had gone, she pushed the incident out of her mind.

On Tuesday morning, Carole was already in the hospital office typing some letters for Ryan when he came in from surgery. "Sorry, can't sit down to talk to you today," he said, stopping by her desk.

"That's all right, doctor," Carole replied, her fingers continuing to skip quickly around the computer keyboard.

"No, it's not OK," he responded. "I can't sit down."

The way he emphasized *can't sit* caught her attention. "Something's wrong?"

"You could say that." He seldom spoke of his own infirmities, and now that he had her attention, Ryan didn't seem able to find a good way of explaining what was bothering him.

"Did you hurt yourself?" Carole asked.

"Well, in a way, I suppose. I didn't get home until after the generator was off last night."

"Oh?" After his evening hospital rounds, Ryan frequently went with Lloyd over to the farm shop where they checked on the evening crew. While the generator was on, mission wives came to have their corn ground at the flour mill, the carpenter used the electric saw to cut pieces ahead for the school desks he was building, and other workers did repairs requiring power tools. "What happened?"

"Nothing. I mean, it doesn't take much to get ready for bed, so I didn't bother to put on my solar lights—or to get a flashlight." Telling about it later, Carole commented again how, for Ryan, he took an unusual amount of time to get around to saying what he wanted to say and that he seemed to be detouring through a tedious series of incidentals. "Then I went into the bathroom and sat down. Then I got up again. Fast. And got a light. And saw that a scorpion had been sitting on the toilet seat first."

That event as well as causing Ryan some temporary discomfort reinforced the mission women's maxim: don't get up in the night without a light.

Tuesday noon when George came in for lunch, he handed Kate a slip of paper. "You're good at puzzles, what do you make of this?"

Kate looked at the paper. "Where'd you get it?"

"Talked to Rene on the radio this morning. He says his trip here to visit Loma is off till at least next week, maybe later."

"That's OK with me," Kate replied. "Shimba said he won't be back with the rest of the forms till Friday." When Shimba had returned from his second try at getting information about the Loma children for their Kids for Kids project, about two-thirds of the applications had been properly completed. Little by little he was completing the rest. "But what's this?"

"That's what Rene said when he was talking about Loma—then he said to tell Lloyd."

"The bees are buzzing. Don't pick the flowers." Kate read what George had written on the paper. "What's that supposed to mean?"

George shrugged. "That's why I'm asking you."

"Have you told Lloyd?"

"Yeah. And he didn't say anything one way or another."

"Well, obviously Rene's trying to tell you something—the local people say that if a swarm of bees passes overhead and doesn't land on your property, that's the sign of a blessing."

"And if they land?"

"You might get stung." Kate's suggestion was half in jest. "Obviously someone's angry, and they shouldn't be disturbed."

"But who are the bees? And what are the flowers? What do they have to do with Loma and Lloyd and us?"

Wednesday morning George received another message. Rene's plans had suddenly changed. He was already on his way to Mbinda.

CHAPTER 27

"What should I do? Oh . . ." Carole looked up with puffy eyes, her usually vibrant bronze complexion dull, and Kate watched as her neighbor struggled to make sense of what had happened that morning. "That man!" The usually gracious and efficient and in charge person had disappeared into a confused girl who sank back into the softness of the couch. "I thought all the gold in America would be safe in his hands. And here. I don't know whether I should just kill him. Or if I should just leave! Or what!"

Kate, herself shocked with the suddenness of the news—and the charges—was glad for the comfort and seclusion of her study, which she could now share.

"I trusted him. My Lloyds of London, I called him. Safe as the Bank of England—I thought! Oh, Kate. I'm mortified. Mortified. Missionaries. Examples to everyone. And look." She shook her head, "I can never tell my folks what's happened." She leaned forward and braced her chin in her hands. "Lloyd's always said that we can manage for ourselves. And we can. He's so generous, though. Kate, I love him because he's such a generous, caring person. And now look."

Kate waited, not speaking.

"That's just the problem. Too generous," Carole continued.

"What's going to happen to us now? I don't want to have to leave Mbinda. I thought this is where God could use us."

"God still can use you here." Kate searched for the right words to reach through Carole's confusion. "No one says you have to leave."

"But . . . we will. They'll send us home. How can we stay on as missionaries after this? How can God . . . ?" Confusion and hurt filled her voice, and tears brimmed her eyes. "Kate, I'm afraid. Afraid of what might happen. Afraid I . . . I . . . Oh, God. God, help us." Her shoulders started to shake, and she covered her face with her hands.

Kate slid closer and slipped an arm around her neighbor's shoulders. "Cry." Her voice was quiet. "That's best. Just cry." She wished she could honestly tell Carole that a good cry would cleanse her emotions then and there and that would make everything settle and be as it always had been. But it wasn't all that simple.

Everyone liked Carole—missionaries and nationals. A black American, she'd first come to Africa immediately after college graduation as a single missionary and had worked two years in the office of the president of the neighboring mission area. During her first furlough she'd met Lloyd at the university she'd attended. He had transferred there into graduate school to finish his masters in education and was doing a special project showing the importance of agriculture in the elementary school curricula of developing countries in sub-Saharan Africa. As she told everyone when she returned to the mission office, they'd "clicked" from the beginning and were already making plans for after his graduation. "He's like nobody I've ever met," she raved, showing folks photos of her fiancé. "Handsome, polished, intelligent, a world traveler—and a thorough Christian," she'd add. "The Lord willing, after our wedding, we'll be back in Africa. Africa's home for him, you know."

And then she'd explain about how he'd become an MK—a missionary kid—telling how his folks were missionaries from France at a station about a thousand miles to the north. One morning they heard a scuffling at their front door and the sound of a baby crying. His mother went and found a little boy baby wrapped in a rag and lying on the doormat, kicking and crying. Beside him was a scrap of paper torn from a school notebook and on it a message in a smudged pencil scrawl: "This is Lloyd. Please take him and train him in God's way."

"And that's what Mom and Dad Parmer did. They're the only folks he's ever had—it's a pity they never lived to know what a fine man he's become." Carole would add, then continue telling how his mother had grown up in the States—her father was an executive with an international company—and that his father had finished his ministerial training in England and they'd met at a church missionary conference in France. They never did find out exactly who Lloyd's real mother was, but it seems she probably belonged to a displaced tribal group who had temporarily fled across the border during a political uprising. Mrs. Parmer decided Lloyd should grow up speaking both English and French, so she always talked English with him; his dad talked French. In addition, they encouraged his integration with the local children, and he went to African schools during his early grades and learned two tribal languages as well as Swahili. He later attended school in France, England, and America. "And he's an absolute gentleman with French charm, British good manners, and an American sense of fun," she would end.

In those days Carole couldn't say enough good things about this Lloyd who was to be her husband, and everyone at all the surrounding missions wished her well when she went home the next summer to prepare for the wedding and told her to hurry back so they could meet her Lloyd. Mbinda was their second mission appointment, and Jamie, their second child, was still a toddler when they had arrived. Carole divided her time between the children and her work in the school and hospital offices. Lloyd, as well as being in charge of the teacher-training program, taught a few subjects, but his expertise lay in organizing and directing the agricultural projects that were run in conjunction with the schools. Under his guidance the students, both primary and secondary, had planted acres and acres of gardens and were learning new and better techniques. In the process the teacher-training students were also assimilating ideas of how they, too, could one day spearhead garden projects in their own schools. The latest of Lloyd's undertakings, the pilot project in which Marie was working, was to be the beginnings of an ongoing agricultural seminar for young folk who couldn't pursue academic careers and for adults who wanted to learn techniques that could improve production in their home fields. Nearly all the people of the savanna area were subsistence cultivators, eking out a hand-to-mouth living from their gardens. Lloyd's idea was to develop a sequence of short sessions that would teach area-appropriate techniques to help the villagers organize and plant their fields in a way so they could reap maximum harvests for their work.

Rene was excited about his proposal and had found funding for it from a German church organization. They planned a double thrust for the project, scheduling selected teacher-training students to be seminar instructors as part of their school practicum. These students would thus gain intensive, practical training for eventually setting up their own programs. The Kids for Kids sponsored school at Loma, as well as the primary school on the mission, would both have training gardens. It was an ambitious project, and George had been helping Lloyd with the planning. Even Kate had become involved, doing more than simply organizing the child-sponsorships at Loma, and both of them were surprised at Rene's intense series of questions when he had arrived at about eleven the evening before.

"How's progress with the seminar gardens?" he asked almost as soon as he arrived.

"Good," George had replied. "With Lloyd in charge, our youngsters have some vegetable beds already coming into production."

"Kids have started coming by with greens to sell from their percentage of what they're growing," Kate added.

"Have you taken delivery of all the piping and fittings for the irrigation system—and did you get a stock of roofing sheets for the storage buildings that are to be built?"

George shook his head. "No. That's what we told you on the radio the other day. Didn't you get the answer to the message?"

"Yah. That's just the problem," Rene replied, " 'cause the bees have been buzzing with some strange messages. That's why I thought I'd better get down here and see for myself what's happening."

"The bees?" George was quick to pick up on the phrase. "Who're the bees?"

"Just people," Rene answered vaguely then he said, "I may as well come straight to the point since this project is under the direction of the school, and you both are involved. The financial report your accountant sent up last week includes receipts for roofing sheets, pipes, and things for the irrigation system, and for their shipping costs—and they're all authorized by Lloyd, which is logical since he's in charge of purchasing. I was surprised to get them, though, 'cause I didn't think he'd ordered any of that yet. So I talked to the fellow who does mission purchasing. He said the only thing that's been ordered and delivered like that is the stuff The Chief got for his new house he's building for his retirement. I'd also been hearing rumors that Lloyd was helping The Chief buy stuff for finishing his house, so I decided I'd better go see The Chief. Well, he was very open that Lloyd had told him to buy the stuff and send him the bills."

"Are you trying to say . . . ?" Kate looked at Rene with questioning eyes and shook her head.

"I wouldn't be saying anything, except the evidence is not good, and I wouldn't even be talking to you now, but I need to be sure before I go to Lloyd. Whether his reaction is good or bad, I know I can count on you to be witnesses as to what is the truth of this matter should any further questions develop."

They decided that George would go with Rene to talk to Lloyd first thing the next morning, and if indeed there were problems they couldn't resolve, they'd have to bring in Ryan. Kate had seen Ryan come over to the school office a little after eleven, but she'd heard no details about any of the discussions until Carole's visit.

"Five thousand dollars!" Carole had blurted out when she'd first come to see Kate. "He's taken $5,OOO of project money! And he says it's because of those committees—and the mission president."

Kate had let Carole talk.

"He felt sorry for the man. Like he says, the president has worked for the church, for the mission, all his life, and look what he has—nothing. With the bad times the country's having, his salary hardly buys food for his family, and what's he going to do when he retires? Go back to live in a hut in his village? An old man with nothing after all these years of living in a comfortable mission house in the city? He's been trying to build a house for himself and his wife so they'll have someplace to live. And—during the committees.

"Well, Lloyd understands how these fellows think, and he told him to go order the things he needs for the house, to just send us the bills, and we'd find money to help him." Carole took a deep breath. "Well, I didn't know anything about this. Not till this morning. When Lloyd got the bills, he said he didn't dare say anything to me. He had no idea the president would need that much, and where could we get money like that—on our salaries? He'd just gotten all that project money, so he borrowed it. Borrowed? Hoping the Lord would provide something before anyone found out what he did. The Lord provide? Honest, I've got no idea what was in his head. We've got no savings. We used everything we had to buy the truck. And we still had to go into debt for that. What are we going to do? Kate, what are we going to do?"

That was when the tears had started.

Now Kate patted her shoulder again. "Just cry," she repeated. "You're safe here with me." She sat close to the younger woman, willing her to find comfort in having someone she could lean on, someone she could trust, and at the same time she was remembering the time during their second year at Mbinda that she'd wished, desperately wished, for someone—another woman, someone older, motherly, stronger, someone who could help her make sense out of what was happening. Particulars forced themselves into her mind. And this time she couldn't stop them.

George had gone to the city—a two-day drive during dry season—to purchase supplies for the next school year and to plan with the educational superintendent for the new upgraded teacher-training program that they hoped to implement at the school. A young elementary teacher, wife of the pastor in a mining town about midway to the city, had been visiting with her parents, both nurses at the hospital, and had asked to ride with him.

"Isn't there someone else to go with them?" Mbayo had asked the morning they'd left.

Kate shrugged off her house worker's remark and waved George and his passenger on their way. Then the day before she expected him back, a letter addressed to George was delivered to the door. As she always did with mail that came when he was away, by his request, she opened it to see if there were any messages that needed to be passed on to him by radio. What she saw couldn't have stunned her more if she'd been hit across the stomach with the flat of a board.

"My loving one, oh how my heart has become sad to know that I might not be here when you come again . . ."

Kate's arm dropped, and the pattern on the carpet swirled into a spiraling motion. She stumbled to the couch and dropped down. "No!" Her mind did not want to believe what she had just read. "No! No! This is someone's sick joke."

She held the letter up again—forcing herself to read more, wanting to know, yet not wanting to know the reality of its meaning. "George? And an African?" The more she read, the more she realized that the contents had never in the writer's remotest imagination ever been intended for her eyes. The person's identity was evident. "That . . . That . . .woman!" Kate formed the word "woman" with such vengeance that it grew fouler and more filled with hate than any expletive.

183

Mbayo had the afternoon off, and Kate stalked the house from room to room, her legs wooden, her heart numb, the letter clutched in her hand. Sometimes she flopped herself into a chair or onto a bed, and then the tears would flow. Sometimes she gave in to a burst of anger and pounded the wall with her naked fists. Sometimes she threw wordless pleas toward God, but she had no idea of what she expected or even wanted of Him.

One moment emotions stormed with anger, the next moment she went limp with hurt, with fear, and then the hotter passions urged her to act. She'd get even. She would. She'd leave. By the time he returned, she'd be gone. Vanished. And no one would know where. She pushed into the storeroom and grabbed a suitcase off the shelf. Feeling the hard contours of the handle in her hand made her aware of the concreteness of her actions. "Now what?" Her own question startled her. She stood in the crowded cubicle and looked down at the worn sides of her favorite traveling case. Reason started to mesh into the confusion that filled her mind. George had their vehicle. All the other missionaries were away. She had no way of going anywhere—except on foot. "A white missionary, a woman, carrying a big blue suitcase down the road. And I don't want anyone to know where I am?"

She continued to stand where she was.

"Pack his things. Set them in front of the door."

She grabbed another piece of luggage off the shelf.

"And if I do? What do I want? A divorce? For him to be fired? For us to be sent home? To face family, friends, new jobs? To have to explain?"

184

The second suitcase became heavy in her other hand.

"No . . ." She slowly formed the single answer to all her questions and let the cases slide from her hands. That simple act jolted the new set of tears she'd been stalling. It was already very late, and she stumbled her way in the direction of the bedroom, leaving both suitcases on the floor where she'd dropped them. She fumbled for the handle of the door, and as she found it and started to push down to open the door, her body stiffened with disgust.

"No!" She had screamed the word into the stillness of the house. "I'm not. Not in there! Not! Not! Not!" She flung herself around, her heavy-footed steps carrying her into a spare bedroom, and dropped herself across one of the beds. Scooping the pillow into her arms and burying her head in it, she sobbed. And sobbed. Sometime toward morning she fell into an uneasy sleep that gave only momentary analgesic to her troubled thoughts, for she awoke with a start to find that the sun had not yet moved full-force into the day, but was only a hint of light behind a heavy shroud of mist.

"When he comes, what will I say?"

The seesaw of her self-questioning resumed where it had left off when sleep had silenced the agony of its up-and-down rhythm. Some time during the previous evening she'd stopped pronouncing George's name, even in her thoughts. He'd become *he* and nothing more.

She'd heard stories about other missionaries—both male and female—and affairs, romantic attachments, which had trapped them. She could name names of some who suddenly, without forewarning, had quickly packed their belongings and had left their places of work. On their service records, across from their names in the blank for "reason for departure," was a terse "medical" or in other cases "family."

"And I was so sure the Lord wanted us to come to the mission field, that He had a special work for us to do here." She sat on the couch again, staring at nothing in particular, vaguely wondering why God removed His hedge of protection from around those who worked for Him and allowed them to wander into such foolishness. During their mission orientation there had been talk of that *185* phenomenon called "culture shock" and how it could hit even veteran expatriates and of the nontypical behavior it triggered. "But not this!" She was vehement. And searching within herself for answers, she found none.

It was nearly seven and darkness had already fallen when she heard the sound of their vehicle on Pioneer Way, and then the flash of lights whisked across the living-room wall as it turned into their drive. He was whistling as he came up the walk, and as he opened the door, she stood as if in standing she would have more strength, that she would have better control. He came toward her, a boyish bounce to his step, his face crinkled with a grin like it did when life had given him some bonus. He dropped the bag he was carrying and before she could step out of his reach, grabbed her into a big hug, pulling her close.

With an almost super human force she shoved herself back, out of his arms. "Where did you stay?" she demanded, her eyes snapping. If she hadn't been so full of hurt and anger, and if the numbing ache that she felt hadn't probed to the very core of her person, she would have laughed at his shocked transformation.

"What?" He'd grabbed out for her again, but she quick-stepped backwards.

"Don't you touch me!" she ordered. "Where is that . . . that woman!"

His jaw dropped.

She pointed toward the letter she had purposely left lying open on the near corner of the table.

He blanched.

"Well . . ."

"It . . . She . . . I . . ." Words that could have contained meaning and might have been formed into sentences of explanation seemed to be out of the reach of his mind.

"Should I load the car? And leave? Now?" She spoke forcefully.

"No! Kate!" There was a pleading in his voice as he spoke her name. "Kate. I can explain."

186   "I doubt there's much to explain that the letter hasn't already told me." She herself was surprised at the calmness with which she spoke now. "And I doubt that the brethren are interested in us staying here any longer."

"No one knows." George looked at her squarely now.

"With a woman who writes details like that. And no one knows?" She could hear the sarcasm of her words, but again her feelings had assumed a woodenness.

"That's the only letter."

"How can you know?"

"I saw her yesterday. She told me."

"You were with her again!" She spit the words toward him.

"I . . . NO! Not like that. Kate!"

His hand reached out to her and she knocked it away with her fist. "Stay away from me. Don't you touch me." The woodenness had come alive, and she knew a solid rage, a strength of emotion such as she had never before experienced. Yet she spoke her words slowly, calmly.

"There's nothing. It's all . . . all a horrible mistake." And George's body seemed to sag, and he slumped to the couch. "She's married. She can't talk." His words were muffled. "If she did . . . in her culture . . . her husband could beat her to death . . . or his family." He looked up, and the haggard sagging of his face surprised her. "God knows I'm a married man, with a wonderful wife, three wonderful kids. I don't want . . . I didn't want to hurt them. I . . . I . . . No one else knows. Kate, you've got to trust me. No one knows."

Kate stared at him. "Trust? Now?" That's when she started to laugh. And it was a dry, hard, disgusted laugh. "Trust?" She shook her head. "Mbayo's left some food on the kitchen table." She turned toward the hall. "I've moved into the spare room." And the wooden soles of her sandals had clapped briskly against the cement of the hall floor.

But that was years behind now. George had vowed there was nothing. Nothing more. That the woman . . . His head had sagged as he tried to put the whys of what had happened into words. *187* "It . . ." Tears stopped his efforts. "It was all a horrible mistake," he finally repeated.

It had taken months of talking and tears and pretending that life was fine when it wasn't, until at last they had made their peace. Now, as she sat beside Carole who was suffering with her own problem, a very different problem, Kate stared down at the wedding ring she wore. There never had been anyone in whom she could safely confide or turn to for help in dealing with the ache and the hollowness, the hurt and the anger, that followed her discovery of what had happened. She wasn't sure how they managed to maintain a cover of normalcy during the ensuing months, but they did. They and God, as George said. Then the church in North America had sanctioned the use of rings for those whose consciences required them, and when they passed through Johannesburg, it had been the perfect time for them to buy their rings and to make a new beginning.

From that day, Kate had trusted that the problem was settled and completely behind them and that her feelings were buried and done with—that is, until that day of the previous year when one of the mission workers had casually mentioned George's stops at the pastor's house each time he passed through that same mining town.

"What are we going to do?" Carole's sobs had subsided, and she had blotted her eyes dry with another tissue.

Kate shook her head and drew a deep breath. "Somehow." She spoke softly, confidently, and lay her hand on Carole's arm. "You'll find the right answers."

Then, a sudden doubt struck through what she had said, and she was searching her own conscience again. *But will I?* she wondered.

CHAPTER
28

"All of you know why we're here this evening." Ryan looked around the room from Lloyd to Rene to George to Kate to Carole, and then back to Lloyd. "We have a problem—all of us."

A silence had fallen, and each individual seemed to sit on a private island under the latticelike shadows scattering across them. Encased in a woven bamboo shade, a single bulb hung from the heights of the old ceiling and lighted Lloyd and Carole's entire living room. Kate studied the scroll pattern of the rust-hued carpet that didn't quite reach from wall to wall and followed it with her eyes to the edge where a highly-polished strip of red cement blocked the space between it and the wall. Then she focused on the well-filled built-in bookshelves that stood across from her. She hadn't seen anyone after Carole had left her place, not until the messenger had called for her to come.

"In my years of being a doctor I've found that when someone falls and gets hurt I can never help that person get better by my yelling and shouting because of whatever foolish thing he or she may have done. Oh, I'll say plenty if I think it may prevent a repeat performance, but healing is helped along only with medicines and bandages and care and treatment. This afternoon, I've talked to Lloyd. I've talked to Lloyd and Carole. They understand the seriousness of the situation in which they are involved, so there's no need for any of us to go into any more detail about that.

"In medicine if we catch a disease before it spreads, it can sometimes be cured with rather simple treatment—in the situation we have to deal with now, I believe we can keep the treatment reasonably simple and not have to institute any radical procedures. Lloyd and Carole have agreed to the treatment I'm proposing, and Lloyd's going to explain it to you."

Lloyd stared at the floor for a long moment, and when he looked up, his dark-bronze features were very sober. "What I've done is wrong—very wrong—and before God I want all of you to know that I'm glad Rene caught what was happening. I wanted to pay the money back. But how?" He spread his hands. "I made some very ambitious promises. I couldn't wait. I guess I thought because I was doing what I thought was kind and good—and because of that—God would open the windows of heaven and drop the money down into my lap. But He didn't. And I had to make good those promises, and . . . well, this is something that affects all of you. I've already asked for Carole's forgiveness." He reached for her hand. "And now I'm asking the rest of you. Doc. Rene. Prof. Kate. Please forgive me."

Heads nodded around the circle.

190

"In this case, though, having forgiveness isn't enough. I have a big debt to make right. A debt that I myself am not capable of paying. Praise the Lord, though, He has made provision for me this time." At this point Lloyd looked at Ryan and Ryan nodded as if in signal for him to continue the explanation. "He has put it in our doctor's heart to make us a personal loan. The money will be paid back to the project immediately—thanks to the doctor's loan—and I will pay him back bit by bit each month. And before all of you, I want to thank him for this wonderful help he's giving us. Thank you, Doctor. On behalf of myself and Carole and our children, thank you."

Everyone was looking at Ryan now, and Kate felt a sudden respect for the man who so often irked her.

"The loan's one thing," Ryan replied. "A temporary bandage to clear up the symptoms. The other part of the cure will be as Rene and George and I have discussed. You, Lloyd, are still in charge of the project as you always have been—and that includes purchasing." Ryan drew a deep breath before he continued, as if it was not all that easy to say what he had to say. "But, for the duration of its installation, you'll have to have a double signature on the invoices and charges for all purchases or moneys paid out to verify that goods or labor has actually been received. That means either George or I will have to countersign everything, or Rene will not accept it—which little, extra job neither of us needs but which we are very willing to do because we know you, Lloyd, and because you are valuable in the Lord's work here in Mbinda."

There were nods again all around the group, but no one else volunteered to speak.

"Well, I hope this will be the medicine that will bring the disease under control and that you will come out strong and healthy. As I see it, that's about it, and . . ." Ryan looked around the circle again. "I don't see that anyone else needs to know about this—so none of this will be mentioned outside these walls. God doesn't see man's mistakes as we see them, and I think this is one of the cases where the truth is in not telling others all you know."

Ryan stood and crossed the room toward Lloyd. "God give you strength," he said, holding out his hand.

Lloyd was quickly on his feet, but instead of reaching to take the hand that was offered, he held out both his arms and embraced the doctor.

CHAPTER

29

Little puffs of dust squished from under Kate's sandals, marking her steps along Pioneer Way. She'd just spent another two hours in the school office helping George with more forms for the Kids for Kids project in Loma. When she reached the memorial, the broad, bench-like base was for once empty, and she eased herself onto it, facing toward the mission entrance, and watched the crazy-patching of light and shadow cast by the afternoon sun's angling through the mango trees. The rains had held since the weekend, and a mudhole in the center of the road had dried, leaving a scooped hollow with hard, mud-gray ridges. Sitting back against a boulder under the memorial plaque, she let her mind drift, and she considered what Mbinda might have been for those who had come to the mission in the early years. She supposed that folks then expected mission life to separate them by time and distance from the rest of the world. *I wonder*, she asked herself, *did they ever struggle with the same worries or frustrations or even feelings like . . . ?*

She pictured the earlier generations of missionaries as a hardier folk, more dedicated, more willing to leave family and friends, more pioneer in spirit. *Did the women ever cry with loneliness, aching for security of the homes they'd left behind? Did they hurt for their adult children? Did they want to be close to parents and comfort them still, like . . . like I want for Karla and Jamie? And Kimmie?* And she imagined that they must have. That they had to have been normal, feeling parents. That being Christian, they wanted to protect their children from the world's evils, and . . .

And their men. The next thought shouldered its way in. *Did they worry about them, traveling, staying close and with the Africans—and their women? Did they ever learn that . . . ?*

She felt her hands tense around the edge of the cement base where she sat. Suddenly she realized that her right hand was balled into a fist and that she was bouncing it against the sun-warmed, unyielding cement, and her mind came alive with thoughts that she struggled against for the past months. And she was glad no one walked the road, no one was near to see her face, no one was coming who would expect her to speak, to say any words of warmth as one must in greeting those who passed.

Liar! Liar! The word pulsed along the currents of her emotions. *A liar!* The suddenness, the fury, the intense surety of her thoughts, startled, almost frightened her. *If he were to walk out of the school. Now. I . . .*

She broke off, midthought.

How can I? The one who just the other day spoke such encouragement to Carole. And Luanne? Who sees our marriage as so good? Oh, God . . . The words continued voiceless, but she heard them shouting within herself. *I've asked you to take all this. God, Why? Why won't you take my anger? Now!* And then she was on her feet striding toward the house, and then she was in her study with pen in hand. And paper. Seated at the desk.

George. She intended that the message stride to the point. Then she looked upward. *This isn't right. Give me good words.* And she added a "Dear" before the name. *You have lied to me—again.*

The round, even letters of her teacher's script soon filled the entire page as she poured out her heart, her disappointment with her husband, a disappointment she had held within herself for more than a year, telling how she had learned, accidentally, about his stops at the pastor's home when he had gone to the city.

I don't know if there is any significance to this, she admitted; *all I know is that you asked me to trust you, and I gave you my trust. You told me not to worry, and I pushed my worries about us aside. The other day, when I heard you talking to Lloyd, saying words that were right and good to encourage him, something happened inside me. And I realize that I do not trust you anymore. That I am angry, very angry. That . . .*

She wasn't sure she wanted to put onto paper what she really felt—that it was up to him. That he had to choose whether or not he wanted their marriage to continue. And she sat at her desk confused, worried that she was thinking such thoughts, wondering why God didn't take away her anger when she had pleaded so many times for Him to take it, to give her a new heart and a right spirit. She reached out and pulled her journal from where she had left it that morning and, without stopping to read anything, found a certain comfort in just leafing through it—knowing it was full of texts and suggestions and quotations she'd copied from those who'd walked the spiritual road before. Then her eye caught one of her favorite snatches from Romans as Phillips had translated it. "We can be full of joy here and now even in our trials and troubles" (Romans 5:3).

194

She let the book slide from her hands. "God," and her thoughts pled with Him to listen to her, to hear her even in her silence. "I want that joy. I've been trying to find it. You know I've been trying to find it—I've been trying hard—and I'm all worn out from trying."

CHAPTER
30

George and Kate sat on their camp stools at the front of the reed enclosure. Since the mission group had started holding meetings in the village, the congregation had completely outgrown its tiny church building, and Chief Loma and his friend, the chief from a neighboring village, had supervised construction of this temporary shelter. Now they sat on cane chairs at the back, the rest of the congregation filling the space in front of them—women on one side, men on the other, the children crowded between the adults and where the speaker stood. Some sat on stools, some on old pans or jerry cans, some on bricks or on the small solid cylindrical cases the termites built everywhere in their fields, and one man sat on an upended section of a large coil spring that had obviously come from some piece of very heavy machinery. From the ranks of those makeshift church pews all looked up at the speaker.

"Those who practice such things will not inherit the kingdom of God."

The old pastor laid his Bible on the bare wood table that served as pulpit, and it was still open to the fifth chapter of Galatians. He stepped to the side, and Kate noted how his suit jacket bagged from his shoulders. Flecks of faded red and yellow traced a subtle plaid through the well-worn material, and his tan slacks hung heavily around his knees, suggesting that they had been patched and repaired many times over. He wore shoes, though their polish could no longer hide their age and their laces were strands unraveled from a flour sack. But he wore no socks.

"Sorcery, hatred, jealousies, selfish ambitions . . ."

Kate followed the list in her English Bible as he repeated acts of the sinful nature.

"Before we talk more, let me share with you a story." The pastor rested his hand on the edge of the table, and he looked around to where George and Kate sat with the nurse and the visitors who'd come from another district church, and Kate noticed his serious intensity. Then he again faced the rest of his congregation. "In a certain village," he said, "there was a man and his wife, both Christians, and the time came that the woman had their first baby—a little girl. They were both very happy with their child. One day when they went to work in their fields, the mother, in order to work better, untied the baby from her back and put her in the basket that she had brought and left her to sleep by the edge of the field. After awhile, they heard the baby cry, and the mother, as mothers do because they love their children, dropped her hoe and hurried to the infant.

"The father heard a gasp of surprise. 'A snake!' the mother cried out. 'I saw the tail of a snake hanging from the baby's nose. And then it disappeared inside.'

196

" 'We will tell no one about this,' the father told his wife. "And so they went home and the mother prepared food for them as she usually did. And the baby ate as usual. The parents saw nothing more of the snake, and the child grew as all normal children grow, and then the day came when she was of age."

Kate listened keenly, taking in details as the pastor unfolded the tale.

"One of the village boys had been watching the girl from a distance, and he saw that she was very beautiful. Being a Christian boy, he went to the pastor of the church. 'I would like to marry that girl,' he told the pastor. And so the families were brought together, and they and the elders of the church gave their blessing on the marriage. On their wedding night, the young man took his bride to his house and while they were both sleeping, the snake, which had been living in the girl all these years, crawled out of her nose and bit the young husband, then crawled back inside. In the morning when the girl awoke, her husband lay quietly. Thinking he was still sleeping, she attempted to awaken him. And then she realized the awful truth. She ran crying from the house, and that day they buried her young husband.

"A few years passed and another young man fell in love with that girl. He went to see the pastor, for he, too, was a Christian, and again a wedding was arranged. On their wedding night, he took his new bride to his house and while they were sleeping, the snake crawled out of the girl's nose again and bit this young man. When the girl awoke, she found her second husband dead. And they buried him.

"After this, the girl went back home to live with her family. Now," the pastor asked, "if you had been the pastor in that village, would you have given your blessing if another young man had come and asked to marry that girl?" He pointed to the church elder who sat on a wooden chair near the chiefs.

"No!" the elder exclaimed, shaking his head. "I wouldn't."

And the chiefs and all the others in the enclosure shook their heads in agreement with his reply.

"Well, the years passed, and another young man did come, *197* a man well known for his Christian ways and for being a man of prayer, and he went to the pastor and asked him to bless his marriage with that girl. The pastor refused. The young man insisted, saying that he understood the problem, that he knew what had happened to her first two husbands, that he loved her very much, and that if he married her, he was sure nothing would happen to him. Finally, the pastor and the elders and the family agreed to his proposal, and the marriage was arranged.

"The first night, instead of going to his home village with his new wife, the young man told her they would stay in her village, and, since they were Christians, they would spend the entire night in prayer so nothing would happen. And so they began to pray. The girl, though, became tired, and after awhile he told her to go to sleep, that he would continue to pray by himself. Toward the middle of the night while he was still praying, he saw the snake emerge from the girl's nose and crawl along the side of the room and return. And then he understood.

"The next day the young man went into the woods and picked the kind of reeds the men used who make traps in which to catch fish, and he wove a trap, the kind in which if something goes in, the reeds are slanted in such a way so it can't get out. And he took the trap back to the house with him and set it in the place where he had seen the snake go the night before."

The sun had come out and was shining down brightly into the roofless church shelter, but the congregation sat spellbound. Even the small children were engrossed in the tale.

"That night the young man said to his new wife, 'we will pray again tonight. Then tomorrow we will go to my village.' And again they began to pray together, and again the woman became tired, and again the husband told her to go to sleep, that he would continue to pray by himself. The woman went to sleep, and in the middle of the night, as it had the night before, the snake came out of her nose and crawled along the edge of the wall and into the trap. And then the young man was able to kill it. The next day when the parents of the girl saw the dead snake, they recalled the time when their daughter was a baby in the basket in the garden and how the snake had crawled into her nose. With the snake dead, the young couple could now safely go to the husband's village.

"How many of you have snakes in your lives?" the pastor asked. "The serpents of witchcraft or of jealousy or of hate? Or maybe you have a snake you don't even know about, and bit by bit, because of your mean tongue or your bad actions, those about you are being killed because they do not see Jesus in your way of acting, and they are not being drawn to Him?" As the pastor drew further parallels, pointing his congregation toward the saving power of Jesus Christ, Kate began to examine her own heart. "Jealousy. Ambition. Pride. The snakes within ourselves may be so well hidden that we don't recognize them, that we need to ask God to point them out to us so they can be killed.

198

Mean thoughts. Anger."

Anger? Kate began to feel uncomfortable, and within her heart she began to ask God to show her what she must do.

"Are there those who wish to come forward, those who for the first time wish to accept Jesus into their hearts and to have the snakes of sin in their lives killed?"

"Yes, Lord," Kate whispered to herself. "Take it." She neither moved nor stood. A missionary did not respond to calls in an African village church—the questions such a move would raise would disturb the self-examination going on in the minds of the villagers, but she did bow her head. And she was aware the Lord had heard. When she finally looked up, she was surprised to see a crowd of people standing at the front, among them Chief Loma and another man she recognized—a man who was conspicuous by his absence from the previous baptism.

"His wife has categorically refused to let him be baptized," the elder told her when she'd asked why. At the time, she found the reply rather startling. *A woman? Refusing to let her husband do anything? And he bowing to her wishes?* She kept those questions unspoken though.

"Her uncle is one of the strongest witch doctors in the area," the elder continued. "A Christian in the family would weaken his power."

199

And then Kate had understood the meaning under the words "categorically refused." They covered the not-to-be-mentioned-to-a-missionary fact that witchcraft was involved with threats of fetish and retaliations. A person would have to be very strong in his relationship with Christ in order to endanger his life by being baptized under those circumstances.

And here that very man was back in church for the first time since the day of the baptism, standing with those who had come forward to show they were inviting Christ into their lives to kill their serpents of sin. Kate was beginning to realize the deeper significance to the meaning and power of the sermon they had just heard. "Witchcraft. Jealousy. Anger."

And her thoughts turned inward again.

CHAPTER
31

Rene's announcement sent a wave of shocked Nos around the small group gathered in the Shayne living room. He had arrived unexpectedly just after dark and had asked for a meeting of the missionary staff. "But he can't do that!" Kate's reaction had been immediate. "He can't send you away—just like that!"

"What seems to be the problem?" George's question was more to the point.

"Well, you know about mission committees and how all our projects have to be approved through the proper channels. I try to keep everything in front of The Chief, to keep him informed, and to do things right. But there's been such an explosion of projects that I'm sometimes not sure myself which way I'm goin'. Overworked. Understaffed. What's new. . . ?"

They all nodded, each knowing a personal version of the frustration of trying to keep the operations under their direction running in a way their professional backgrounds, their sense of responsibility, and their common sense, dictated.

"Kids for Kids brought things to a head. It was all approved. We had funding for two more projects—schools—and I thought I was OKd to put one here in Loma and one at a village near the city. The city project's fine. Then when I mentioned to The Chief about the evangelism, the baptisms, and the school in Loma, he hit the ceiling, yelling that George and I are running our own programs, that we have no respect for him, that we missionaries are all alike."

"George?" Kate was shocked, but she said nothing aloud. "The mission president angry at George?"

"Then he said I could go to my house, pack my bags, and leave—for all he cared. Well, I just let him go on. He was angry. What he was saying wasn't official. But several ears were standing around. There are bad feelings about us these days. Too many of them. Afterward I did some listening around. A tribal clique has a village where they want a school—an out-of-the way place no missionary'd ever go, and they'd been pushing The Chief to get the place voted. If he could do that, well, it'd be a case of you scratch my back, and I'll scratch yours. Kids for Kids, though, would never accept because . . ."

They'd all heard stories about goods, equipment, and money donated by various organizations that disappeared before arriving at its intended destination. And of mythical projects. One company even sent photos of the road they'd built. When the funders came to inspect, the road didn't exist.

"Kids for Kids wants its projects under missionary administration: no expatriate supervisor; no funds. The Chief understands that, and I think he'll settle down. If he doesn't, well . . ." Rene shrugged. "Loma project is still on. I have a check with me, and you'll deal direct with the funders."

"We'll certainly pray it doesn't come to that," Kate heard George saying. "What you are doing is vital to church growth, and what we see happening at Loma now matches reports we've heard from other projects—baptisms, increased tithes and offerings, new churches."

As George spoke Kate was thinking that of all the missionaries, Rene was the one who understood the Africans best, the one who got along with them so well and who had a way of encouraging them to make the best of what they had, the one who was the—and she almost laughed at the incongruity of what she was thinking—that of all the missionaries he was the most Christian.

"I see Loma as a living example that development and evangelism do go hand in hand," George was saying. "The Africans involved say the same things—that because people eat better and live better, they see the projects as real Christianity in action."

"When it touches them," Ryan interjected. "But those who have no projects—we've all seen the syndrome. Jealousies. The outrageous stories they fabricate. Their letters of false accusations."

Ryan himself had been the target of a series of hate letters. After he'd blocked the promotion of an instructor to directorship of the nursing school—because of incompetence—letters began circulating. Most were addressed to the mission president, with copies going to various church leaders and government authorities. None came directly to him, though a copy of one addressed to the Canadian Ambassador mysteriously appeared on his desk at the hospital. It demanded his immediate repatriation to Canada, alleging that not only did he perform illegal abortions but that he grossly insulted his African staff and colleagues by repeatedly alluding to the fact that they had tails like monkeys.

Ryan had shrugged the matter off, saying that he had no time to waste on defending himself against such absurd charges. The mission president felt otherwise. Ryan's medical and surgical reputation had put the mission on the map. Patients came from many parts of the country to be treated by Bwana Lyan—as he was often called by villagers who still used their L's and R's interchangeably—and many referred to the church in general as the Mbinda Church. The president called for an internal investigation, and it soon became apparent that all the letters had come from the same typewriter and all bore signatures of fictitious names. By comparing characteristics of the type styles, those carrying on the investigation traced the typewriter to the school, and corroborating testimony proved that particular machine had been borrowed by the church pastor about the time the letters had begun circulating. Blame was placed on a son of the pastor—the same son who was barred from the mission and who triggered the colorful dispute between Ryan and the father. The other interesting fact was that the pastor's wife and the nurse's father came from the same family. No charges were laid, but the matter of the letters quietly faded away.

"Really, I feel sorry for The Chief with all the pressure he's under," Rene replied to Ryan's comment. "With all the other would-be chiefs, especially in this culture where the church provides the perfect climbing ladder for those who want power. With traditional focus on outwitting or manipulating the forces of evil in order to destroy competition and to get what you want. And all the tribal friction." He shook his head. "It doesn't necessarily pay to be too successful. Then add our insisting things be done 'right'—OUR way! Well, we don't make his life any easier."

As the discussion flowed back and forth, thoughts from the recent Loma sermon flashed into Kate's mind.

"For now we're still here," Rene was saying. "And I want you to know that I, personally, intend to stay as long as the Lord makes it plain that He needs me and my family here. These days it's more important than ever for us to rely on the Lord. Which brings me to the real reason for meeting with you this evening. Rumors are increasing. My friends say the secret service has uncovered a plot against the governor. This ethnic thing has split the military, and political sympathies follow very obvious regional and tribal lines. Total ethnic cleansing may become a fact. Several embassies have sent out warnings to their citizens living here."

Kate glanced around the room. Ryan, Lloyd and Carole, Luanne, Rene, she and George, the two young Parmers playing at the table were together within the walls of their house as they had been on many earlier occasions, and the evening sounds of the mission, subtle with hummings and whirrings, filtered through the window as always. But she no longer found reassurance in the ongoing insect songs, nor did she feel the security of the walls. Rather, she was very aware of being a stranger in a country where the government was losing control of a population who harbored the concept that democracy gave individuals the right to do as they pleased—regardless. She was also aware of forces—invisible and intangible elements—burrowing into, and infecting, tainting, and corrupting the hearts of normal, everyday men, women, and young people, even hearts of those who lived and worked on their mission, filling them with hatred and jealousy and anger. Inflamed with a passion for rights, those infected could . . .

And in your own heart? The suddenness of that near-voice caught her thoughts and for a brief moment turned them inward, and she did not like what they found.

"What are the real possibilities, and what do they mean for us?" Lloyd directed his question to Rene.

"The current discontent could mean civil war. It may mean confrontation among the military themselves. It may simply simmer and continue more or less as is indefinitely. Nobody I've talked to has any good answers. Whatever, the so-called 'foreign elements' still here on this mission can easily become a target at any time."

"Wouldn't they be safe here? On a mission?"

Rene shook his head. "The undercurrents of agitation are building, and if you have any families with suspect ethnic origin who'd like to cross the border back into their home territory," Rene took a deep breath. "Well, it'd probably be in the interest of everyone's safety to help them go now."

Kate's thoughts, trying to make sense of everything being said, found temporary focus on one name—Marie.

"Embassies are watching what's happening, and there's talk that if the situation gets too touchy, troops may be brought in to evacuate foreign nationals. They're telling their citizens to be prepared—that includes all of us—and to keep a bag packed with sleeping bag, clothes, passports, travel documents. What you can carry is what you can take, they say, and at the same time all of them say they expect things to blow over without any real trouble. But you never know—it's best to be prepared."

When the others had left and the generator had been turned off for the night, George and Kate continued to sit on the couch. In the darkness she felt him reach out to take her hand. She tensed and pulled it back.

"What's wrong?"

"I don't know."

"Something's been bothering you, and it's more than what's been said tonight."

"Maybe."

"Kate. You know I don't like guessing games."

"Ummmhhh."

"Kate!" He spoke her name sharply now. "What is it?"

"I don't know, George. I'm not sure." She wanted to talk, to tell him how she really felt, but she'd held back for so long that she couldn't find any easy way to begin. She sat silently, keeping to her side of the couch, searching for words. At last she spoke again. "I don't like the way I am lately. Frustrated. At every little thing. Angry. Besides, if Rene goes—what's the sense of us staying?"

"Especially if he goes—which I doubt he will—there's gotta be somebody who stays."

"But what's the use?"

"Of what? Us staying?"

"Yeah. With the ethnic tensions and church leaders who want us out."

"Just look at the challenge."

"Of what? Of having to send Marie away?"

"Of Marie who we may be able to save because we are here so we can send her away—if it becomes necessary," George corrected. "And the challenge of working with the teachers. The students. The Kids for Kids project. The families. Kate, we're doing a work no one else can do. God needs us here—especially in these troubled times. He needs someone who can point them away from all the guff and all the evil."

"Us? George. Us?" Her voice wavered. "How can God use us when . . . when . . ." She hesitated.

"When what? What are you getting at?"

"You should know."

"What?"

"Us."

"Us?"

"George. Where did you stay the last time you went to the city?" There. She'd said it. The question was out.

"In the guest house."

"And where did you go in the evening before you went to the guest house?"

He took a few moments before he answered, and even in the dark she knew he had that little crinkle between his eyes that he always got when he wasn't exactly sure of how he should reply. "I don't know what you mean."

"George. You've been lying to me. That's what I mean. Lying." She paused, and even in the darkness she could feel his shock at her accusation. "I know where you've been. I've been told—in innocent conversation—that each time you go, you stop to see her." She paused again, but not long enough to let him form any words of defense. "And I'm angry. Very angry." Her voice was calm. She didn't feel any rush of passion as she had on the day she'd written that letter—and put it away—but her words tended to follow the text of what she'd written. "Angry because you told me I could trust you. Angry because . . . well, I don't know what you still feel or don't feel. I don't know why you stop there. I don't know if I even want to know. That's your problem. I never intended to say anything, ever, but . . ."

206

"I told you that you didn't have to worry."

"Thanks for the easy words." She was tempted to become very sarcastic, and she caught herself and stopped speaking for a moment, and in her thoughts asked for the right words. "Since we worked things out back in the beginning, you've said that." Her voice was calm again. "You've told me not to worry, and I accepted that as your way of saying that you were sorry for what had happened. And I know you wouldn't intentionally become involved in something that would cause us to have to be sent home, because . . . well, sometimes I think you like the Africans too much—because of her, maybe."

"You mean, that's what you've been thinking? All this time?" The incredulity in George's voice almost triggered the anger that had to this point been under control. "But they moved. Sweetheart. They moved. Three years ago, at least. I don't even know where. Oh, Kate. You silly little thing. I said you didn't have to worry."

"But why didn't you say so? Why didn't you tell me?"

"Because we agreed never to talk about it. Because I assumed you knew."

"Then—why do you go to the pastor's now, and stop and not say anything about it?"

"Sure. I stop by there. To drop off mail. To pick up mail for the kids in the dorm. To . . . Oh . . . Kate . . . I'm sorry. So sorry for what happened so long ago to make you think this." And George slid close to her and reached out and drew her into his arms, and she felt like both laughing and crying, but she did neither. She simply let herself lean against her husband, relaxing into this new understanding. And as the awareness settled into her thoughts, her heart became infinitely lighter—not because of what George had said but because of what she herself had said, and because at last she had been honest enough with him and with herself to tell him how she felt and why.

After some minutes, she lifted her head away from his shoulder. "Do you think there's any truth to what Rene said tonight?"

"About having to evacuate?"

"Mmmm-huh."

"The possibility exists."

"Do you really think we might have to leave here—to leave Mbinda—like that? To leave everything behind?" Suddenly as she heard her own questions, she realized that down deep she did not want to go. "And never come back?"

"I hope not. But we should be prepared—in case."

"Then I guess we'd better pack some emergency bags tomorrow."

CHAPTER
32

Thursday afternoon Kate heard the unmistakable roar of The Beast, as Rene called his battered Land Rover, pulling into their yard. He had stayed on at the mission, occupying their spare room, and every morning he drove to Loma to oversee preparations for the new school building. The previous day he'd hit the side of a deep hole too hard and had come home with his tailpipe strapped to the roof rack. "Lloyd and I'll help you weld it on Sunday," George had promised. Kate waited for Rene to come into the study, as he usually did, with the report of his day's activities, but he didn't come. A few minutes later Mbayo appeared at the door.

"Madame. It's Pastor Rene. He's . . ."

Kate jumped to her feet and hurried into the living room. Rene sprawled on the couch. He made no attempt to move when she came in. "Only the Lord knows how I made it back." His words slurred, and he groaned and tried to roll onto his side.

"Send Jonas for Dr. Ryan." Kate spoke quickly to Mbayo as she bent and put her hand on Rene's forehead. It was hot, very hot. Minutes later Ryan arrived with Maurice, and Kate left them their privacy. Before long Ryan came to the study.

"Malaria. Bad." He leaned against the doorframe, and Kate could tell by his face that he, too, was very tired. "I've sent for a nurse to bring medications; then we'll get him into bed. Hope you have plenty of blankets, because the chills'll start soon. Luanne and I've been going day and night this week—but if he gets worse, call me. I've treated this boy for malaria before. He's been working too hard again, and we may need to set up an IV for him."

When George came in, Rene huddled under at least four blankets—and the entire bed trembled with force of his chills. An hour later, Ryan looped by their place on his way home from treating another emergency that had come in. By then the fever had rocketed higher. "Call me if he seems at all worse," he instructed.

At one o'clock George got up to check on their patient. "I'm going for Ryan."

At the sound of his voice, Kate bounced fully awake. The glow from their fluorescent light filled the hall and momentarily framed George in the doorway. Then Kate heard his quick steps leaving the house. She jumped out of bed, pulled on her robe, and hurried to the room where Rene lay. He moaned weakly, and in the light filtering in from the hall, his features took on a ghastly pall. The minutes dragged. At last George returned with Ryan. A nurse followed them. "Get Mademoiselle Luanne." Ryan's instructions to the nurse were quick and concise, and about fifteen minutes later both he and Luanne came in, arms full. Kate slipped away and crawled back into bed. Rene had plenty of medical help, and she considered it expedient for at least one person in the household to get some rest. In the background she could hear the murmur of quiet voices as the IV was being set up. Footsteps came and went, and George told someone to build a fire and to heat some water. With her mind, she sought divine help for those who tended Rene. Then she slept. At six she awakened. The house was still. Too still. She hurried to the sick room and saw that Rene slept, an IV needle taped to his arm. Beside his bed sat an African nurse. She whispered a greeting. The nurse nodded. "Pastor Rene is sleeping," he said, his voice low. "He is very sick, but God is great. He will make Him well."

209

Kate had nursed George through a few attacks of malaria—they came on fast and hit hard, but if he started treatment right away, he usually, though still quite weak, would be up and about by the third day. Malaria was like that—somewhat cyclic—and she expected the same pattern for Rene. On the third day, though, if anything, he seemed weaker. "You're very fortunate to have chosen to get sick here, young man, and not out in one of your villages." Ryan spoke cheerfully to his patient. "I'll guarantee that not only are you getting better service than you'd have in any village, we're also treating you better than they would in any of the city hospitals."

Rene almost smiled. "Thanks, Doc," was all he managed to say.

"That boy's too sick," Ryan confided to George and Kate. "Going too hard, traveling too much, besides all the stress. Even if we can get him back on his feet, he'll not be in shape to drive back to the city."

"Should we get authorization to have him flown out?" George, as usual, was helping Ryan to think out the options of what could be done. "Does he need to be taken elsewhere where they have better facilities?"

210 Ryan shook his head. "I think we can handle the medical part here as well as anywhere. What concerns me is that as soon as he starts to feel better, he's going think he's invincible and go off in that Beast of his and collapse somewhere where there'll be nobody who can do a thing to help him."

"What do you suggest?"

"I like your idea about the plane. Talk to the president when you're on the radio this evening. Tell him that Rene may be well enough to fly next week and that I suggest they arrange an early furlough and medical leave for him. He needs to get out where he can be given a thorough workover to be sure nothing else is going on."

"Do you think we should suggest that Charles, the volunteer who's been working out of Rene's office, be flown in at the same time so he can drive The Beast back? Rene was talking of him coming to help with project construction."

Chapter thirty-two

"Sounds like a good idea."

That's how it was that the next week a thinner, much less energetic Rene left his prized vehicle sitting under the avocado tree beside the Shayne garage and flew back to the city with a MAF Cessna, and Charles, the volunteer project worker who had arrived on the same plane, stacked a collection of boxes and bundles in that same garage. Rene had recovered enough to be up the last two days before he left, and he had spent three rather lengthy sessions at the radio discussing with Charles what he should bring and what he should do when he arrived in Mbinda. "Are you still studying for your amateur radio operator's license?" he asked Kate.

"I gave that up long ago as useless," Kate replied.

"Times are changing." Rene sounded almost like his old self. "I've got friends . . ."

Kate laughed. "I've never known anyone else with so many friends," she teased.

"Yeah." He shrugged. "When you got too many good friends, though, you also got too many good enemies. As your man George says, that makes the challenges." Rene spoke with a smile, then he suddenly became serious. "George is a good man, Kate. A very good man, a good missionary. He has a way of being able to get along with almost everybody. Take good care of him. He's a good man; he'll be going places."

Kate laughed again. "Sure, Rene. I always take good care of him. I've also heard folk say before that he'd go places—even back when we were first married—only then I didn't realize that it'd be to Africa.

"Rene." She spoke his name a bit hesitantly as if she weren't sure if she should ask the question that was in her mind. "Do you think you'll be coming back after your furlough?"

"Ya." He said just the one word, then waited before he said anything more. "Even if there's trouble. In my own heart I say that I'm coming back. It'll take more than an angry Chief and a little malaria to keep me—and my family—away. And when we're back," this time he grinned, "Like I started to say, I got friends—some in Europe are sending equipment for two communications bases—one in the city, the other here. Charles is bringing the letter that authorizes you to set up an international ham radio right here at Mbinda. He'll put up the antenna and get everything ready so that when you're back from furlough . . ."

Kate feared she wasn't hearing right. "Do you mean. . .?"

Rene nodded emphatically. "You'll be all set to talk with home any time you like—right from your own house. The hospital makes Mbinda a logical choice. More than that, George and you are doing a work for the people that . . . well, you deserve it."

CHAPTER

33

George worked at his computer; Kate sat with a book. Charles had left the morning before with Rene's vehicle, driving it back to the city. Rene and his family, as Ryan had suggested, would soon leave on an extended furlough to give Rene time to regain his health. The radio antenna was up and a stand sat to the side of the desk for the radio they were to bring back after their own furlough, which was to begin in only six weeks. "Imagine!" Kate exclaimed. "Being able to talk to the kids. From Mbinda! If we can convince one of them . . ."

George pushed his chair back from the computer table and swiveled toward her. "I'm sure that'll be no problem. If I remember rightly, one of the many pluses about our Kimmie's Ron is that he's a ham."

Kate looked surprised. "I'd missed that. You mean he has his amateur radio license? That man seems too good to be true. If only . . ."

George stood and walked over to stand beside Kate's chair. "They need us to give them time to find their way together."

"You're right." She let the words draw into a sigh.

"Wasn't it Kimmie who invented the maxim about not being either too bad or too good?"

Kate nodded.

"Well, somehow, I have the idea that her Ron fits the mold—that he's not too bad—rebellious—nor too good—self-righteous. Knowing our Kimmie, she'll be helping him to understand things he's never thought about before."

"I hope you're right."

Silence fell between them for a few moments; then Kate spoke again. "That night when . . ." She hesitated to speak aloud exactly what she was referring to, but she knew George would understand what she meant. "I wish now I'd talked to you earlier. I . . . I feel . . ." She searched for the right words. "I feel like someone who's been chronically sick and then after months and months, maybe years, of searching for the right treatment has finally found it." As she spoke, she realized that was exactly the way to describe the difference in attitude she was experiencing. That it was like she'd tried a new medicine and then one morning she'd awakened and the pain had been replaced by a sense of well-being. "The anger is gone." A confidence replaced her hesitancy. "And in its place I have a joy and contentment—even happiness—like I . . . well, being with you, being here at Mbinda, in spite of all the headaches and problems and being so far away from the children, I know now this is where we belong, and I'd be happy to stay here forever—if this is where the Lord wants us."

214

George reached out and cupped his hand over her shoulder. "You're more like the Kate I used to know—a long time ago—only better."

"I . . . I'm learning." She looked up at him. "I didn't want to be angry. I'd prayed and prayed—and I couldn't understand why God didn't take it away. It's clear now. I needed to go to the person—to my brother against whom I had aught—and let him know that what he was doing . . . well, what I thought he was doing. Let him know how it was affecting me. And . . ." Her voice faded, and her confidence disappeared, and again she was groping for words.

"Yes."

"Remember the night I fell."

"Mmmm-hmmh."

"Well . . ." She struggled to say what she knew she had to say. "Woody . . . he . . . well, there was nothing to it—really—because . . . because . . . I fell."

George let the silence hold them before he replied. "I was worried. I wasn't sure, but I suspected. Then I thought maybe I was too jumpy because of what . . . what I'd done."

Kate shook her head. "You were right, and it's good I fell, because . . . Because that's what kept me from—from falling." A short, embarrassed giggle interrupted her words. "I'd prayed. The kind of prayer you call a dangerous prayer. I . . . I kinda knew before. I didn't want anything to happen. And I did. And I was angry with you. At the same time, I was afraid of myself. So I told the Lord that if I ever started to do anything stupid, He should knock me down. He must have taken me at my literal word. Because I fell. Oh, it hurt. But I'm glad now. So glad."

"Katie." George eased himself onto the wide arm of the chair beside her. "My sweet, silly little Katie." And he pulled her against his side.

"Even then, I wanted . . . well, I'm glad Woody's return visit was canceled. Now . . . I can tell you that no matter what, it wouldn't make any difference—and that's the honest truth."

He squeezed her again. "I believe you. And that's the truth!"

Suddenly Kate realized that she felt comfortable just being beside her husband, comfortable in a very comfortable way. And she realized that she could be open and honest and unafraid all at once. Then an old question pushed its way in, but it too had changed, and in her mind it was tugging playfully at what he'd just said. And with a rush of mischief, she spoke the three words. "What is truth?"

"Us."

"Us?" His quick answer caught her off guard and made her pull back. "What do you mean?"

"Our relationship. Our honesty with each other. With our own selves. With God." He spoke quietly. "Truth is the willingness to examine what we are and who we are. To . . ." He slipped his arm from around her and let it drop onto his knee and leaned away from her, and again they became two people sitting in their own separate worlds. "You don't know how I suffered . . ." His thoughts chopped into short bits and he, too, appeared hesitant as he reached down into that part of him that had been so long shut away. "That time when . . . I hurt—how I hurt. And I knew I'd hurt you. That I'd broken trust with you. And even if we outwardly appeared to be walking side by side, on the inside, I knew that we were both going our separate ways. And that made the hurt even worse. And I didn't know what to do."

The silence that fell between them this time was no longer one of the tense silences to which they'd become accustomed but a silence that belongs to two individuals who are experiencing a new growth of understanding and of caring for each other.

"I'm sorry, Katie. Very sorry for what happened then. And for now. For the misunderstanding."

She reached over and laid her hand over his. "I'm sorry too. Sorry I didn't realize I should tell you what was happening inside me. Sorry. But now . . ." She looked up and their eyes met, and both of their smiles were sudden and spontaneous.

George nodded. "That's why I said truth is us. Truth is a relationship—a relationship where neither person has to be afraid. And it's only when we are totally honest that we each can help the other and that we can grow in closeness."

They continued to sit on the couch. And the songs of the insects and the distant evening sounds and the voices of the occasional persons coming or going along Pioneer Way formed a background, distant and separated from the haven of the study. The glow of the lamp spread softly through the room to include the carved chairs and the hippo and the African baskets, symbols from the culture they'd been called to serve and that also belonged to this tiny piece of world that was theirs and theirs alone. For the moment there were no hungry people, no possible wars, no ethnic purges, no theft, no school duties, and no concerns for their students who worried because they had no one to provide the money for their next installment of school fees. It was their time to be together, to be alone without interruption and to sort through and to evaluate and to make known their innermost thoughts and concerns to each other.

"We both grew up being told what to believe," George was saying. "We took those lists of dos and don'ts as the truth, but they couldn't keep us—from falling." He grinned, and she was happy to see the hint of mischief that now lighted his eyes. "Maybe we're some of the lucky ones," he added quickly. "Our tough times didn't break us. Instead we're learning from them—and among other things, we're learning how to believe—and because of that I think our marriage is growing better than ever."

"I think so too," she agreed, and she absent-mindedly ran her finger back and forth across his wedding band. Then she realized what she was doing. "This was so important to me. Back then." She stopped and tapped his ring. "I'd always wanted us to have rings—even when the church said we couldn't wear them. Then that day in Jo'burg when we made those new promises to each other—for me these were a symbol of what I wanted our marriage to be. Now . . ." Her thoughts led her to consider what they had in their possession at that very moment. "I think we have that kind of marriage—and it's caught me by surprise." There was an almost laugh in her voice. "I see now that at its worst—and at its best—marriage is symbolic of God and His people. Seeing that . . . knowing the relationship we have, well . . . these rings . . . they're not really that important, are they? I mean, whether we wear them or don't wear them makes no difference to the truth of who we are, does it?

George tugged playfully at a wisp of her hair. "I've always said that my wife has a special gift of insight." With a sudden move of mock gallantry, he lifted her hand and brushed his lips against it. "The truth has set us free," he said, and his voice became totally serious. "And let's keep that freedom of truth."

CHAPTER

34

The next morning the reality of school brought the usual mixture of problems and petty grievances and work and laughter, and in the midst of it the mission messenger delivered an envelope to Kate's classroom door. "I got a letter from Andre today," she reported to George at the dinner table.

"Which Andre?"

"The fellow who kept coming for help to raise money to free a friend of his from prison—I finally gave him about ten dollars a few weeks ago."

"Oh?"

"He profusely thanked me for helping so his friend can begin life again with his family. With it he sent, of all things, a tiny papaya leaf saying it's symbolic of the growth of hope and trust. He's also offering to help us get school supplies at great savings—if we're interested."

"By all means," George responded. He was always looking for ways to save money for the school. "If he comes around, send him down to my office. By the way, I got a letter too." Smile lines crinkled at the edges of his eyes. "Remember Mitombo?"

Remember! Mitombo had sat for three years in the senior class before he managed to pass the state exams and qualify for his diploma.

"He's actually made it into university, and he wants us to know that he's seriously studying, that he seriously needs money—of course—and that he's seriously improving his English. Here, see for yourself how serious he is." George pulled a letter from his pocket and handed it to her, pointing to the last line.

She read it aloud. "I am seriously thanking you from my very bottom."

That weekend both Kate and George went to the Loma meeting. The crowd was even larger than usual—over thirty adults had already been baptized—and after the service, the chief came to them with the local lay evangelist. "He wants to be baptized," the evangelist told them.

"Praise the Lord!" George exclaimed.

"But there is a little problem yet," the evangelist continued, and, knowing that time pressed the Shayne's to return to the mission, he did his best to come directly to the point. "The chief wishes to have your counsel." And he pointed George and Kate toward the woven cane chairs that two young boys had carried to the shade of a mango tree. They sat down, and the boys brought other chairs for the chief and the evangelist.

"What does the problem seem to be?" George asked

"The situation of the chief's second wife has not yet been resolved."

By tradition a chief was expected to be the husband of several wives and the father of many children, and although current economics made having several wives impractical, they often had two or three. The church, on the other hand, had during the early days agreed with other Protestant missions to take a decided stand against polygamy. In order to become a baptized church member, a man must be husband of only one woman. Some had argued that the Bible did not clearly indicate that polygamy was wrong. They urged that the Christian thing to do was to take the family unit intact into the church and in that way protect the junior wives and their children from the social and cultural stigmas that result from the breakup of even polygamous marriages. "We don't understand all the fine points of their traditions," they warned. "And we can unwittingly condemn innocent women and children to unnecessary suffering by breaking up the family stability." At the same time, they suggested that accepting such families into church membership should be done with clear directives that the husband would take no further wives and that no plural marriages would be tolerated among those who were already church members. The hard-liners, though, won out, and everyone hoped that their approach would put an end to polygamy.

It hadn't, Kate and George learned soon after their arrival in Africa, and plural marriages remained in rather common practice. Several village men had two, some even three, wives. Merchants often had several—one wife to run each business establishment. One they knew had seven stores in seven towns and seven wives—one to run each of his stores. Even some women, they were surprised to find, accepted polygamy as a good thing, saying that with women outnumbering men as they do, they would rather become a second wife and risk the inevitable jealousies involved than to remain without any husband at all. The chief's problem, though, was one he had inherited. As part of the initiation rites through which all hereditary chiefs are expected to pass, he was required to take the widow of the previous chief as his own wife, to provide for and care for and to be to her a husband for the rest of her life.

"Has the problem been discussed with his second wife?" George asked.

"Oh yes," replied the evangelist. "She also is in the baptismal group and is willing to accept a reasonable settlement that will care for her needs."

"Then the problem is settled."

The evangelist looked at the chief, and the chief cleared his throat and began to speak for himself. "Since I have no other means, I have offered her a share of the crop when the corn is ready. She has agreed, saying that will be enough to establish herself. But the next baptism is before the harvest."

"There'll be another baptism later."

Kate noticed that at George's response both the chief and the evangelist seemed to become interested in studying the ground to the side of their feet.

"We already have had the problem of one of our newly baptized Christians who has died," the evangelist finally said. "This has helped us to realize how quickly our life on this earth can be over, and this week the chief has come to me with a question. We know that baptism purifies us before God, that it washes away our past sins. If he has to continue to wait until he has solved the problem of his second wife, what if he should die before he can be baptized? On the day of judgment, would God allow him to enter into heaven?"

A simple "of course" sprung quickly to Kate's lips, but, realizing the sincerity of the question, she held it back. The concept of a literal purification had become very evident during a question-and-answer period after the last baptism when one of the candidates had asked, "But what if we drink the water from the river—after all the evil spirits have been washed away from the lives of those being baptized? Can the evil spirits get back inside us?" The religion of their traditions offered no savior. The ambivalent behavior of the gods, the demi-gods, and the spirits of their ancestors—sometimes benevolent, sometimes treacherous—made it necessary for the living to constantly protect themselves by appeasing and satisfying the quirks of those shadowy beings that belonged to the nether world, which they believed was on the other side of life. Thus religion had become a part of everything they did. Their legalistic notions of appeasement were easily transferred to the supreme, all-powerful God of the Bible and His handling of their fate for the hereafter.

"In your heart you have chosen to follow God, haven't you?" George asked.

"I have seen that God's way is good," the chief replied. "The Bible shows how we should love one another and keep the commandments; then God can help us."

"And you are making arrangements for caring for your second wife?"

"We have made an agreement," the chief replied.

"Then in your heart, you are doing what is right and good for her. And doesn't God look into our hearts to know if we are pure in a way so He can take us to heaven?"

"That's right. People look at us and accuse us because of what they see, but God knows how we are inside. Even so . . . I don't want to wait to be baptized." As Kate listened, she felt sorry for the man who found himself caught between the rules of the church and his heritage of tradition.

"There is another problem." As the evangelist spoke, he looked to the chief as if to verify whether or not he had the permission to continue. The chief made no sign to stop him. "The chief's mother is not in agreement with the arrangements that have been made."

Despite the burdens they were forced to bear and the dowry system that could give outsiders the idea that wives were just another chattel of a man's property, women had more influence than showed on the surface. They managed the family money and properties, and in privacy they counseled their husbands. In their clan, by tradition the chief's mother was his closest advisor, and her wishes were seldom ignored.

222

"She favors the second wife and wishes for the first wife to be the one divorced. Here in Africa our life becomes very complicated, especially when it involves the ways of our ancestors." Again the reversion to a generalization to cover the actual meaning of traditional practices that the evangelist was not sure missionary ears could comprehend. "The mother is behaving in a way that would make you think she has forgotten she is a Christian." The chief's mother, as well as his first wife, had been among the first group baptized after they had begun holding meetings in Loma. Even at that time the chief himself had requested baptism. "There are whispers of what might happen if the chief does not do as his mother says."

The allusion left no doubt in George and Kate's minds about what kind of threats were involved. Sorcery and witchcraft had, if anything, become more widely and more openly practiced. "But why?" Kate couldn't refrain from the question. "The chief's wife seems a very fine woman, active, and a good mother."

Again the evangelist looked at the chief as if checking to see if he had permission to continue. "Jealousies. For example, if he had a job with a regular income, the mother would expect him to give his salary to her; then she would in turn give an amount to his wife for running the household and keep the rest for herself. The chief's wife is a strong woman who doesn't easily let herself or her household be cheated and therefore is labeled as a troublemaker by the mother." The evangelist paused, and Kate wondered if his explanation were complete and if George might have an answer that could be of some help. "And then there is the other problem." The evangelist spoke toward the ground again. "His wife's family is not of his own people but come from another tribe.

A sudden ache pierced Kate's heart. "In the name of Christianity, what have we done?" The silent question throbbed in the wake of this last bit of information. She looked at George and saw that he, too, understood the choices the chief faced. Life in Africa could be complicated, too complicated. A chief who didn't have a wife from his own people could be considered as not being a real chief.

CHAPTER
35

"Madame, I tried to come sooner." Andre stood on the porch, looking distraught and making his excuses. "But the truck we are to use to transport the supplies we wish to bring to you . . ." He spread his hands in that expression that Kate understood too well. The impossible had happened again. The truck, as he explained it in his expressive French, had fallen into disrepair along the way when they were many kilometers away from everywhere, and he had hiked on foot all that long distance to come to her and to tell her.

George was away—in Loma—for the day to visit the project and to see how construction was progressing on the school. By coincidence it seemed that every time Andre came George happened to be away.

"As I showed you on the list of prices for supplies we can get for you, we can save you very much money—but now our truck has acquired this problem." Andre looked at her and sighed and again spread his hands to emphasize the hopelessness of the position in which he found himself. "It can be repaired, but we still lack about a hundred dollars to pay for the pieces we need."

"I'm sorry," Kate returned. "But the director is not here."

"I cannot wait," Andre replied. "I have a ride back to where the vehicle is—it is stopped exactly in the center of the road in such a way that no one else will be able to get around it. If you can just help me with this money now, we can get the parts and be on our way and have the vehicle repaired and running again, and that amount will be deducted from the price of the supplies we'll bring. If I don't find the money now, then we'll no longer be able to get ourselves on the way quickly enough to get these things for you."

What Andre was saying made sense. According to the prices he'd quoted, the one hundred dollars would save them several hundred dollars on purchases for the coming school year. She'd shown George the list he'd brought, and he and the accountant had agreed to order the supplies—cash on delivery. "I wish the director were here," she hedged. "Maybe he could help you."

"Please, Madame. We want to aid the school. We know how difficult it is for you to buy everything you need. If you can just give me the money now, then we can have the supplies back to you before you go on furlough. You'll see."

"Well . . ." Kate easily had the amount he wanted on hand in the house. They'd just cashed a big check so they could pay the students they were supporting—Kate had also set aside a large sum for Marie, since rumors were becoming more insistent that something was about to happen. A hospital family was preparing to leave. If necessary, they would take Marie with them because their home village was near her mother's family.

"Madame. We have all the money except . . ."

"Very well," she replied. And she went into the study to get the money and to write out a receipt for him to sign.

"Oh, thank you, Madame. You'll never regret that you have helped," Andre exclaimed. "You will be seeing us again in two weeks with all the supplies." And as he walked down the walk with the wad of bills in his pocket, there was an extra bounce to his step.

George drove in about an hour and a half later. "This Andre that you talk about—how does he usually dress?" he asked almost directly when he came in.

225

"Well, sort of like one of the more fashionable school boys, she replied. "You know, in those baggy kind of plaid pants. And . . ." There was something unique about his outfit that she'd noticed. "Every time I've seen him, he's worn white sport shoes with bright green laces. He's the only boy I've seen wearing green shoelaces. Why?"

"Well, I think we've just discovered the ring leader of the Loma theft and con artist ring."

"What are you saying?"

"I checked in Loma about this fellow after you had given me the list of school supplies he said he could get us at a discount. The chief warned me to be careful. He said that we were maybe being sold stolen goods. Then bits and pieces of other stories started coming out. It's very useful to ask questions, Katie. Especially to folk such as two of the chief's counselors who have recently had their sins washed away by baptism. Complaints had come to them about a Loma boy who had been visiting another Protestant mission near town. A young fellow in baggy pants who wears green shoelaces had collected quite a sum of money from two of the women—he'd asked for help for a friend of his in prison. Then something made them suspicious, and they went to the prison—the prisoner they thought they'd helped did not exist. There was also some careful talk that indicated that this same young man might know the whereabouts of the hospital microscope and that he keeps the village market supplied with kerosene and fuel oil and bananas and pineapples. Another interesting fact is that he's from the same family as the guard Zamu."

As George shared his latest discoveries, Kate experienced a very strange and very uncomfortable feeling. And the longer he talked, the worse she felt.

"It seems the fellow goes by several different names but that he consistently wears green shoelaces when he goes out. The chief warned me never, under any circumstances, to give him money for any reason."

"George."

"Yes?"

226

Chapter thirty-five

"You're not going to like what I have to say. I don't like what I have to say. In fact, I'm feeling rather . . . well . . ."

"Kate, what's happened?"

"Andre—or whatever his name is—was here this afternoon."

"And."

"It's a very long story, but he convinced me he needed help to repair the truck on which he said they're bringing the school supplies and that we can deduct the money from what's owing when they deliver the goods."

"How much?"

"A hundred dollars. George! I've just given away a hundred dollars of the money we'd saved for Marie!"

Sometime in the middle of that night Kate awoke and thought she heard someone singing. She reached over to George—and found that the bed beside her was empty. At that she sat bolt upright. Small crises—like the time Zamu pounded on the window grilling—easily awakened her, but seldom fazed him. But at the first indication of something of real consequence, he was immediately awake and on his feet. As her eyes adjusted, she realized that he was standing to the side of the window. She could still hear the singing, only now it seemed to be getting louder. "What's happening?" She hissed the question out on a whisper.

227

"Not sure." he whispered back. "Lloyd said this evening that some project workers were discussing a political rally and something about foreign parasites."

The music became louder yet as if a chorus were marching along Pioneer Way from the direction of the river. Then the words and melody became distinct. "Onward Christian soldiers!" She crept out of bed and tiptoed across to stand beside George. "They're singing 'Onward Christian Soldiers'!" Her vision was adjusting, and in the light of the partial moon in the cloudless sky she could now easily see a long group of people moving quickly along the road. All seemed to be carrying things over their shoulders.

"Hoes?" She heard the question in George's whisper.

The singing column marched past their house without hesitation and then past Parmer's and on in the direction of the church.

"Are you going to do anything?" Kate asked.

"Like what?"

"Find out what they're doing?"

"Not for the time being. If . . ."

Sounds of shouting broke out in the distance—someplace vaguely in the direction of the church. Shouting and screaming went on for what seemed a very long time to Kate, but George said it was maybe fifteen minutes. A few minutes later, the singing resumed, and the marchers soon reappeared and made their way back along the road in the direction of the village. "I'd better go get Lloyd," George suddenly said. "I'll try not to be too long."

He returned about an hour later. "What we expected. Riff-raff from the villages, stirred up about this tribal thing. At the teachers' housing. The gist of their message was that if the 'elements' from our mission are not gone within a week, they'll be back. And they'll do more than just sing. They carried hoes and spears and mpangas—Lloyd suspects a good deal of their weaponry are from the garden tools that disappeared from the project stock here a while back." George dropped down onto the side of the bed and sat with his head in his hands. "And I thought we could get through the school year without this. Joel and Joshua. Both of them come from the wrong side of the border. Excellent teachers. In the Bible study group, they were among the best. If they want to leave—now—I can't stop them. Before God, I can't. Oh, Katie."

Kate reached out and caught George's hand in hers. "Of course you can't."

"The school will suffer. Can't those people see what they're doing to themselves and to their youngsters? Chasing away some of the best teachers. Because their parents or grandparents were born in the wrong place and to the wrong tribe."

"George."

He didn't respond, but she continued anyway.

228

"Haven't you been encouraging the mission to open a school on the other side of the border?"

"Yeah."

"Well, maybe God can work for good—even in this."

The morning dawned clear, with skies a depth of brilliant blue. A few wisps of mist caught the sun's rays and were transformed into streamers of light tracing the river's meanderings. It was one of those near-perfect, exhilarating mornings that come when the seasons are changing from the time of rains to the long six-month time of drought, and the temperatures are neither too warm nor too cool. Despite the idyllic weather, the students seemed edgy and unable to concentrate on their lessons. During break they gathered in small clusters. Kate sat at the desk in her classroom.

"Madame."

She looked up to see Marie standing in the doorway. "Come in," she invited.

"Did you sleep well last night?"

Kate shook her head. "And how about you? "

"No. Madame. It was very frightening—in the village—they—those people—passed by Papa Clement's house and they said very awful things. It was as if the evil spirits were speaking. Madame. Do you think I am cursed?"

"Of course not, Marie."

"But I ran away from my village to come here, and now the trouble has come to the mission. The curse has followed me."

"Of course not," Kate repeated again. "It's not you. It's . . ." And she searched for the right thing to say. How do you explain the love of God to a child—an orphan—who has been chased from her home because she has the blood of her mother's people in her veins? And who is being pursued again. "It's because of the spirit of evil that gets into the hearts of people who refuse God's truth."

"But, Madame. I know these people, and they know me. Many of them sit here in church every Sabbath. They're Christians."

And Kate felt a terrible ache in her own heart, for she understood too well the truth of what the girl was saying. "The devil, the evil one, works hard to blind the eyes of those who think they know God," she said as she held out her arms toward the girl. "No matter what happens, don't let him trick you into the same mistakes. Don't let him cause you to lose your faith in God's love for you." And she held the girl close and couldn't find the voice to say anything more.

CHAPTER
36

That weekend all the missionaries stayed on the mission. After the church service, while Kate stood outside talking with some of the teachers' wives, a little grandmother made her way through the others toward her.

"Madame."

The voice was thin and pathetic, and Kate recognized the woman as a widow who lived in Kato village. She had, they said, come there long ago with her two children and had worked her fields for many years selling tomatoes and peanuts to earn the amount necessary so the children could attend school. Now she was too old and too weak to work, and both children had grown and married: the girl later died; the son lived in the far north, and even if he had money to help his mother, there was no safe means in these times of political upheaval for him to send it to her. Frequently the woman walked the two kilometers to worship at the mission church. Kate took her proffered hand, and the leathery skin felt rough against her own, and the hand trembled.

"Madame, I want to die."

The dark eyes looked up, and Kate saw how the aging features sagged too close to their bones and noticed the brittleness of the gray

231

hair that wisped around the edges of the faded head-cloth. "What is it, grandmother?" she asked. And she cupped her other hand over the hand she held and cradled it, as if in so doing the trembling would stop.

"I'm too hungry, and I want to die."

Kate looked politely down at the ground as the woman spoke and couldn't help seeing the cracked and broken plastic shoes that gaped around the worn feet—it seemed an unwritten law that the mission church was not like the village churches, and no one came into its services without wearing footwear of some kind. Nor could she evade the tattered edges of the faded cotton wraparound.

"I have nothing anymore. Nothing at all."

"Come with me to my house," Kate replied.

At the house Kate brought out some bananas and bread, and the grandmother took the gift and laid it in her lap then held both hands over it and bowed her head, and her lips moved in a silent blessing. While she sat on the steps and ate, Kate put together a package with cornmeal and oil and a little salt. The woman stood to receive the gift and clasped it against her thin body. "Thank you, Madame. May the God in heaven bless you with a long and peaceful life and give you strength to continue the good work you are doing here."

232

Kate could see tears in the old eyes, and she resolved to send more food later in the week. The rest of the day passed quietly. At about two the next morning Kate roused.

"Wake up!" George hissed.

"Huh!" She rolled over and sensed, more than saw, him standing by the bed.

"The military are on the march!"

"What?" Suddenly she was wide-eyed and alert. "Where?" She jumped from the bed, her usual worries about stray insects and the risks of touching the dark floor with bare feet not remotely in her mind.

"The Peace Corps rep just drove in. Troops are in town. There's shooting and looting. And general confusion. The Americans are sending a plane in at daybreak to their maize project about fifty Ks south of Loma. He's on his way to evacuate a couple of volunteers and take them down. If we want to go with him . . . well, we've got thirty minutes."

Kate was already pulling into a pair of slacks and a sweatshirt. "What does he advise?"

"Go. He's in radio contact with the consulate in the city. All American citizens have been told to leave."

"And what do you think?"

"It's best."

Kate was glad for the bags they'd packed.

"Be sure to get your passport and money." George ran through a quick list of small items they needed to add as though he'd memorized it long ago. "Then I'll run to see Doc."

"Are the others leaving?"

"Except for Doc. Says the folks need him more than ever now." George had a drawer open and was stuffing his personal documents and business papers into the side pocket of the gray bag he always carried when he traveled. "I'm taking him my school keys and things."

Kate pulled her backpack out of the closet and, in the light of the solar lamp George had hung over the bed, momentarily regarded its bulging sides. She'd promised the kids that no matter what happened, she'd do her best to bring out the albums with family pictures.

233

"Better bring some water," George called back to her as he hurried out. In the background she could hear the motor of a Land Rover.

"Pictures," she was thinking. She ran into the study and grabbed three books—ones in which she'd consolidated photos from the highlights of their lives for each of the children—and with effort managed to force them into the already full bag. Shadows from her flashlight's beam staggered against the wall as she dragged her bags out to leave with George's and hurried on into the kitchen. She propped the little light on the cupboard—George still hadn't put in the solar light he'd bought for the kitchen—and filled two bottles with water, pulled a loaf of bread out of the fridge, and a small container of dried mangoes and dropped them all into a plastic bag. Just then, someone pounded on the door.

"Are you ready, Madame?"

Having Jonas arrive at that moment seemed, at the time, to fit perfectly into the normal sequence of events, and without hesitation she pointed the flashlight toward the bags. He shouldered both backpacks then picked up their two carry bags. Their eyes met as he swung past her, and she saw that they looked puffy and worried. "Thank you," she said quietly. "Thank you for . . . for everything. When you see Mbayo, tell her . . ." She faltered momentarily. "Tell her we'll be back," she completed hastily.

She flashed the light briefly around the room, and it swathed across the large oil painting of an African river village, bathing the water with an almost moonlight effect. It was her favorite of their African paintings, quiet and restful, and she had always planned to take it with her when they went home to stay. She gave a half-laugh, picturing the impossibility of trying to fit it under her arm and drag it along.

"Katie?" George called from the open doorway. "Coming?"

234

"Two minutes!"

Her quick footsteps echoed along the hall and into the study where she closed the windows. She needed one last moment alone in this place that had been her haven, her sanctuary. There could be no goodbyes, none that could be formed in real words, to Marie or to the others, and as she stood in the middle of the room, a prayer filled her heart. In that instant the beam of her light caught on one of the mask faces, the one on the chair with the carving of the lady pounding. Those chairs, too, she'd always planned to take home, and the hippo. The eyes of the mask face were as they always had been, blank and unseeing. Blind. Then, with a start, she realized that she understood. The ones left behind faced hunger and many dangers, but they did not have to be trapped by blind traditions or by the blind senselessness of what was happening. In the morning the plane would carry them above the mists and beyond, and she would have more than the ache of memories, more than the sadness of leaving. She would have truth. The truth that here in Mbinda she had come to see. And those they left behind would have the truth she and George had shared, a growing truth. And for that she was glad.

She turned and went to where George waited.

"Ready?" He reached for her hand, and together they hurried into the night.